Queen's Pawn

Queen's Pawn

VICTOR CANNING

HEINEMANN : LONDON

Willam Heinemann Ltd

LONDON   MELBOURNE   TORONTO
JOHANNESBURG   AUCKLAND

First published 1969
© Victor Canning 1969
434 10758 1

Made and Printed in Great Britain by
Morrison and Gibb Limited, London and Edinburgh

Queen's Pawn

ANDREW RAIKES STOOD checking his hotel bill. The girl behind the desk watched him, liking what she saw . . . the crisp white shirt, and just the right shade of blue in the silk tie to go with the small-patterned herring-bone tweed suit. The blue of the tie was almost the blue of his eyes; nice eyes, crows'-feet crinkling them a little at the corners as he scanned the bill. Tallish, well-built, he'd be well into his late thirties, she guessed. In imagination she ran the tip of her finger down the line of his jaw, across the firm, hard, sun-tanned skin. He had the kind of face she fancied, square, honest and with a lot of intelligence. The lips were generous and the mouth long and firm. She shut her eyes for a moment, trying to hold the impression of the face, but the whole suddenly became misty. A good face, but hard to carry in the memory. She couldn't know it, but it was one of Raikes' minor assets.

Raikes filled in a cheque and signed it—*John E. Frampton.*

The girl made out a receipt and stuck it to the bill.

"Thank you, Mr. Frampton. I hope you've been comfortable with us."

"Of course. Thank you."

He smiled. Suddenly she felt the day lift up, pleasure spring in her, and knew that she would like to do something for him, would like to share something, anything, with him. That was another of his assets. She couldn't know, though, that if the circumstances warranted it—which they never had yet with anyone—he would have killed her without a touch of remorse.

Raikes picked up his case and went out into the London

I

sunshine. A nice girl, he thought. In a way she was unique. She was the last person for whom he was ever going to write a bad cheque. Today was the end of almost twenty years of careful, efficient cheating, twenty years untouched by conscience, untouched by suspicion. Andrew Raikes who had stood for so long behind all the false names was now consigning them into limbo. With him now was the satisfaction of having done what as a youth of nineteen—as the red Devon soil had rattled, dry from summer drought, on to the oak lid of his father's coffin and he had watched the grave diggers spit on their palms to grip their shovels—he had sworn he would do.

It was a beautiful day, hot, with a warm smell of tarmac coming up off the road. A pigeon planed down the narrow chasm of the street, dropped its flaps, braked, and touched down a few yards ahead of him. Its neck feathers were lacquered with oily iridescence in the sun. Cock bird, blue chequer, silver ring on its leg, wanderer from some backyard loft, no true-bred London vagrant.

He turned into St. James's Street and moved, unhurried, towards Pall Mall. At home the river would be high and coloured with recent rains. No use for a fly. He wanted some more Mepps and a few small Tobies for spinning. Hardy's was just round the corner. Just spinners, he told himself. No wandering around the place letting his eye be taken by some expensive rod or reel. A man should keep his mania within bounds. The big sea trout were in the river. A good run this year. A six pounder leapt and line went whipping off the multiplier with a thin, heart-stopping whine. A young girl in a miniskirt went past him quickly. The movement of her bottom lifted and swayed the skirt like an ice-skater's. He watched her legs, unmoved. The girl was quickly lost in the crowd. Brown tan shoes, skin-coloured tights, yellow miniskirt, a small stain marking the bottom right-hand edge, white blouse and sloppy green cardigan, black hair, lank, no shine, neck length, height around five-foot three, weight a hundred and twenty odd. Five years hence if something reminded him of her he would be able to

2

recall every detail. Life was all detail. Detail was survival.

He went happily into Hardy's. The assistant who usually served him was whipping a backing on to a line. He gave Raikes a grin. He wandered the length of the shop. A soft amber light came off the racked rods. He ran a finger down a length of Palakona split bamboo, took down a small brook fly rod, handled it, felt it, moved it, sensing the play from butt to rod tip. The assistant looked across at him and nodded. From under a low arch of alders he flicked a pheasant tail upstream to the edge of an eddy, and tightened smoothly to the hungry take of a Taw trout. Always hungry, but not always foolish . . . the brown torrent like pale beer, and upstream a dipper flirting his white waistcoat on a moss-covered boulder.

He bought some Black Fury Mepps, some four-gram golden Tobies, and the rod. He made out the cheque from another book on his Exeter bank and signed it—*Andrew Raikes*. The bank had had a Raikes account since it was first established in 1790.

He walked across the road to the R.A.C. for coffee. Berners was waiting for him. They sat at a small corner table, and Berners produced the final papers, the completed statements, the meticulous summing up and balance sheet and profit distribution of fifteen years of work between them. Unequal partners. Seventy-five per cent Raikes, and twenty-five Berners and both of them well content. Berners was not his real name. Raikes did not know his real name. It was the name that Raikes had given him when they had first met. Berners would never know why he had chosen it. In return Berners had given him the name of Frampton. Of Berners he knew nothing except their work together. He did not know whether he was married, where he lived or what he intended to do now. Neither of them had ever shown the slightest curiosity about the real identity of the other.

Berners said, "All you have abroad has been moved into a Swiss account. I know the number naturally."

"I'll change it in the next few days."

Berners tapped his folder. "Over the years we've had an average growth rate of just under sixty per cent."

Raikes grinned. "We've taken bigger risks than most business men."

"By the way, I sent an anonymous donation to the Prisoners' Aid Society."

"How much?"

"Two hundred and fifty."

"I hope it's not tempting fate."

"We could have gone on to bigger things." Berners smiled. "We're young and —"

"Know when to stop. Never be too greedy."

Berners shrugged and began to tidy the papers away into the folder. He did it neatly. That was Berners; neat, methodical, nothing ever overlooked; a head that held and processed figures, facts and possibilities like a computer. A small, round-shouldered man, narrow-chested, but with big strong arms, oddly out of proportion with the rest of his body; white-faced, with a dull marble shine to the skin; grey cloudy eyes; blue serge suit, black tie and a striped shirt; fair hair with a crescent of baldness running across the high brow, he looked like nothing. Somewhere, he had another life, slept, ate, dreamed, and knew people. But where or how had no concern for Raikes.

Berners, fidgeting to go, said, "I suppose we should have a bottle of champagne or something?"

Raikes smiled. "It's a bit late for us to start being conventional."

"Then that's it."

Raikes stood up, taking the file. They went out together and stood in the entrance while the porter went to find a cab.

Berners shuffled his feet a little, and Raikes waited for what he knew was coming. Knew because it was in himself, too.

"What happens if anything goes wrong in the future?"

Raikes shrugged his shoulders. "We handle it on our own. From now on you don't exist for me."

The taxi drew up and Raikes went towards it, Berners

4

lagging with him a little. No goodbye, no firm handshakes. A partnership had ended, the books had been closed.

To the cab-driver and for Berners to hear, Raikes said, "Charing Cross station." The porter opened the door for him and he got in, half turning for a moment to smile and nod at Berners. Then he was away. As the taxi took the corner to swing into the Mall, Raikes slid back the glass behind the driver and said, "Not Charing Cross. Paddington."

He was in Taunton by mid-afternoon, walked to the garage for his car, and drove the forty miles home without hurry. He lived alone in the house. There was Mrs. Hamilton from the village who came in and looked after him when he wanted her. She'd left a note that she would be up at six for an hour to prepare his dinner. He went upstairs to change into old clothes, looking forward to a couple of hours on the river. Car tyres slewed over the gravel outside and a horn blew. Through the window he recognised the car. He went back to his dressing table, heard the front door open, the sound of shoes in the hall, the opening of other doors as she searched for him and then the hard trot of her heels on the polished oak boards of the stairway.

She stood in the open doorway and said, "Why didn't you shout?"

"I wanted you to have the pleasure of finding me. Where are you off to?"

"Meeting in Barnstaple and then dinner afterwards."

He moved to her and took her hands, looking at her, grinning.

At once she said, "Oh, no you don't, Andy. That's why you didn't shout. To get me up here."

"Any room would have done. Mrs. Hamilton isn't here."

He lifted her suddenly, kissed her, and carried her to the bed.

She said, "You going to carry on like this when we're married?"

"Why not? Only more often."

She shut her eyes, smiled, and sighed, "Good."

She came from this county as he did. Her father owned three thousand acres, eight hundred of it woodland and moor. All

5

that would go to her brothers and meant nothing to him. She had the right name. She moved with the right people as he and his family had always done. She *was* right. She was what he wanted and had been prepared to wait for. There were twelve years between them. They had known each other for seven and he had made love to her four days after their first meeting on a pile of bracken, six hundred feet up on Dartmoor with a moon brighter than any golden guinea in the sky. Her father had a two-inch entry in the *Directory of Directors*. Once, he and Berners had defrauded a group whose board her father was on for three thousand pounds. He had spent some of it on a diamond-set watch for her and put the rest in English China Clay shares which now stood him in at a handsome profit. If he didn't love her it was a matter of no importance. The feeling he had for her was as near to love as he would ever come. Mary Warburton. A good sound, honest name. Good breeding, good background. She would throw the kind of children he wanted.

She pulled off her dress, swearing as some button or hook caught for a moment in her hair. As she lay back he caressed the soft inside of her right thigh and unslipped the fasteners of her girdle. He came to her, ready as he always was once his hands had touched the soft hidden places of her body, and they made love with the vigour of two healthy animals.

Lying with her afterwards, close, yet detached, he said, "You name a date. Next year some time."

"Why next year?"

"Because I'm taking possession of Alverton Manor from the New Year. That's always been the place I wanted to take you to."

She leaned over him, touched the hollow of his upper lip, and said, "You mean that's the place you've always been going back to. In a way you've never left it."

"Maybe not. Keep the Alverton Manor part to yourself for a while."

"Why?"

"Because I want it that way. I want it to be something you

6

and I can get used to ... the idea of it ... on our own for a while." He slid his hand across her stomach, let it rest lightly on her pubic hairs and said, "Was it all right?"

She said, "As though you didn't know. Sometimes I think the top of my head is going to come off." She looked at her watch, the one he had given her. "Christ, I've got to make Barnstaple in thirty minutes. I'll phone you tomorrow morning."

He watched her dress, using his hard brush to tidy her dark hair, and he liked everything he saw. She was almost as tall as he was, her body brown-skinned from a recent trip to the Bahamas; good, firm breasts, no scragginess ... you put your arms around her and you knew you were holding something worth having. He lay there, completely relaxed and hardly knew it when she kissed him and ran down through the house and roared away.

This, he told himself, was the real beginning. He was back. John E. Frampton and all the others were dead. Enter Andrew Raikes, a gentleman of the County of Devon, a man of substance and property. Christ, it sounded like something from a Victorian novel. Well, let it. He was going back to Alverton, and soon he would carry a bride over the doorstep, a wife who would give him children, sit beside him when he chaired the local Conservative meetings, hunt with him, shoot with him, and manage the luncheon basket at point-to-points. ... Yes, it was pure Victorian. But that's how he wanted it. So far as he was concerned the twentieth century had only provided the means for return.

CHAPTER TWO

Two months later—mid-November and the fishing season over—he came back late in the evening from a walk by the river. It was the river where his father had taught him at eight to tie on a fly, to cast, to switchcast and to Spey roll and had hammered home the lesson that impatience had never unravelled any line tangle.

He walked back to the house knowing that he would have missed Mrs. Hamilton, moving leisurely in the dusk that was spreading indigo shadows under the trees. Going up the drive a little owl suddenly screamed in the orchard below the house.

A car was parked on the gravel under the broad cone of light from the lantern over the front door. It was a blue Rover 2000, the TC model. Looking inside he saw that the driver must be a woman. There was a pair of comfortable women's driving shoes down by the control pedals. A half-length suede jacket was thrown over the back of the driving seat. On the dash shelf was a bottle of nail varnish, some emery files, and a small packet of tissues. Going up the house steps he saw that there was a light on in his sitting room.

The sitting room door was six inches ajar. The car had a Kent number plate. MKE 800F. The woman had to be a stranger. He didn't like strangers in his house.

Moving up to the door he saw her hand resting on his small chairside table, the long fingers toying with the fluting of a cut-glass tumbler which was half full of whisky. No rings. A long, slender-fingered hand, the nails painted a dark cerise.

He went in. She sat in a chair facing him. For a few moments

8

they looked at one another without speaking. She had a long, pale face, attractive, but coarsened by the thick lining of lipstick and heavy eye-shadow. The hair was auburn, faintly wavy, and drawn heavily to one side so that her left ear and the pale sweep of left temple seemed over-isolated, vulnerable. She wore a single row of pearls around her neck, a plain white jumper and a green skirt that came well above the turn of her knees. The shoes she wouldn't wear while driving were white leather with long, thin heels.

She stood up, almost as tall as he was, and said, "I hope you don't mind. Your Mrs. Hamilton let me in to wait as she was going. Also . . . well . . ." She gave a nervous laugh that went with the voice, a little coarse under the careful manner. "I helped myself to some of your whisky. You are Mr. Raikes, aren't you? Andrew Raikes?"

"Yes, I am."

"I'm Belle Vickers. A least, I've always been called that. Mabel exactly. Ghastly, isn't it?"

"Oh, I don't know. It's quite a nice name." He gave her a smile and sensed the nervousness begin to drop from her. He went round her to the sideboard, poured whisky for himself and, siphon in hand, I said "What can do for you, Miss Vickers? Please sit down." He waved her back into her chair and then splashed soda into his glass.

She sat down, sipped at her drink and said, "Well, it's just that I've sort of got a message for you."

"What is it?"

He came round, facing her in the chair.

Suddenly, she said, "Christ, this is awful. I don't like doing it at all. He just said that I was to give you the message and also this which was to make you understand that it was all genuine."

He sat down, resting his elbows on his knees, nursing his glass in both hands, watching her fiddling about in her bag.

She handed him an envelope, thick manilla, sealed with red wax in five places, the cover plain.

9

"I don't know what's in it. I have to hand it to you, sealed like that, and also—" she was fumbling in her bag again, "—I've got to have a receipt from you that it was delivered with the seals unbroken. Here."

She handed him a piece of paper and a ballpoint pen. He put them down on the side table and broke open the envelope. Inside was a small sheet of white paper. On it was written—*John E. Frampton.* He stared at it for a while, then he lifted his glass and drained it. Miss Vickers watched him nervously.

He got up and went to the fireplace. With his lighter, he set fire to the paper, held it by the corner as it burnt away and then dropped the ash into the fireplace and stirred it with a poker. He came back, signed the receipt and handed it with the pen to Miss Vickers. She avoided his look. He gave her a warm smile and took her glass.

"I think we could both do with another drink, don't you?"

She nodded and started her clumsy fumbling in the bag again. This time for her cigarettes and lighter. He let her get on with it and refilled her glass. Nervous Miss Belle Vickers. One day he was going to kill her.

He brought her drink back. She gave him an apologetic smile, her hand shaking a little as she took the glass.

"And the message?"

"Tomorrow morning I have to drive you to an appointment. It will take us about three hours."

"I see."

The shock was deep in him, but he was handling it easily, the long years behind him, all training for this moment which he had hoped would never come; would have wagered could not come, because he and Berners had been so careful. Somewhere there must have been a conjunction of time, place and personality which they could never have foreseen.

"I'll call for you just after nine."

"Where are you staying tonight?" For a stupid moment he entertained the idea that if a thing were to be done then it should be done quickly. At once he rejected the stupidity.

"At Eggesford. At the Fox and Hounds."

She smiled. She was easier with herself now. One hand went up and smoothed the sweep of auburn hair. Then, less from sympathy but, he felt, almost claiming some kinship in misfortune with him, she went on, "I'm sorry I had to bring the news. Don't think I don't know how you feel. At least I think I do. Something like it happened to me."

"It's a man, of course?"

"Yes. But don't ask me questions about him. About anything. I just have to take you to him. Maybe it won't be anything like as bad as you imagine. I mean . . . well, with me it wasn't. In some ways it was a good thing, except . . ." Her voice trailed away.

"Except what?"

"Well, except that ever since—no matter how good parts have been—I've never been my own person. Me, I mean. But maybe it will be different with you. You're a man, and men aren't easy to possess, are they? Not like a woman. In a way, it's almost what we want to be . . . Oh, I don't know. I guess I'm just talking. Knowing how you must feel. Seeing that it was me, too, that had to come here."

She was trying to comfort him. He didn't need it. He was right out of the range of comfort. It was a waste of time. There was only the future sliding towards him and he standing, preparing for it, knowing he was going to bend it his way.

He gave her his warm smile, automatically, knowing that she would think he had been grateful for comfort, and he reached down and helped her to her feet.

"Don't worry about me. But tomorrow, don't come up here. I'll be on the road down below, waiting for you."

He walked out to the car with her and opened the driving door. As she bent to get in, the nape of her neck was below him, defenceless and vulnerable. One hard chop with the side of his hand could kill. But it would do no good now. She was not the one, not the first one.

She reached for the ignition key, her head turned sideways

II

to him, the pale, over-dressed face sympathetic and she trotted out for him the comforting clichés which she thought would help. "I really do know how you feel. Not that men show it like women. With me there was almost a panic. But it was all right in the end. Anyway, better than it might have been."

He watched the car clear the drive and then went back into the house.

She lay in the hotel bed, remembering him and the room. At first she had thought she wasn't going to like him. He'd looked at her and it was all there. Not liking or, maybe, not approving of her. She knew his type, knew that voice, the way they were so sure of themselves, that something they had right from the beginning which even when they came down in the world they never lost though you might meet them serving behind a grocery counter. But even so, she had been sorry for him. He was probably having a horrible time at this moment. Didn't she know, hadn't she gone through it herself? Anyone in his position would have to be afraid. If he were to come into her room now, she would take him into her bed and give him the comfort of her body and the warmth of a few minutes' oblivion. Then, moving her long legs under the sheets, she knew that she was a liar. To hell with comfort and oblivion . . . She would have liked him here as a man. What she wanted was the hardness of a male, the long, rapacious spasms of passion. He was her kind of man. He had to be to be in this fix. He wasn't the first she had handed a wax-sealed envelope to. But he was the first that had taken it without showing one moment of weakness. Yes, he was different, and because he was different, she knew that there was a lot she would like to give him. She thought of the hard, contained length of him, the blunt, composed, intelligent face, that smile that slowly embraced you, and the steady, seldom blinking blue eyes.

She sat up, switched on the light and found a cigarette.

Smoking, she stared at the untidy dressing table, seeing herself in the mirror.

Mabel Vickers. Born, 7th February, 1945. (That made her Aquarius). Today in the *Daily Mail* her horoscope had read, 'There is harmony in the air; you will make new friends and cement old ties.' She didn't care a damn about cementing old ties, but new friends were always welcome if they had something to give, something one wanted.

Her father—a gunner in an A.A. regiment—had been killed in a lorry accident in Italy a month before she was born, which was a good thing really because, much too late for her ever to care about it, she had learned that he wasn't her father. Still, she thought of him as her father, though he was only a name and face in photographs and a lot of vague and contradictory chat by her mother. Her mother had married again in 1947; a vigorous, full-bodied woman with little thought in her head for anything which did not concern herself; a cheerful, happy woman, the life and soul of any party that revolved around a crate of stout and a couple of bottles of gin. She'd married a publican and they'd moved to a small pub at Headington, just outside Oxford. From there, when she was seventeen, after some indifferent schooling and six hard months at a secretarial college she, Belle then for many years, had gone to work as a typist in the Morris Cowley Works. Six months afterwards her stepfather had taken to coming into her bedroom at night, usually a little tight, talking to her, teasing her with happy horseplay that had slowly turned into mucking about with her. When she had complained to her mother, her mother, highly amused, but wanting no trouble, had given her fifty pounds out of the till money at the end of a week, and she had gone to London.

During 1962 she had shared a flat with two other girls and worked at the Prudential Assurance offices in Holborn and had begun—she didn't know why—to do a little shoplifting in her lunch hour. It had been at Marks and Spencers and Woolworths at first because they were easy, and then the more expensive stores. She had sold the stuff mostly to her flat mates and their friends, explaining that she had contacts in the trade and got things cheaply. She had never been caught. Her first really complete and satisfactory sexual relationship had been with a married man at the beginning of 1963. He took a room at a West End hotel once a week, arriving at six, stripped, did his exercises in front of the window, and then made love to her until seven o'clock. Between them, in the next quarter of an hour, they drank half a bottle of whisky, and then he went. He thought her shoplifting a great joke, had encouraged it, and had taken over the marketing end. In the middle of 1963, she had changed her job and gone to work as a secretary in the City offices of the Overseas Mercantile Bank in Cannon Street. A month later she gave up shoplifting because she suddenly discovered that she had a head for figures and accounts and a right hand that was extraordinarily facile at forging. Her married lover was delighted with her new talent, rewarded her by staying one complete night a week at the hotel and, every two months, a long weekend at Brighton. Between them they set a target of twenty thousand pounds and then they were to leave for the Lebanon where he had contacts. He was a little annoyed when she insisted on keeping her fraud-gained money in her own account. During this period she was frequently unfaithful to him, mostly from curiosity and a feeling that a woman's experience should not be narrowly limited. Love she knew nothing about, but she was growing up fast. At the beginning of 1964 the married man had disappeared off the face of the earth. (She had always thought, still did, that this had something to do with Him, but she had never been able to confirm it.) Him, among other, many other things was the Chairman of the Overseas Mercantile Bank. He had called her into his private office, locked the door, and complimented her on her skill with figures and accounts, and the talent she possessed in her right hand. Her moments of panic had not lasted long and she had accepted the contract offered to her. The endorsement had been made, after she had removed her panties,

14

on the thick pile of the office carpet and was witnessed by a long line of photographs of past chairmen of the Bank from the panelled walls. It had not occurred to her to take, even for a fleeting moment, the other alternative which meant the simple picking up of the office telephone by him. She was promoted to be his private and personal secretary—one of many—and changed her place of work. From then, until now, she had served him efficiently and faithfully, submitted to him when he needed her, and had seldom paused to consider whether she was happy or otherwise. For the last four months he had shown no need of her body, but his consideration, affection and discipline over her remained the same. He was not the kind of man to throw away anything that still might have some use.

Tomorrow she would take Andrew Raikes to him. She might never know what contract would be made between them, but she knew that Raikes, whatever he thought he was now, would never be the same again.

He met her on the road below the house just after nine. She wore now a navy-blue dress with tan collar and cuffs. Pinned above her left breast was an old silver two-franc piece converted into a brooch. She was still too heavily made up.

She drove fast but well and he watched the roads, knowing them all. No attempt was being made to conceal their destination from him. Somewhere, a long way east of Exeter, he said out of the blue, over the low sound of the car radio which she had switched on when their desultory conversation had withered, "What do you know about me?"

"Very little. Your name, where you live. Before I came, a few photographs . . . description. But really of you, nothing."

"Whoever he is, I imagine he's waited a long time?"

"Probably. It's a kind of talent in him. Knowing and waiting."

A passing signpost gave him the name of Winchester somewhere ahead. He had a picture of chalk streams, waving weed

15

beds, ranunculus, stiff water celery stalks and the bulge of a
brown trout nymphing just below the surface. Fishing, of course,
had been his pocket nirvana. He had always known that.
Something to shut some part of the world out. With his father
it had simply been the gentle pursuit, the mild and happy com-
plement of a country life. His father, a gentle old man, had let
the world take and cheat him, and had then done what had to
be done, dispossessed himself and, that over, had quietly died.
Not from shock, or a broken heart, but out of pure contempt for
a world that no longer held anything for him.

An hour later, from a side road she turned into the open
gates of a secondary driveway. Far away, over parkland, he
caught a glimpse through elms of a large, grey stone mansion.
He saw her look at her wristwatch. She had an instruction to
have him here on time. Ahead of them a small lake appeared.
She drew in at its side. The surface was dense with water lily
pads. Ten yards from the bank a water hen jerked its way
between the pads.

She said, "There's a waterfall at the end of the lake. You
go up the steps at the side. At the top there's a summer house.
He'll be there."

"And you?"

"I shall be here when you come back."

He got out and moved away, pushing his hands into the
pockets of his tweed jacket. Going up by the waterfall, the
sunlight making a small rainbow in the mist of the spray, he
felt the flick of water on his face as the slight breeze fanned it
over the steps. The summer house was built with a pagoda
style roof. A teak verandah ran along its face.

He went across the verandah and stopped just inside the
door. The whole floor plan was one large room. Windows broke
all four walls and in the spaces between them were murals, one
long design running the full lengths of the walls; a tropical
landscape, green, blossom-thick jungle, the blue, yellow and red
of macaw and parrot, the chocolate pelts of monkeys and the
tawny hides and black-and-white stripes of animals. A glass-

16

topped table supported on white-painted wrought iron legs filled most of the centre of the room. A smaller, similarly designed table stood against one of the side walls, holding bottles, glasses, a pile of magazines, a brown-paper wrapped parcel, and cigarette and cigar boxes. An electric clock, large faced, with bronze hands and bronze stars for the hours faced him from high in the wall opposite. His eyes went round, taking everything in, recording, filing, never to forget.

Standing near one of the side windows, watching him, was a man about five feet high. He wore a white silk shirt, blue linen slacks and white shoes. The man's face was ugly, the skin red, the features squashed as though at some time an immense hand had been clamped on it to screw and deform everything. Parts of the skin had a high, glabrous shine, and both ears stood well out from the skull. The hair was a grey-white fuzz, cut short and laid evenly over the top of his large head like a cheap, dirty carpet, white once, trodden flat and worn filthy now. Breaking the distorted planes of his face was a large, untidy, scruffy, brown moustache, theatrical and comic. Under one arm he carried a slim, yellow leather brief case.

Without moving, he said, "Sit down, Mr. Raikes."

Raikes sat down on a chair at the end of the table. The man opened his brief case and slid a folder over the glass top to Raikes.

"You can study that while I get you a drink."

Raikes said, "Who are you?"

"The name is Sarling. John Eustace Sarling. You've heard of it?"

"Yes."

"Then we needn't bother with any more for the moment. As a name it is a good name. It's a pity that it carries such an ugly face. Just look through the file. You usually drink brandy and ginger ale at this time of day—correct?"

"Yes."

Sarling's voice was quiet, evenly-paced. He could have been

17

a doctor tactfully and skilfully allaying the rise of alarm in a patient.

Raikes opened the file. There were some sheets of lined foolscap inside clipped together. The first page was covered, in red ink, with a neat handwriting, widely paragraphed.

Raikes read—

Andrew Ferguson Raikes. Third and only surviving son of Anthony Banks Raikes and Margaret Raikes (née Ferguson). Born 14th May, 1930 at Alverton Manor, Eggsford, N. Devon. Prep. school. Dragon, Oxford. Pub. school. Blundell's, Tiverton.

It was all there, baldly laid out. Two elder brothers, both killed in the Second World War, Royal Navy, Submarine service. Death of mother, 1945. Sale of Alverton Manor, 1947. Death of father, 1948. He read it all, mechanically, not letting memory or emotion play any part.

A brandy and ginger was put at his elbow. He read on, glancing up once to see Sarling sitting at the other end of the table, a glass of milk in front of him.

The last paragraph on the page read—

Two years with investment analysis department of Grubb, Starkes & Pennell, Moorgate. Left Jan. 1950, voluntarily. From this point never in legitimate employment or business again, and never used his real name for any operation.

Raikes flipped through the following pages. Each one was headed in block letters with one of his aliases or the name of one of the companies, businesses or projects he had set up. Martin Graham, the P.P. Trading Company (that had been mail order stuff), John Hadham Properties (that had been only a short time after he had brought Berners in), Felix S. Snow, Beauty Pack Ltd., John E. Frampton, Billings, Hurst & Brown, Silverton Suppliers (that had been their first venture in the wine business), Angus Homesteads ... almost the whole roll call came up before him, and with it the memory of one-man offices, rented warehouse space, derelict, vacant lots with Berners going down first thing in the morning to stick up a phoney notice board and he arriving in the afternoon with some client who had been lunched and wined well and thought that he was chiselling him into a cheap option. At one time they used fifteen different lots without the slightest claim or title to them.

Without a glance at Sarling, he went back and read in detail one or two of the accounts. Somebody had done a good job for him. He read the John Hadham Properties details. Berners' name was mentioned, but no information about him was given. He moved on, checking the others. Berners was mentioned again and again, but no comment was made against his name, no biographical facts given. Almost as though Sarling had been reading his mind, his voice came from the end of the table—

"I have a separate file in here of Berners." He tapped the brief case in front of him. "Take your time, read it all through."

Raikes closed the file. "There's no need. You've made your point. So what?"

"So now we can come to an understanding. Let me make two things clear, Mr. Raikes. First, I have an enormous respect and appreciation of your powers, your industry and your intelligence—but above all of your ability to organise not only people but affairs." He nodded at the file. "That record must be unique. Any other man, any other brilliant man, would never have had half the run you've had. That is why I need you. And, secondly, let me assure you, I mean you no harm. But you must know this already, otherwise it would have been the police who visited you and not my Miss Vickers." He smiled and the face was grotesque, but there was a warmth, almost a kindness, in the cloudy brown eyes. "As a matter of interest—because of the Bank Act I couldn't check it of course—how much have you made over the last fourteen or fifteen years?"

Raikes smiled, too, the professional smile, the first move to some relationship which was going to serve him better than Sarling. There was no alarm in him, no anxiety. All that remained was the handling of the situation—and that must go only one way, to his own advantage. There was a lot he wanted to know before he could frame the first positive move.

19

He said, "Somewhere around three hundred thousand pounds."

"How much did you give for Alverton Manor?"

"Thirty-five thousand."

Sarling nodded at the file. "That's what most of that was about, wasn't it?"

"Most of it. My father trusted his friends, particularly his City friends. He believed what they said, because he thought that was how friendship was. Even in disaster he accepted their explanations and their solutions for recouping his losses. In the end he lost everything, even the house where the family had lived for over four hundred years. I'm not sentimental about it. It's a fact. He lost everything, and then he died. What did he have to live for? I just told myself that I would get it all back from the kind of people who had taken it from him. I didn't reason or argue with it. I just saw it as the thing I had to do before I could take up the kind of life which I really wanted."

"Which was?"

"To be a rich man, to live again in the house which was ours, to enjoy simple things but to know that I could have the luxuries which might now and then appeal to me. I believe in continuity, Mr. Sarling. A very different thing from survival."

"Did it never occur to you that you've done all this for different reasons? That you've done it simply because you are the kind of man who could have no satisfaction from life unless he lived dangerously? Have you ever considered that?"

"I've considered it."

"And?"

"I want exactly what I've said I want. To go back to Alverton and live my way. Why else do you think I took so much trouble with all this?" He tapped the file. "If the police had come to me, I would have killed myself. Now, perhaps you'll answer some questions of mine."

"So far as I can."

"What was it that led you to all this? What mistake did Berners or I make?"

"In a sense there was no mistake. Only the result of two manias—yours and another man's. He died six months ago. But he compiled your file, that of Berners, and those of quite a few other people. People who have something to hide, people who have never been touched by the police, never been suspected by the police . . . people, some of whom I have used, some I will use and some, quite a few perhaps, who will never be used, and never even know they could have been used. You see, Mr. Raikes, I collect certain sorts of people in the way other wealthy men collect paintings, sculptures, rare books, what-you-will. I've found it very profitable. The man who investigated you for me was in my regular employ. He was a German. His name Wurther. He came here after the war. During the war he worked for the Gestapo. He had a mania for detail. Set him a problem and he was in torment until he had solved it, and when he had solved it he was in torment until he had a new one to solve. He was fifty-four when he died, burnt out. You remember, of course, Silverton Suppliers?"

"Of course." Raikes got up and went to the small table to get himself another drink. He didn't ask; he knew that already their relationship had moved fast, beyond small preliminary courtesies.

"You sold it—and a brilliant, shameless fraud it was, cooked books, false receipts and contracts and a warehouse stock which was three hundred per cent overvalued—to the Astoria Wine Company. They were expanding fast and in a hurry to grab small outfits before their rivals got to them. Greed makes most men careless. Well, the Astoria Wine Company was a subsidiary of a large holding concern of which I was chairman. When the fraud was discovered I put Wurther on to an examination of Silverton Suppliers. Not an official one. My own personal one. You remember your small office in Duke Street?"

He remembered it well. A good address and all the solid, expensive office furnishings on hire-purchase, but sold with the business as assets. A warehouse in Camberwell and seventy-five percent of the stock rubbish. He and Berners had worked a solid seventy-two hour stretch to set up the stock display. He came back with his drink. "We made a mistake?"

"Not that the official investigation revealed. But in one of the desk drawers, amongst all the fraudulent, faked official correspondence and so on, there was a copy of that year's Anglers' Catalogue from the House of Hardy. I don't think you would have left it there knowingly. It must have got hidden between the other stuff. The catalogue had been handled quite a bit. Wurther loved nothing better than such a trivial detail to start from. There was only one mark in the catalogue, and that was a small red ballpoint dot against a rod. A man who makes a mark against an item like that probably wants it, probably will get it. Hardy's is in Pall Mall, five minutes from Duke Street. All he had to do was to get a list of everyone that year who had purchased such a rod and then begin to sort through and investigate twenty, maybe fifty names. It was the kind of work he loved, the kind he fed on."

"I'm sure a firm like Hardy's wouldn't have given you access to their books." He knew the rod all right. It had been a Hardy-Wanless spinning rod. He could see the details on the page now with a photograph alongside it of a ten-pound Spey Springer caught by . . . J. L. Hardy it must have been. A red ballpoint dot, and a ferretting man called Wurther.

"No. He didn't even ask them. Wurther likes things to be difficult. His Gestapo training had taught him that there were always ways and means. He once broke into a stockbroker's office for me three nights running and got photocopies of a month's dealings which I wished to have. No one in the office even knew that there had been a break-in. In your case it took him five months to get what he wanted—and I never knew how he did it. But he got the list of names—and then he checked every name, and photographed each person, unknown to them of course. We had four descriptions of you, not all agreeing. Wurther eliminated the list down to about six possibles. You were amongst them. To a man like Wurther, it was from then on just a matter of time before he isolated you.

Would you call the red ballpen mark a mistake on your part? I suppose you would. For his own amusement Wurther went back into some of your past operations. Making up the file on Berners was a comparatively simple matter after all that."

"Have you got hold of Berners too?"

"No. I'm leaving that to you. But I need you both."

"Can't you leave him out of it?"

"No. I want you both."

"For what?"

"At the moment I don't propose to tell you. Let me make it clear that this is one operation only. After it is done you will both be free to go back to the lives you want to lead and never be troubled by me again. Also, you'll be paid handsomely. You may need other help. For that you can draw on the people who are on my files."

"This is some illegal operation?"

"Naturally."

Raikes slewed round in his seat and sipped at his drink. Through the window he could see a fold of parkland with sheep grazing and beyond that a long run of red brick boundary wall. He put his glass down on top of his file and said quietly, "You've Berners' file in your brief case. I've got mine here. I don't care a damn about the rest. Why shouldn't I kill you now as you sit there, then go back and kill Miss Vickers, burn the files and disappear?" He took his right hand from his jacket pocket and laid an automatic on the table top.

Sarling ran one hand over the disfigured, patched-up face, flexing his mouth to tauten the skin over his chin. He said, "You would do it?"

"Yes."

"Have you ever killed anyone before?"

"No."

"Yet you know you can do it?"

"Yes. It would be no more to me than tapping a trout on the head with a priest."

"Good. Well, to put your mind at rest—I have photostatic

23

copies of all the files. They are in an envelope addressed to my lawyers with a message stating that in the event of my death by violence or in ambiguous circumstances the envelope is to be opened. If I die naturally the envelope and contents are to be burned unopened. So you see I am well covered."

"Just one job, but for the rest of our lives we will be in your hands?"

"Except that you will know what we have done together, so I shall be placing myself in your hands, too. Surely that's an equitable arrangement?"

"Is it?"

"You have reservations about it?"

"You know I have. What is more, you don't need me to name them."

"You must take my word for it. I am the exception that proves the rule." He stood up. "I think that's all we need to say to one another at the moment. I shall be in touch with you very soon." He went to the side table.

From behind him, Raikes said, "How much does Miss Vickers know of me?"

"Nothing of what is in the file."

"Or what it is you want us to do?"

"No." Sarling came back to him. "Berners' real name is Aubrey Catwell. He lives at No. 3 Princess Terrace, Brighton. You'd better get in touch with him. Here." He held out the brown paper parcel which Raikes had seen on the small table.

"What is it?"

"A present. Something I thought you would like. Don't bother to open it now."

He went out of the summer house ahead of Raikes and, without turning or saying goodbye, walked away from the top of the waterfall, taking a small path that disappeared into a yew walk. Raikes watched him out of sight and then went back to the car.

Belle Vickers was behind the wheel, waiting.

"Straight back?"

"Straight back."

She drove off. After a while, she said, "It's a curious thing about his face. After a time you don't notice it."

Suddenly angry, he said, "So far as I'm concerned it's going to be clearly in my mind until the day I see him dead. And you needn't bother to tell him because he knows!"

They were back by five o'clock. She left him at the bottom of the drive.

In the house was a message from Mrs. Hamilton that Miss Warburton had telephoned. He didn't care who had telephoned. He was in a rare mood of real anger and he knew that there was nothing to do but to wear through it before he could think straight.

He opened the present from Sarling. It was a copy of Dame Juliana Berner's *Treatise of Fishing with the Angle*—the first book on fishing in the English language, and also the first book on fly fishing. This was a facsimile of the 1496 edition, published in 1880. Inside it on a separate piece of paper was a note in Sarling's handwriting. It read—*Please collect your instructions on Monday next (27th) at Flat 10, Galway House, Mount Street, W.1.*

The ugly-faced bastard could just as easily have told him this during his visit. He poured himself a large glass of whisky and the anger roared on inside him. Until this day he had been his own man. Now he was somebody else's and it hurt. He jerked a copy of *Who's Who* out of the bookshelf and slammed it open, ripping the pages over until he found him. All right, all right, he told himself, ride with it for a while, get it out of your system now, here in this house, and finish with it, and then begin to think.

Here it was. John Eustace Sarling. His master. And all because of a red dot in a catalogue. Leaving the catalogue *had* been his mistake. The only one in over fifteen years. He had the rod still. The first time he had used it he had taken a six-pound sea-trout, fresh run over Colleton Weir, on the

25

Fox and Hounds water. Betrayed by the thing you loved best. Irony in that. Well, there had to be something that Sarling, John Eustace, born 21st December, 1908, had to have, too. Something he loved, something that would betray him, something that would let him get his hands on the files and the photostatic copies and then put a bullet through the skin-grafted forehead. Nothing about where he was born, no parents mentioned, no education, no sons, no daughters, no wife, no trivia listed, just a straight jump from birth to *Chairman: Sarling Holdings; Stanforth Shipbuilding Co. Ltd.; Suburban & North Investments Ltd.; Overseas Mercantile Bank Ltd.;* a great string of companies, running through to *Is also Director of a number of public companies engaged in commercial and industrial enterprises. Address: Downham House, Park Street.* Maybe that was where the photostats were kept, or perhaps they were at Meon Park, Wiltshire which was his country address.

He put the book away and sat down, staring straight ahead of him.

He heard the front door open and footsteps down the hall. Mrs. Hamilton put her face round the door.

"So you're back." She looked at the glass in his hand. "Isn't it a bit early for that?"

Suddenly he felt sane and calm. "Don't you start bullying me."

"That'll be the day. You rung Miss Mary yet?"

"No."

"Then do it."

"I will."

She went through to the kitchen, leaving all the doors open and he heard her begin to clatter about. She was sixty-five and her black hair showed few traces of white. When he had been seven years old and she the cook at Alverton she had taken his trousers down and leathered his backside because in a moment of rage he had called her a 'bloody old bugger'; and old Hamilton, her husband, had carried him home the first time he had ever got drunk on cider, harvesting.

He reached out for the phone and called Mary. The following evening he took her out to dinner in Exeter and told her that from the beginning of the week he would be in London for a while. He gave her no details, offered no explanation. He never had with her. When he had been away before on his various projects with Berners he had merely been in London on business where it was understood that he had a large number of property interests. She showed no curiosity about his London life largely because she came from the kind of family in which the menfolk seldom discussed their business affairs with the women. In the past, too, whenever he had been staying in London, although he used hotels, he also booked a room at his club and stayed there the odd night and always looked in during the day to see if there were any messages for him. If he wanted to speak to her he always called her from the club.

In the train going up to Paddington on Monday morning everything was settled in his mind. Sarling had to go, and after Sarling, Belle Vickers had to go. There would be no peace or security for him or Berners until they were both dead. But first a way had to be found of getting the files and the photostats.

He took a taxi to the Connaught Hotel and then walked slowly up Mount Street. Galway House was almost opposite Scott's Restaurant. He went in and walked the plum-carpeted stairs to the second floor. Number 10 was at the end of the right-hand corridor and on its right-hand side. Before he went in he knew that its main windows would overlook Mount Street. On the entrance door was a small brass card-holder. The pasteboard slip in it read—Mr. and Mrs. Vickers.

He rang the bell and the door was opened by Belle Vickers. The sight of her made him feel belligerent and ungracious.

She said, "I thought you might get here about now. I looked up the Taunton train times."

She went ahead of him and showed him round the flat. It was like a hundred others, a hallway, cloakroom, a large lounge with a small dining recess at a far window that over-looked the street, two bedrooms with a bathroom and toilet between, and a small kitchen. To anyone who knew their way around and had the money it could have been completely furnished in an hour's visit to Harrods. He came back from his inspection and began to make a drink at the sideboard in the lounge.

She said, "I'll have a gin and tonic. I've fixed some cold meat and salad if you feel hungry."

"Thank you."

He gave her her drink and made himself a brandy and ginger ale. The brandy was Hines and it was sacrilege to put ginger ale in it, but there was no other. Only the best for Mr. Sarling's colleague.

Looking round the room, cataloguing it, docketing everything away, he said, "Rented, furnished?"

"Yes."

"For how long?"

"I don't know."

"In your name?"

"Yes."

"Tell Sarling when you see him, that I want full details of the agreement."

She said, "It's going to be difficult if you're going to go on being angry."

He shook his head. "It's a luxury I'm allowing myself until I know what I'm expected to do—and be."

He walked over to the far wall. There was a picture on it showing a stampede of white horses against a flat, marsh-like, Camargue background. He straightened it the half-inch that it was out of true and said, "What's behind it?"

"The safe."

She began to fumble in her handbag for the key.

"Don't bother. You can give it to me later." He walked to the telephone and looked at the subscriber's number in the centre of the dial. Turning, he said, "When does Sarling arrive?"

"So far as I know he doesn't."

28

"What do you mean?"

"There's a sealed letter from him in the safe. You'll have to give me the usual receipt. After that, if there's anything you want then you have to ask me."

"And how often are you going to be here?"

She hesitated for a moment, and then said, "My instructions are that I am to live here with you and put myself entirely at your disposal. I can fetch my things in this afternoon."

He looked at her. The long, narrow chin was tipped a little defiantly, but not very convincingly. He knew that from the moment he had entered he had been upsetting her but it didn't matter. He could reverse all that in a few hours if he wanted to, and he almost certainly would. She hadn't been quite so heavy with her make-up but she was wearing her hair pouffed up on top of her head so that it looked like a ridiculous bird's nest affair. She wore a tight black jumper that left her arms bare from just below the shoulders, and long, close-fitting pink trousers. He followed the long line of her legs, marked the flat stomach above the slight pelvic thrust, and the press of her large breasts against the jumper. She had a good body.

He said, "If I should object strongly?"

"Those are my instructions. You would have to take it up with him. Do you want to eat here ... I mean alone if you want? I could go and get my things."

"There's no need. You can get them after lunch." He walked over to her. "I'm sorry if I've upset you. But this kind of situation can put you in a bit of a bastard mood. All right?" He smiled, picked up his case and carried it into one of the bedrooms.

She went into the kitchen, put on a small apron and began to make a salad dressing. She found herself wondering whether he would like it the way she was doing it. He'd got her disturbed right down to the pit of her guts. That bastard Sarling. "*You live with him, do what he wants, and watch him.*" What was she, some bloody detective, or a woman who just wanted out of the whole stinking trap? She caught sight of her face in the small mirror over the kitchen table. It was such an unhappy face that she had to laugh at herself. Whoah, Belle. Always darkest before the dawn . . . Christ, why is it that nothing I ever do for myself turns out the way I'd seen it? Look at that hair. That bloody little hairdresser had said it would make her look so good. It made her look like a freak. She began to peel two eggs she had hard boiled for the salad. One of them, still soft, broke in her hand and covered her fingers with yolk. That bastard in there, making her feel ten inches high . . . She wanted him to be nice to her. She wanted to be nice to him. Any kind of niceness he wanted. But all she'd got—without a chance for her to give anything—was this nervousness in her.

CHAPTER THREE

BEFORE SHE WENT he gave her a receipt for the contents of the safe. They were a sealed letter from Sarling and a bulky brown-paper parcel. The parcel held, in notes of one, five and ten pounds' denomination, two thousand pounds. He didn't bother to check the amount. Where money was concerned he was sure that both she and Sarling would be meticulous.

With the girl out of the way he sat down, lit a cigar—there was a box of Bolivar Regentes on the sideboard—and opened the envelope. Clipped together were some sheets of lined quarto writing paper covered in Sarling's large script. He read:

Conduct of operations and communications from Mount Street. Miss Vickers will take care of commissariat and all incidental financial aspects. All communications with me will be made through her.

Payments to outside people for operational duties, or retainers pending operational duties, will be made in cash from the two thousand pounds provided.

Chain of command, some security notes. At no time will you, in dealing with subordinates, let it be known that there is anyone in authority over you. At no time in dealing with subordinates will you use your real name or reveal your Mount Street address. The only people known personally to one another will be me, you, Berners, and Miss Vickers.

Selection of operators. There are in existence at Park Street—Downham House—the files of over fifty people—men and women—who have, to choose an all-embracing

31

word, certain *discrepancies* in their past. On indication to Miss Vickers of the type of person required she will supply a selection of files from which a choice can be made.

Raikes leaned back in the chair and blew a cloud of smoke towards the stampeding horse picture. He read on, almost bored now, anger and belligerency long gone from him.

There was some more stuff about security details and the need for the minimum appearance of himself and Miss Vickers in public together. Why that, when the whole of Galway House would know within a fortnight that they were living together up here? Didn't Sarling know the world held porters, postmen, chars and nosey neighbours?

The last sheet of paper was headed PRELIMINARY OPERATION, and read:

1. All the relevant facts appertaining to this operation are listed below. The success of this operation is vital to the main one to follow. It will be planned by you and Berners. Only one condition is imposed by me. The operation must be completed within the next two weeks.

2. There is an Army Supply Depot at M.R. 644550. Ordnance Survey Sheet No. 171 (One-inch map). Hut 5 contains six crates, painted green, with usual War Department markings, and all stencilled in white paint with the identification BATCH Z/93. SERIES GF1. One of these crates is to be stolen. All their contents are similar. The crate is to be lodged in some safe place.

3. The operation will be carried out with the minimum of violence. Either you or Berners will take an active part in it.

Raikes folded the sheets of paper carefully and put them in his inside breast pocket. Batch Z/93. Series GF1. It all sounded a far cry from the kind of operation which he and Berners had carried out.

He went out and bought himself the Ordnance map. The

Army depot was in Kent, near Wrotham. Just after he got back, Belle Vickers came in carrying a large suitcase. He got up, took it from her and carried it into the other bedroom. She took off her coat and he saw that she had changed into a plain green dress with the silver franc piece pinned to her breast.

He said, "If you make us a cup of tea we can have a chat. There are some things I want to get straight."

Over the tea he said, "Where did you go for your stuff—Park Street?"

"Yes. I'm either there or down in Wiltshire. It was more interesting, in a way, when I was in the City with him."

"You sleep with him?"

"I used to. Not now." It was so unimportant it roused no feeling in her.

"What happened to his face?"

"So far as I know it was burned when he was a young man. I don't know how."

"Have you any idea what he's after? This collecting people and using them?"

"I think it began just in a business sort of way. You know, get the dirt on someone, and then use it to swing a deal."

"And it's grown from that to something else?"

"If you say so."

"He warned you, of course, that I would pump you?"

"Yes."

"And you'll tell him that I have."

"Yes."

"You'd like to be free of him, wouldn't you?"

"Yes."

"So would I. We might do something together."

"He said you would suggest it."

"So, what's the answer?"

"I don't know."

"Well, take your time. Now let's get down to business. Have you any idea of the instructions I have received?"

"No." She was easier with him now, even though she could

33

not help a certain curtness in her tone; and, anyway, she suspected him, she just had to. He didn't care a damn for her. Just himself. How he was to get out of whatever fix it was that he was in, was all that bothered him.

"These files. I can have what I want from them?"

"That's what he said. But he'll know which ones you get."

"Right. You've got a good memory?"

"Yes."

"I want a man, somewhere in the forties, English, and who's been in the Army or the Navy. Someone who can wear a uniform and knows the drill. Someone who knows about cars and not an educated type. Someone who could look after himself in a fight. Got it?"

"Yes. Today?"

"No, tomorrow will do. I've got two weeks to work with. We'll begin as from tomorrow. That leaves us the rest of the day. Are you a good cook?"

"No. Nothing turns out right."

"Then I'll take you out to dinner."

With a touch of alarm, she said, "You can't do that. He told me we're not to be seen in public together."

He grinned. "His own words are 'a minimum appearance' in public. Once is as minimum as you can get."

He got up and moved toward his bedroom. From the door, he said, "If there's a film you would like to see we could take that in first."

They went to see *The Sound of Music* at her choosing. Within a few minutes she was completely absorbed in it. That pleased him. No matter what she'd done in the past to put herself in Sarling's hands (and it must have been something that had aroused Sarling's respect which meant that she had a courage and hardness of her own) she was at the core a romantic. He wasn't going to have any trouble with her at all. Perhaps this was Sarling's big mistake, putting her with him.

Afterwards he took her to the Pastoria in St. Martin's Street;

34

whitebait, fillet steak, and a bottle of Château Beychevelle of of which he drank little.

Walking across Leicester Square afterwards to find a taxi, he said, "I want a car tomorrow morning by ten. It's got to be a station wagon. Hire it in your name, but don't use Galway House as an address. You'd better say we want it at least for a month. I'll be back sometime in the late afternoon. Could you have the files waiting for me then?"

She nodded and he took her arm and steered her across the road. She was still probably dancing and singing somewhere with Julie Andrews. (Actually she was telling herself that he had decided to be nice to her, to play her along, and that meant, of course, that he had decided to have her gang up with him against Sarling. She enjoyed it when he was nice to her. He'd been amusing and attentive—only just now and again a touch of curtness coming in, like about the car and the files. Whether she would play along with him, she didn't know. Sarling might be odd at times but he was no fool. He had money, power, his own intelligence and the brains of other men that he could call on. This man might not have a chance against him, and for the sake of her own skin she had to be on the right side. She would have to think about it. Anyway, there was no need to make a decision yet.)

He sat and had a nightcap while she went off to bed. Down in Devon he had scores of male acquaintances and friends, but nobody who had come really close to him since school. Berners was his only friend. They were two of a kind. He smiled as he thought of the first job they had ever done together. A simple operation directed from one room in the Strand—*The International Sportsmen's Directory*; a mailing list of sports celebrities, bought from a legitimate mail-list agency for a few pounds, and then a first-class brochure to catch the eye, and a form for filling in biographical details—to be returned with a three-guinea subscription which covered the entry and a copy of the directory when published. Simple and as old as the hills, and they'd netted two thousand pounds and cleared out within three weeks. God, his father would have turned in his grave.

She was back with the car at ten minutes past ten. Quiet, efficient, no fuss, he liked that. In the flat before he left, he handed her twenty pounds.

"Buy yourself a second-hand wedding ring. We don't want any unnecessary talk about us. Have a chat with the porter sometimes, and mention your husband. And twice a week post some letters to us here. Separately and both together, Mr. and Mrs. stuff. I don't have to tell you to change the handwriting and postmarks, do I?"

Stiffly, she said, "I hadn't thought about the ring, but I'd already decided to arrange the letters. You'd like me to say something nice in the ones to you?"

He chuckled. "Plain paper will do. Sorry if I'm a bit brusque, but you know the reason why. Nobody likes a half-nelson on them and their face pushed into the dirt."

He drove down into Kent, along the A.20 to Maidstone. At Wrotham Heath he turned right past the golf course along the Mereworth road. The Army depot was two miles down the road on the right-hand side. It stood in a small wood, the trees and brush cut down to form a twenty yard ride all along the road perimeter railings. He went slowly past the entrance gate, had a glimpse of Nissen huts, decorated with fire hoses and stirrup pumps, roads lined with white washed stones, and a small hut just inside the gate. The gate was closed and there was no sign of a sentry, no sign of anyone.

He drove past it as far as a pub called the Beech Inn. He turned and went back. A hundred yards from the gate he checked to see there were no cars on the road. He slowed to a crawl and dropped the car's nearside wheels into the shallow road ditch close up against the railings. Holding the car with the brake he spun the back wheels, digging them further into the soft ground.

He got out and surveyed the car. She was nicely canted over

36

and securely held in the ditch. A car came towards him, slowed momentarily as though to stop and help and then accelerated by. He was glad. He wasn't in need of any good Samaritans. He knelt down by the bogged rear wheel, scooped up some of the loose earth, rubbed it on his trousers and face and worked it into his hands and then headed down the road for the main gate of the dump.

There wasn't the slightest nervousness in him. It was just as it always was with himself and Berners when they got under way, a cold sustained sense of confidence in their own ability and an unforced manner that made truth out of every falsehood they developed.

There was a middle-aged civilian clerk in the office. Raikes told him that he was stuck up the road and wanted to phone a garage for a breakdown truck to come and pull him out. The clerk obliged with the number of the nearest garage and in-dicated the telephone. Raikes went to it and called the garage, at the same time making a mental note of the subscriber's number on the telephone dial. While he waited, he lit a cigar-ette, chatted over his shoulder with the clerk and casually studied a layout map of the site that was pinned to the wall. It showed the roads in the dump and the huts, and obligingly each hut was numbered. Hut 5 was on the main road into the trees from the camp entrance, the third on the left. The huts on the right-hand side were even numbered.

He got the garage and arranged for them to come out and pull him from the ditch. Ringing off, he turned to the clerk, held out his filthy hands and said, "Anywhere I could have a wash-up?"

He knew there was. It had been marked on the site plan. An ablution hut between numbers six and eight up the main site road. The clerk told him where it was and he strolled up the road.

He washed up in the hut. There was no one else there. From the window he studied Hut 5 across the way. It lay end on to the road, and was entered by a normal sized door. Small

37

windows flanked the sides of the door. There were no bars across them and the door had a simple mortice lock. A soldier in battledress cycled up the road whistling and went out of sight.

Raikes went out of the back door of the ablution hut and around the back of Hut 6, which was a Nissen hut of the same style as No. 5. It had a door in the rear as well as the front. He went back down the road to the gate hut.

He thanked the clerk for his kindness and then walked up the road to the car to wait for the garage truck to arrive.

He was back in London by half-past four.

Belle Vickers was there. There were three orange-covered files on the table. On top of them were two pound notes and a two shilling piece.

He picked up the money. "What's this?"

"The change from the ring." She held out her left hand, with a plain gold band on the third finger. "You'll be glad to hear it was a very simple ceremony. Just the jeweller's assistant who patted my bottom once. He was damn sure, of course, that I wanted it for a dirty weekend. Sarling noticed it, too. He laughed. At least, I think he did. It's difficult to tell."

He gave her back the money, thrown for a moment by her mood.

"Buy some cheap brandy. I don't like using Hines with ginger ale."

"So that's it. Now we're married we have to economise?"

He gave her a grin. "You'll be surprised at what we're going to have to do—once the honeymoon is over."

He sat down and picked up the files. Apart from Berners—and he could be left in peace for the moment—he wanted one other man.

He went to visit him the next morning.

George Gilpin threw an old tyre on the bonfire, then stepped back, waiting for the black rubber to begin to frizzle and fry

38

and burst into flame, thick, smoky, sulphur yellow flame, black trails of oily smudge whirling high into the sky. Someone would phone from the bungalows up the road in a moment complaining. They always did. Every Thursday when he had his bonfire. Well, let 'em. A garage always had junk to burn, cartons, crates, old tyres, oily rags. A sword-shaped tongue of flame slashed in a great curve from the edge of the fire. He watched it grow, delight on his red, sweating face. Wonderful thing, fire.

His wife came round the corner across the garage yard and out to him on the waste plot. A wave of smoke, billowing in the wind, made him move back a few feet. He saw her coming. Someone must have phoned already. She'd got on her sky-blue office overalls with Gilpin's Garage embroidered in red across the front. Even the overalls did something for her. Shape, that's what she had, shape; and no matter how she dressed it came out and shouted at you. A jolly, rollicking, plump, plumper than it needed in places, kind of shape which was one of the delights of his life. He laid a big hand on her bottom as she stood beside him and then slid it up around her waist. Her coarse blonde hair tickled the side of his face.

"Who is it, old girl? One of the old tabbycats got her washing out. All her woollen drawers getting smuts in 'em. Which is all they ever will."

"No. Some bloke out front. Interested in a car."

"Then tell Dickie—oh, he's out, isn't he? What car?"

"The Zephyr station wagon."

"Nice to get that off me hands. O.K. Some fire, eh? Got to get rid of the rubbish." He gave her breast a squeeze. "Save us a slice of that for tonight, love."

She thumped him in the middle of his broad back and he went into the rear of the garage. He washed up in the toilet, straightened his red and white spotted bow tie and slipped on his jacket. He jerked a little more of his breast pocket handkerchief into view and gave himself an approving nod in the mirror. Good old Georgie, nice little business, always a wallet

39

of fivers to flash in the pub, have a drink everyone and meet the wife but keep your hands off her, not that I mind normally, but we've just come back from Majorca and she's a bit over sun-kissed in places. . . . The Zephyr, eh? Three hundred and fifty quid, perhaps; stood him in at two-seventy. Anyway, not a penny less than three twenty-five.

He shook his head, chiding himself in the glass. You're doing too well, Georgie; eating too well; hardly pushing forty yet and putting it on. Must be the beer.

The man was standing by the station wagon. Nice enough looking bloke. Gent. Shouldn't think he was pushed for a hundred quid ever. No crumby haggling and fencing with him. Some of them were the limit, cutting it down in half-crowns at the end and wanting you to take in a couple of old peram-bulators and a Lambretta in part exchange, and then what about hire purchase arrangements? Lived beyond their income they all did, keeping up with the bloody Joneses. Colour television in No. 1 at the beginning of the month and there was colour television all down the avenue by the end. The women shopping round the supermarkets for twopence off, bloody harassed, working themselves up for a good scream at the kids when they got in from school. Yes, a bloody hard life for some, and mostly their own fault.

"Mr. Gilpin?"

A good voice, educated. That's something you can't buy late in life.

"That's me. Not a bad looking bus, eh?"

"Smith's my name." He put out a hand.

"Glad to know you, Mr. Smith." He pumped the hand briefly. "Kind of thing you're looking for? Not a lot on the clock. But you know and I know what that means sometimes. However, we've been right over her. Nothing wrong."

"Could I try her?"

"Why not? John o'Groats and back if you like."

Chuckling, George Gilpin removed the placard from outside

the windscreen which read—GILPIN'S BARGAIN OF THE WEEK. £400. ONE OWNER ONLY.

They moved off, Mr. Smith driving.

George Gilpin chatted away. Mostly you had to because there was usually something to hide and you wanted to take the customer's mind off things. But it wasn't necessary with this car. Habit kept him at it.

"Only one owner, you know. Schoolmaster in Watford. Looked after it like a baby. His school was just around the corner, so he hardly ever drove it, 'cept once a year he used to take it abroad for a month. Great camper. Used to sleep in the back." He was going to add, "Probably with a different French tart each night," but decided against it. This bloke wasn't that kind.

They went up the road towards Hemel Hempstead, then swung away left-handed, George Gilpin giving a direction now and then, and finally hit the common at Chipperfield. George nodded at the pub on the edge of the common and said, "Hot morning. Care for a jar? They keep good beer in the Two Brewers."

"A good idea."

Ah, he was all right then. Not too toffee-nosed to drink with the hoi-polloi.

Mr. Smith sat on a bench in the garden of the pub, and George Gilpin went and fetched the beer. He raised his glass to Mr. Smith and said, "Well, here's how."

"Cheers."

"What you think of her?"

"It's quite a reasonable car. But not at four hundred." Mr. Smith smiled and went on, "If I really wanted her I'd give three-twenty or thirty. No more. But I don't want her."

"You don't want her? Then why—" What had he got here, some screwball, an awkward customer, wasting his time?

"What I really wanted was to have a quiet talk with you— well away from your wife and the garage."

"Oh. What about?"

"About you."

"That so?" He was cautious now. Nobody had anything on him, and his record was clean, and the garage was clean—that was one thing he had determined on from the start. But this bloke suddenly gave him an unquiet feeling. Sitting there, easy in his tweed suit, pulling out a silver cigarette case and lighting up, and in no hurry at all.

"You used to live in Wolverhampton, didn't you, Mr. Gilpin?"

George Gilpin decided to play it politely until he knew what it was all about. "That's right. I was a bloody good engineer. Still am. What's your business with me, Mr. Smith? Time's money, you know."

Mr. Smith nodded agreement, and said, "I imagine you remember a firm called Nardon Baines Ltd., in Birmingham. Paint and varnish manufacturers."

"Name seems familiar. But I didn't know Brum well."

"You should do, Mr. Gilpin. There was Harris and Leach— Distributors Ltd., and the West Midlands Furnishing Company."

A moment of panic struck George Gilpin and he could feel the beer turning sour in his stomach.

"Here, what the hell you getting at?"

"You were a good engineer, Mr. Gilpin. Good at anything with your hands, engines, clocks, fuses—and explosives. The three firms I've mentioned all went up in smoke over a period of a year. Nardon Baines was the last one. That went wrong. Only three quarters of it burned. The caretaker and a fireman lost their lives in the blaze, and one of the three devices you made to start fires in three separate places at once failed to work."

George Gilpin stood up. If there was fear in him, there was too much else also for him to bother about it. He said, "You're asking for trouble, Mr. Bloody Smith. I don't know what you're talking about, but I do know this—so far as I'm concerned I'll take you back to your car at the garage and after that, if I ever

42

see you again, you can take the consequences. You're a nut case."

Mr. Smith shook his head. "Sit down and don't draw attention to yourself. The Birmingham Police still have your little device and also very good records of the fingerprints on it. You were such a good craftsman, Mr. Gilpin, you would never believe that anything you made wouldn't work—so you didn't wear gloves. I know you haven't got a record—I wouldn't be here otherwise—but all I have to do is to give the police an anonymous call and you'd be in trouble. Just you, because the man who hired you and worked with you is dead. Finkel was his name. Herbert Finkel. And you never knew who he worked for. You were just anxious to collect two thousand pounds for the three jobs and come south to start your garage."

George Gilpin sat down. He was a practical man. He recognised spilt milk when he saw it and didn't bother crying over it.

He said, "You're playing a bloody dangerous game. How much?"

Mr. Smith smiled. "I want about two days, maybe a little more, of your time—and I'll pay you five hundred pounds for it and then forget that you ever existed."

"You'll pay me?"

"Yes."

"No thanks. I'd rather pay you. I got a good business, nice wife, plenty of friends. I don't do any jobs. Fact, I never did any but those three and I think I was crazy to do them 'cept I wanted some cash to start with. I hope Finkel is in hell."

"You'll do a job for me, Mr. Gilpin. Not a fire-raising job. Something quite simple. And you get five hundred."

There was no way out. He knew that. One phone call would bring the police and that would be the end and he didn't want any bloody ends. There was a lot of years of kick left in him yet and he meant to have them. He said quietly, "Well, it looks like you got me, don't it? What's the job?"

"Let's drive back. We can talk in the car."

Two hours later George Gilpin and his wife were sitting in the living room of their flat over the garage, a bottle of whisky on the table between them. George Gilpin was in his shirt sleeves and had jerked his bow tie free and opened his collar.

"I tell you, old girl—I don't know anything about the job or him. He's going to phone me when he's ready to put me in the flaming picture. All he says is, get a Land-Rover, Army type, paint it khaki green and muck it about a bit." He tapped a sheet of paper on the table in front of him. "And then he wants all these numbers on it, and them markings. Royal Artillery they are. I'm going back in the bloody army."

"Oh, no you're not. You know what you are going to do, don't you?"

"Of course I do! I'm not having him on me back for the rest of my natural. First this job and then another. I know his kind. I'm going to do the bugger. He may make me do this job, but he won't ever make me do another."

"George—you got to be careful. How you going to do it?"

"Dunno. I got to think. Depends how things are. But I'll do 'im." He drained his whisky glass and pushed it to her to refill.

She shook her head. "You've had enough."

"Maybe. Comes of feelin' sorry for oneself." He got up and went to her, standing behind her. He slipped his hand down the front of her blouse and massaged one of her big, loose breasts. "Don't worry, old girl, Georgie will fix him." He bent and kissed the top of her head. "Wonderful, ain't it? Bloke can be right down in the dumps, but one good feel of you and the world's a good place."

That evening, Belle Vickers came back to the flat just after six. Raikes was sitting by the window. He gave her a nod, watching her go into the bedroom to take her outdoor clothes off. The bird's nest hair-do had gone in favour of her old style. After a while she came back to the room and went to the sideboard to get herself a drink.

44

"Would you like one?" she asked.

"Not yet, thanks. Where've you been—Sarling?"

"Yes, I took the files back. I've also found a lock-up garage where we can keep the car. It's got a small loft over it with one of those sort of ladder affairs ... you know, that come down from the trapdoor when you pull a rope. I paid six months' rent in advance under the name of Smith. It's a turning off the Edgware Road. A bit of a walk."

"Good. How was Fu Manchu?"

She looked at him in surprise for a moment, and then laughed. "That's how you see him?"

"Why not? He's not real, is he? Some green fluid instead of blood in his veins."

"He wanted to know which man you picked."

"Did he? Well, I don't intend to tell him."

"You mean, you want to protect him just in case he isn't a man of his word?"

"Could be. Could be just bloodymindedness."

"Could be both. Though from what I've seen of you it's more likely the last."

"That's how you see me?"

She sat down and sipped her drink. "Now and then. I don't mind. Suppose I must seem the same sometimes. We're both hooked—that makes us touchy, difficult."

"If I asked you how he hooked you, would you tell me?"

"Not now. Sometime I might. What about you—would you ever tell me?"

"No. Anyway, you know enough about me. I was all set to stay where I was—then you came along with a sealed envelope. All that back there in Devon is my real life. This—" he stood up and waved a hand round the room "—is the nightmare. And it's a nightmare that will last so long as Sarling and his files are around."

"And the photostats."

"Where does he keep those? In the country, at Meon Park?"

"Yes."

45

"Did you ever consider leaving him . . . just disappearing?"

"I suppose I have. But it wouldn't work. I gave up thinking about it. Some day he'll die."

"Rich people can live for a long time. They've got the money to buy time from doctors, servants . . . places in the sun. For some people, death should be hurried."

"You're not . . . well, sort of serious about that?"

He turned, standing above her. The glass in her hand was silvered with bubbles coming up from the tonic water; the hand that carried their wedding ring, a broad, dull band of gold. There were times when just the way she spoke, her "supposes" and "well, sort ofs," irritated him, when just the sight of her roused dislike in him. But all this had to be suppressed. He needed her.

He said, "You'll see how serious I am. You think he doesn't know what kind of man I am? You know he does. He's even said it to you, hasn't he?"

She didn't answer. He put a hand down and took her chin, the grasp firm, turning her face up to him. "Hasn't he?"

"Yes."

"Well, then—let's be honest about it. I want him dead. Just that would be easy. But I want those files and those photostats. All of them. I want to see them burn. Killing him without them would be useless." He smiled. "Do you like your nice cage so much?"

"It isn't all that bad. Particularly now that he doesn't come into the cage and muck about with me. You're not really serious are you, though?"

"About wanting to kill him?"

"No. About thinking that I would . . . well, sort of help."

"Why shouldn't you? It's the obvious thing to do."

His surprise was genuine. She could tell that. Suddenly, she had a sense of sheer fright that came from looking at him, seeing him there, tall, hardset, all strength and health, talking of death—no, for God's sake, murder—as though he were discussing the day's racing form. Given security about the files

46

and photostats, he would kill. Swat Sarling out like a fly against the windowpane.

She said alarmed, "But it would be murder."

"You want to stay tied to him until he dies naturally? He's a bit crazy now. He could get worse. You might find yourself having to do something which could end up by destroying you. Anyway, I wouldn't be asking you to do much. Just a little information."

He went to the sideboard and began to mix himself a drink. She watched him. Everything he said was true. Sarling had changed since she had first known him. God knew she wanted her freedom. But even for that there could be too high a price. That was where she was different from this man. He wanted freedom and he didn't care how much he paid, or what he did. That came from the self-confidence in him, the hard certainty of his own strength and intelligence. Why, she thought, did I ever put my hand out and take that first tin of talcum powder from Marks and Spencers? A first wrong move, and me blissfully ignorant of where it was all going to lead.

She said, "What would I have to do?"

"Very little." He came over and gently drew the back of his knuckles across the long line of her chin. He was deliberately working on her. She knew that. Deep down, she wanted him to work on her . . . she had nothing, nobody . . . only a kind of urge in her, drawing her guts out, to surrender to somebody, somebody who would take her in, wrap themselves about her and give her peace.

"First of all we'd have to be loyal to one another." He gave her his warm, fear-chasing smile. "Put ourselves in one another's hands. Seem reasonable?"

"Well . . . yes."

"You'll do it then?"

"I don't know. What would I have to do . . . I mean apart from being loyal to you?"

"It wouldn't be much. It could mean your freedom. Don't think—" he laughed "—that I'm going to ask you to poison his

47

milk or stick a knife in him. You wouldn't know anything about that kind of thing."

She stood up suddenly, drink slopping over the edge of her glass.

"I don't want to hear any more. What you're talking about is murder!"

He shrugged his shoulders. "Sorry. I didn't mean to upset you. Let's forget it. You'd better mop up that stain on your dress."

She looked down at the mark the drink had made, and then went into the bedroom, closing the door.

Nothing came easily, or quickly, he thought. Anything that was too easy had to be suspect. But she would come his way. The outburst marked a stage. She had to have time to get used to the idea of murder. She'd come round, she'd help him, and Sarling would be murdered . . . and after Sarling, she would have to go. Back in Devon, Alverton and Mary were waiting for him. His country, his birthright, his woman, waiting to have his children sired on her . . . his destiny, marked out more surely in his mind than anything else. Only Sarling stood in his way.

48

HE LEFT EARLY the next morning to drive to Brighton. Aubrey Catwell, No. 3, Princess Terrace. He would never be able to think of him as anything but Berners. He remembered their first meeting. He had been sitting in the American bar at the Dorchester one evening, having just wound up one of his fake property option deals, when Berners had come over to him. Fifteen years ago, Berners much younger then, with only the shadow of that crescent of baldness beginning to eat into his fair hair. Without any introduction, with only the hint of a shy apologetic smile, Berners had said right out of the blue, "I should guess you're the kind of man who could put his hand on two or three thousand pounds."

"I might."

"If you were prepared to pay me ten per cent I could show you how to make a fifty per cent profit on three thousand within the next two weeks."

"If you could show me, I might be interested." Already he'd marked Berners down as a confidence trickster, some gentle, hesitant shark cruising through the rich waters of the Dorchester.

Berners knew a company, importers and exporters of chemicals, offices in the City, whose shares stood at thirty shillings. Within the week a take-over bid would be made and the company, since the directors held the majority of the shares and wanted to be taken over, would accept the bid, which would be made at forty-five shillings a share. All Raikes had to do was to buy now and sell when the shares moved up on the announcement of the bid.

49

Afterwards Raikes realised that Berners had been with him less than ten minutes, given him finally the name of the company and had gone, saying, "If you do it I'll be here in two weeks' time. This day, this time. If you're not here, of course. . . ." It was the first time he'd seen that vague, amorphous smile and the gentle, hesitant movement of shoulders and hands expressing resignation. No names had been exchanged. Berners had picked him, trusted him, and had gone. Later he was to know how shrewd a judge of men Berners was. He could sum up their qualities in exact percentages, accepting or rejecting them with the detachment of a computer.

The next morning he checked the company. The price of their shares was low compared with their price-earnings ratio so there was no loss in buying them anyway.

Two weeks later, in the bar, he handed Berners two hundred pounds in notes.

Berners said, "It can't be more than a hundred and fifty."

Raikes said, "How much a week do you make now?"

Berners said, "Fifteen."

"In the offices of Allied Chemicals Ltd.?"

"Yes."

"Making so little that you couldn't afford to speculate on this yourself? What's the point? The extra fifty is your first week's salary with me, and I'll also make you a partner—twenty-five per cent share. The work is congenial, interesting, but entirely unorthodox. I don't want to know your name. I'm not going to tell you mine. Just hand me back fifty pounds if you're not interested."

Berners had put the two hundred into his pocket. They had had dinner together, become Berners and Frampton, and had set up their first operation together. He had never asked how Berners had got the take-over details about his company. They worked together and that was all. They knew no more about each other than was necessary for their work. But now he was going to see a man called Aubrey Catwell. He resented it because it would be like looking on the nakedness of a stranger.

Brighton. The sunlight cat-dancing on the blue sea beyond the pier. The horizon a smoky smudge marrying sea and sky. Along the oatmeal coloured stretch of shore the waves, dirty olive, foam and froth meringued, spilled themselves upon the smooth sand lick, teasing at the plastic containers and the dark mess of dead seaweed. Above it, topping the parade and the tamarisk- and veronica-studded gardens, was Princess Terrace, a creamy, elegant white cliff holding out its arms to the sea, the sky and the winter sun. No. 3 had little red-and-white striped metal awnings over its first-floor windows to throw shade on the narrow balconies. The door was white, flanked with black-painted curves of ironwork to mark the rise of the steps. The letterbox mouth was highly polished brass and so was the number three. Nothing of the polish had so much as touched the surrounding white paint. He rang the bell. After a long interval, a woman opened the door. She was in her sixties, black dress high about the neck, her flesh firm, her hair grey with a thin interweaving of white, and she stood on the threshold in exactly the same way as Hamilton would have stood, polite and prepared and, no matter what came, never to be shaken.

He said, "If Mr. Catwell is in and free, would you ask him if he would be kind enough to give Mr. Frampton a few moments?" He handed her one of his old cards.

A few moments later she was showing him into a sitting room on the first floor. She closed the door on them and Berners turned from the window. Except for the clothes it was the same Berners, the same bald crescent, the mild and, even now, expressionless face, the faded grey eyes and the overall feeling of almost mournful gentleness. But the anonymous, ill-fitting clothes had gone. He wore a dove-grey suit, a rich claret waistcoat, a pearl-coloured tie over which the sheen of reflected sunlight in the room moved as he came forward. On his feet were brown suede shoes ... Berners who had always worn black, heavy soled shoes.

Berners said, "I've just opened a bottle of hock, which I usually do at this time of day if the weather's bright. Angers will

51

be glad if you share it. She thinks a bottle is too much for me alone." It was the same voice, but the arrangement of words, their cadence, and his control over them were all different.

He went to a small pie-crust side table which held a silver tray, the bottle of wine and a tall Venetian hock glass. Seeing there was only one glass he turned to a lacquered cabinet which stood on a carved gilt stand and opened it. The inside was full of the sparkle of crystal.

Raikes said, "I regret this very much."

Without turning, polishing with a napkin the extra hock glass he had taken from the cabinet, Berners said, "Let us enjoy our wine first. And do sit down."

Raikes, who knew a great deal about furniture from his own buying to refurnish Alverton, sat down on a shield-backed mahogany elbow chair which he was prepared to bet was Hepplewhite. The ornamental centre struts of the back were worked with a wheat-ear design. Close to the chair was a Regency mahogany drum table. Against the far wall, facing the window, was an English lacquer commode, the design on the front matching that of the cabinet which held the glasses.

Berners brought him his wine and they drank. Berners, after his first sip, made a movement of his head taking in the room. "You like it?"

"Who wouldn't?"

The chandelier hanging from the moulded ceiling was probably from Murano and old, the polychrome glass flowers throwing back the sunlight in coloured reflection on to the ceiling.

Berners nodded. "True. I was brought up in a council house, and I lived in pitiful bed-sitting rooms up to a year after I met you. I always promised myself I'd have something like this . . . a house and furniture and decorations, all by craftsmen, by men who loved what they made. Don't tell me that you've come to say I might lose it?"

"No. But you've got to protect it. You and I have not quite finished working together. If I could have done it on my own,

I would. But it was out of my hands. We have to protect ourselves—but to do that means that two people have to be killed.
Does that spoil the taste of your hock?"

Without hesitation, Berners said, "Why should it? If the
police were to ring the doorbell I would kill myself. So would
you. If one can take one's own life, then it is an easy step down
to take the life of someone else." He moved away and sat in a
chair by the window.

"Before I tell you about it, if you'd like me to, I am prepared
to tell you about myself, my real name and background."

"I don't want to know."

"You may find it out . . . there are other people involved
who do know."

"Then I shall find it out. But let it rest like that. Would you
like to stay to lunch? I ought to let Angers know."

"No. It won't take long. What about Angers?"

"I got her from an agency five years ago. She's been in service
all her life. She's honest, loyal and sometimes belligerent on
my behalf. She knows nothing about Berners, only her Mr.
Catwell. Help yourself to more hock when you want to."

Raikes began to tell him the Sarling story, the story of the red
ballpoint mark alongside a spinning rod in a catalogue, the
business of the raid on the depot . . . everything, his relationship with Belle and why she had to be used, and Berners sat and
listened, asking no questions . . . sat just as he used to in the old
days when Raikes had worked out a new proposition and put it
to him, listening, no questions, until everything was laid before
him.

When Raikes had finished, Berners sat thinking for a moment
or two. Finally he said, "First things first. What about this
Army depot affair?"

"I've got it all worked out. I'll meet you in the flat on the day.
Before then there are a few things I want you to get me. Here is
a list." Raikes handed him some notes he had made.

Berners read them slowly, then nodded. "There is no trouble
there. You can put me in the picture when I let you have them."

He put the list in his pocket. "What's your reading of Sarling?"

Raikes stood up. "I think he's quietly mad. When he unfolds his big plan I'm willing to bet it'll be some cock-eyed, hair-raising scheme that doesn't stand a hope in hell. He's got to go. But before he goes we've got to have those files and the photostats." Raikes, moving about in the room now, stopped by a picture. It was a quiet, placid river scene in oils, a slow barge moving downstream under sail, a church tower veiled in early summer morning mist in the distance. The tranquillity in the picture, the comfort of being close to Berners again, gave him a more complete feeling of ease than he had had for days.

Berners said, "Delightful, isn't it? It's a John Varley. I bought it at a country sale two years ago." Then running on, the real current of his thoughts flowing smoothly away from trivia, he said, "I agree. He's got to go. I'll begin to work on him, but there's a lot I want to know—from your end. You'll have to get most of it from Miss Vickers. How much time have we got?"

"I don't know. A couple of months at the least, I'd say, from the way things are going. I couldn't set up anything big in less."

"How far do you trust Miss Vickers?"

"She's afraid of him, and wants to be free. But she doesn't like the thought of murder."

"Most people don't."

"She's going to. But that's my job. Don't you worry about it."

"I won't. But eventually we've got to have a lot of basic stuff from her."

Carefully, he went through all the things he would want to know. Meon Park. A complete layout of the house and grounds. Numbers, names and habits of staff. Sarling's routines down there. Safety precautions, burglar alarms, location of safe. And then the same for the house in Park Street. In addition he wanted a complete list of the principal items in Sarling's wardrobe. His preferences in shirts, ties, cravats, his eating habits, details of his health, illnesses and recurring ailments. Eccentricities. His doctor and his dentist. His office routines. Names of his principal directors, his other secretaries. Entertainments.

54

Habits with women. Types he preferred. Did he sleep well or badly? Languages spoken, travel abroad, houses or flats owned abroad. ... Everything. For him Sarling was a big question mark, and until there was no question left to be answered, he knew that he could not be murdered. To murder a man, he had to be known, almost loved, and then guided easily into death leaving no tell-tale ripple behind. Yes, he, Berners—for with Frampton here he could not think of himself as anyone else—knew all this because murder was no stranger to him. A year before he had approached Frampton with his financial proposition, he had similarly picked a stranger in the Dorchester bar. The man had taken him back to his flat, interested, so Berners thought, in the deal. There, the man had drugged him and assaulted him sexually—he, Berners, who was neither homo nor heterosexual, just nothing, neuter and contentedly egoistic —and then had thrown him out. For the violation, the diminution, no matter how slight, of self, Berners had, unknown to his attacker, studied him in detail and depth for two months. One night he had returned at the exact moment of time when all circumstances, facts known, observations taken, made murder secure. He had walked away afterwards and settled with bun, coffee and the *Evening News* in the nearest café, conceding himself only that vanity, ten minutes more near the presence of murder, before the ghost of the man's last anguish went for ever from him. For Sarling, the process must be the same; Sarling, the complete man, known, loved in his mind as any study so final, so detailed had to be loved, and then Sarling made nothing, so that he could return here and inhabit paradise again.

He said, "When you're sure of her, get her a Minox camera. I want photographs of everything and from all angles. Particularly of the safe at Meon and the one in London. Tell her never to take a photograph when he is in the house with her. Tell her never to carry it on her when he is about, not in bra or stocking top. He's a man with appetites. He doesn't want her now but at some moment the sight of her, some movement of arm or leg, some innocent exposure, might turn him on her. She must never carry it when with him."

Raikes said, "I'm sorry about this. Just that bloody little red mark in the catalogue."

"It could have been me. A little ink tick in a Sotheby's catalogue. The biggest betrayer in the world is a man's mania. You never noticed our office pictures when the front had to be good?"

"No."

"They were never reproductions. I've even got a couple of them still in this house. Given the right conjunctions, they could have been betrayers."

Raikes gone, Berners had his lunch, lightly grilled sole and fresh spinach—no canned or frozen vegetables were used in the house. He ate from one of six plates of a dinner service made at the Russian Imperial factory in 1843, painted with a surrounding wreath of multi-coloured flowers and butterflies and with an exotic bird for centre-piece. He had bought the incomplete set in France three years before. He remembered, with a vividness that was almost elemental, the moment when he had turned a plate and seen through the glaze the green initial N and the surmounting Imperial crown of Nicholas the First. Caught up in a reverie, spurred by the word imperial echoing in his mind, he considered the richness there would be in having a large house (not something small and distinct, unique in its perfectly miniaturised proportions). A grand house with parkland; a small world that one could own, a house and terrain where one walked, not jostled by an aimless flow of seaside visitors, but alone across a landscape, knowing that if the landscape displeased it could be altered and reshaped. A man like Sarling could afford that. How, he wondered, was Meon Park furnished? In time he would know because some of this girl's photographs would show it. Curious about Frampton and his fishing. How could that give a man any satisfaction? But as he thought it there was no overtrace of feeling in his mind that Frampton, through his mania, had set them this problem. Of all

56

the people he had ever known well, and they were few, his relationship with Frampton was the least troubled, the most assured.

When he got back to the flat, Belle Vickers was out, but Sarling was sitting in a chair by the window waiting for him. He wore a starched wing collar that cut stiffly up into his neck skin, giving the impression that it helped to support his large head. The pepper-and-salt dark suit looked stiff, unflexible, the creases down his thin legs unyielding over his bony knees. The light from the window, striking the side of his face, gave the contorted flesh the colour of boiled veal.

Raikes, after they had tossed the shadow of nods at one another, said, "You've got your own key to this flat?"

"Yes."

"You think you should come here?"

"Why not? A hundred people come in and out every day. One of my directors has a flat on the top floor. Not that he uses it much. You've been to see Berners?"

"Yes."

"How did he take it?"

"If it spoilt his lunchtime hock he didn't show it."

"You discussed getting rid of me?"

"Naturally."

"And your decision?"

"We deferred it—to our next meeting."

Sarling laughed. "Let me know what you decide. Meanwhile what have you arranged about the Army depot?"

"It'll be done."

"When?"

"I think it's better if you don't know. Miss Vickers will let you know when the crate is in a safe place."

"Very well."

"When you have the crate, how long will it be before you need us for the final job?"

Sarling pulled at his moustache. "You have a free hand for

57

this job and, quite rightly, you won't tell me about it. I can't tell you anything about your final assignment." He stood up and retrieved from the side of the chair a malacca cane with a silver knob.

Raikes said, "How did you know about this crate?" He didn't expect any firm reply. He was talking him out of the flat, moving to the door to open it for him.

"It just came up in conversation once. You, of all people, would not be surprised at the indiscreet way men in authority can talk when they have been wined and dined well. Generals, brigadiers, colonels, naval captains, commanders, police commissioners, chief constables ... they're all men, and many of them have loose, flabby mouths. Not like us, Raikes. We give nothing away. How otherwise would we ensure success? Don't tell me that part of your pleasure in your past career didn't come from the contempt you feel for most men and women?" He paused in his move to the door. "That's where our strength is, Raikes. In our contempt for them. Just see that Miss Vickers informs me immediately when the crate is in safekeeping." He contorted his face into the ugly travesty of a smile. "And go on hating me, Raikes. That's how I like you ... and I really mean like you ... a dangerous animal that must obey the ringmaster's whip, waiting for the one moment of inattention to fly at his throat. You really would like to kill me one day, wouldn't you?"

"Yes, I would." He smiled. "But, of course, I don't underrate the difficulties."

Sarling chuckled. "I never for one moment imagined that you would." Then, putting up a hand to stop Raikes from opening the door for a moment, he said, "Since I know you will open the crate to see what is in it, I must ask you to handle the contents with care."

Sarling gone, Raikes dropped into a chair and lit a cigarette. Dangerous animal ... and Sarling the ringmaster. That's how he saw himself ... manipulating, dragooning his creatures. That's where his pleasure was. How the hell had he got like that? Because of his face and gnomelike figure that made people turn from him? People hated the physically odd. There was something unholy about it for most of them. But none of the people who turned from Sarling could know how much he was hating in return. It had not been enough for him that in everything he had touched, industry, finance and commerce, he had dwarfed them. He wanted more than that . . . had to have more than that. God knew what . . . but it was there inside that large skull, tormenting him.

He had to get rid of Sarling. For that he needed Belle; needed to make her his creature, not Sarling's. She was the first big fish he had to land. The thought made him smile . . . and memory flooded in of one of his earliest lessons of the patience, thought and stubborn will needed to land the wanted fish. It had been on the Haddeo river that ran down into the Exe near Dulverton, a river not fished much, narrow, overgrown, and the trout running small, three or four to the pound. It had been August with the water low and gin-clear. Himself at fourteen, with his father, and he had been grumbling at the poor fishing, anything of size seeing him a mile away, even a long belly-crawl to the bank giving no results. The old man had said that there were big trout, two-pounders, to be had if you knew, if you had the patience, if you were a fisherman worth calling that. Bad conditions make good fishermen. How often had he heard him say that? With the dusk coming, the old man much lower down the river, he had stood solitary for an hour behind an oak, watching a pool and then seen on the far side, deep down, the brief old gold flash of turning flank and belly. He was angry with ambition to land a big one. To prove he could do it against all the odds. Just as some men, because they were there, had to climb the big ones, so he wanted to land the big one. The fish rose once to something but he was slow to see what it was, and there was no hatch, no fly on the water, that he could imitate. The water told him nothing. The fish told him nothing. He knew that one cast, switched from around the tree, and one rejection by the trout would put the fish down. Give the bugger something big to rouse him, make the bugger think he's only got one chance at a rare mouthful. He'd been a great one for swear words in those days. Hadn't Hamilton tanned his ass for it more than once? He put on a White Moth, tied by his father with wings from a white barn owl, a large cream hackle, and the body white ostrich herl . . . a real mouthful.

It all came back to him. The gentle work out of line and then the only tactic he sensed would succeed. He'd smacked the fly down with a bang, two feet upstream of the trout, and with a jerking of the wrist had made it work, struggle on the surface, kicking like a real moth trying to escape the drag of the water film. The trout had come for it like all hell let loose, in a great rush, body arching over it, mouth drowning it and taking it down while he, still behind the tree, suddenly void of excitement or nerves, had said *God Save the King* slowly and then tightened, felt the hook move home, felt the trout's power and shock pulse through the out-streaming line. Ten minutes later it was on the bank. Two pounds and a quarter. When his father had walked up, he had said to him, "There. I told you so." No more. But he had known the pride in the old man. And he had known the pride in himself. And he had learnt his lesson. If you want something from people then you must learn what it is that *they* want badly, wait for your moment and then give it to them, hook them in the moment of their desire and land them, often never knowing that what they had been offered was only a coloured imitation of their real want. With Belle, since he needed her so much, the offer had to be of himself. All that remained was the question of timing.

The door opened behind him and Belle came in with a shopping bag. He got up smiling, took the bag from her and began to help her out of her coat.

Saturday. Four o'clock. Raikes had left in the station wagon two hours before. It was raining. Even through the windows Belle could hear the whining of tyres on the wet road outside.

Belle sat by the telephone. She was nervous. She couldn't help it. Not that she had much to do. But she was nervous, to her surprise, for Raikes moving now out there in the rain towards an enterprise that held danger for him. Though, God knows, she thought, he'd been casual about it, unconcerned as though he were merely going off to a commonplace appointment.

Behind her was this other man, Berners, introduced to her a couple of days before when she had been briefed by them both. He, too, showed no anxiety, no nerves; a quiet, almost gentle man, offering her nothing but politeness and, like Raikes, completely untouched by this thing ahead. Both of them so bloody sure of themselves.

From behind her Berners said, "All right. Ring now."

She stubbed her cigarette out, clumsily, an uncrushed ember still smoking, and picked up the phone. She began to dial a long-distance call, finished, and breathed deep as the line churred away at the far end.

The noise stopped and a man's voice said, "Yes, hullo?" It was a flat, blurred, bored voice.

"Is that the Mereworth Depot?"

"Yes."

"Hold on a moment, please. This is the Ministry of Defence, Whitehall. Colonel Shrimpton wants to speak to—"

"Colonel Who?"

"Colonel Shrimpton." She made it a bit curt, nervousness gone now, as it used to go in Woolworths the moment she had made up her mind what she was going to take. She added, "This is the office of the Master-General of the Ordnance. I'm putting you through."

She scratched a fingernail across the perforated disc of the telephone mouth once or twice and, changing the tone of her voice, pleasant now in deference to authority, "You're through now, Colonel."

She handed the phone up to Berners.

He said, "Mereworth Depot?"

"Yes, sir."

"I don't suppose Captain Kelly has arrived there yet, has he? He's on his way down with some important supplies."

"No, sir. No officer of that name. Nobody at all in fact."

"I see. Well, look, when he arrives, give him a message will you?"

"Yes, sir."

"Tell him that he's to ring me at once at Whitehall 7022. He knows the extension number. Colonel Shrimpton. The moment he arrives. Is that understood?"

"Yes, sir."

"Good. Thank you."

He put the phone down and smiled at her. His right hand pulled gently for a second at the lobe of his ear, and he said, "You did it well. That's set it in train. Whitehall. Master-General of the Ordnance. It mesmerises them, drives all questions from their minds. Who is the Master-General of the Ordnance, anyway?"

He turned away, taking up his hat and gloves.

She said, memory coming easily to her from the simple research she had done in the purple-covered 100th Edition of Whitaker's Almanac, "General Sir Charles Richardson," then added, God save her, trying to impress him (how childishly anxious could you get?) "G.C.B., C.B.E., D.S.O., A.D.C."

Near the door, he said, "Your memory's good. Now, remember—in half an hour ring again and ask for Kelly. He won't be there. Say I've had to go out and give them the message for Kelly to go on to Maidstone. That will put the meringue on the pudding so they'll swallow the whole Kelly arrival in one gulp. All right?"

She nodded.

He stopped with his hand on the door, and then said, "There's nothing to worry about . . . so far as he's concerned, I mean. He knows how to look after himself. And, let's face it, there's something about a uniform as the old song says. Goodbye."

62

He walked out as though he were leaving the office early, business slack and home comforts calling, and Belle sat there saying to herself ... Men, bloody men ... These two bloody men. So damned calm and sure of themselves.

Nothing that she did or said, she saw, was going to alter them. They were going to have their way. They were going to murder Sarling as quietly, efficiently and unemotionally as they were doing this present thing.

There was no trouble. Raikes came down Wrotham Hill to the roundabout then swung left-handed on to the Gravesend road, climbing the hill, the drizzle-shrouded stretches of Kent opening on his right. At the Vigo pub he turned left into a small lane. The Vigo, what battle was that? The navy was all around here. Rochester, Chatham, Gravesend ... the Thames where, before man crammed it with his filth, the great salmon used to run so freely that London apprentices stipulated that they should be fed it only once a week. Vigo, of course. On the coast of Spain. Sacked twice by Sir Francis Drake. Oh, Drake he was a Devon man. So were his two brothers, both of them locked now in steel tombs on the seabed.

Gilpin, in battle-dress, sergeant's stripes, was waiting in a pull-off down the road with the Land-Rover, army numbered and signed, and in the back a grey-green painted crate, stencilled with its Z/93 GF1 and War Department arrows.

Gilpin gave him a grunt for greeting. Raikes climbed into the back and changed into his officer's battle-dress, captain R.A., and they drove off, back to the Wrotham Hill roundabout and then down the A.20 to the turn-off to the Mereworth Depot.

They drove into the depot and pulled up outside the office hut and the sequence of events flowed evenly, long predicted, trouble free because trouble only came when you were unsure of yourself, when the preparation had not been done, when your confidence in the inevitable responses of other people flagged.

Captain Kelly. Yes, sir. Yes, sir. Don't know anything about this crate, but then things get balled up. And, sir, a message for you from Whitehall. Just had it. Go on to Maidstone? The frown. Annoyance. Mucking his Saturday plans up. Ah, well. The short drive up to Hut Number Five, door unlocked by the office clerk. No one else much about late on a Saturday afternoon. Weekend leave, girls call, football matches—and then the gentle neckchop cutting off the chatter putting him down and out almost, three big scarves for mouth, feet and wrists, enough to hold him long enough, and one crate deposited and another crate lifted out and into the Land-Rover and Captain Kelly and his sergeant driving unhurried out of the depot, and not a word between them as they made their way back to the waiting station wagon, windscreen wipers moaning, arthritic against the drizzle, the operation over, only the credits now to come up on the screen, direction and planning by Raikes, uniforms by Berners, Land-Rover and false crate by Gilpin, extra dialogue by Miss Vickers . . . and not a single fingerprint on the crate at Mereworth or Land-Rover to be abandoned here because both of them had worn gloves and—if Gilpin hadn't taken the same precautions while he worked on crate and car at his garage then he, Raikes, had misjudged Gilpin which he knew he had not as certainly as he knew that Gilpin had not yet finished with him because Gilpin was Gilpin and had to do what was in his nature.

In the empty lane they dismounted and Raikes went to the back of the Land-Rover to unbuckle curtains and get the crate out. Gilpin came round to help, sergeant's stripes bright with pipe clay, blouse partly undone, showing khaki shirt, khaki tie, grease-marked on the knot—a nice touch from Berners.

Gilpin said, "Worked like a bloody charm." He stepped round, putting himself on the hedge side of the road, reaching up with his left hand to help with the curtain buckles and slipping his right hand into the opening of his battle-dress blouse. Raikes knew that the man had been waiting days for this moment. He turned quickly and grabbed at Gilpin's hand as it came out of the blouse, clamping his fingers hard on the wrist and in one ferocious movement shaking the gun free.

"Sod you!"

Gilpin twisted, kicked out and caught his knee and then threw his weight at him. Raikes went down, off balance, on the wet ground, crouching, fingertips touching the soft, wet grass. Gilpin's boot flashed out, scoring brutally across his cheek.

Raikes, angered, disgusted that he should have given even this slight advantage, came up knowing that, if it would have served, he could murder him here and now, but knowing that the limits of need were narrower, easily maintained. He caught Gilpin across the neck with the edge of his right hand, staggered him, and whipped his knee into the bulky forward leaning body, winding, driving the man back into the hedge. He sprawled, flattening the nettles, wet leaves scattered on the battle-dress shoulders.

Raikes picked up the gun and put it in his pocket. He could feel blood on his face, pain in his knee. Anger was gone.

He said, "Don't try anything else, or I might just kill you. Come and help."

Gilpin got up, coughing, half-retching at the pain in his stomach.

They carried the crate to the car, sliding it through the back doors, across the metal runners of the floor.

"Put that blanket over it."

Raikes stepped back, watching Gilpin drape the crate with the blanket that lay in the back of the car.

He went back to the Land-Rover, gloved still, and checked through it. He came back with Gilpin's small suitcase of civilian clothes and his own and tossed them into the car.

Gilpin at his side, he drove on down the side road, bore right and went on through the lanes, the map study clear in his mind, knowing exactly at what point he would come back on to the main A.20, cross it and then by other side roads move deep into the outreaching maze of south London suburbs.

He stopped halfway down a hill by the side of a small pond,

wound down the window, and took the gun from his pocket.

"Nobody can trace this to you?"

"No. Think I'm daft?"

"Just now and again you're not far off it." He tossed the gun into the duckweed water. "Start changing."

They both changed into their civilian clothes behind some bushes on the far side of the pond, Gilpin finishing with a fidget of his fingers at a blue-and-white-spotted bow tie. Raikes made him go ten yards into a field, tear a soft wound into the side of a this year's haystack, push the uniforms in and then seal the wound. He came back, mud squelching under his boots.

Driving on, Raikes said, "Killing me would have done you no good. Little fleas have bigger fleas upon their backs to bite 'em. You'd have signed your own warrant. Didn't you know that?"

"All I know is it would have been good to do it."

Raikes dabbed his face with his handkerchief. "You've got a nice business. The life you want. Nobody's going to come and disturb you."

"Well. ...." Then, the accolade clear in his voice, ungrudging admiration: "How the hell did you know?"

"You've been flying all the signals. I'm letting you out at Camberwell." He smiled, forgiveness not offered but insisted upon. "What alibi did you fix with your wife?"

"I'm meeting her at the Chandos, corner of Saint Martin's Lane. We've been to the cinema. Then dinner at a Jo Lyons and home. Watertight."

Before he let him out at Camberwell, Raikes said, "Your money's in the pocket in front of you."

Gilpin opened the dash pocket and took out the thick envelope. Without opening it, he said, "Five hundred, plus the charge for the Land-Rover and odds and ends?"

"Nine hundred altogether. Enough?"

"Yes. I got the Land-Rover at a car auction, Leicester way. No one could trace it."

"I never worried. That was your neck."

When he let him out in a side street, the drizzle gold-beaded now from street lights, Gilpin leaned through the window, half offered a hand, then withdrew it, and said, "Sorry for the nonsense, guv. You're all right."

He went, tugging up raincoat collar, down the pavement, paused at a corner, turned, raised a hand, then disappeared, plunging into memory.

Thirty-five minutes later Raikes drove the car into the garage off the Edgware Road. He shut and locked the door and manhandled the crate out of the back of the car. Already with Gilpin he had been surprised how light it was. He lowered the trap ladder, then taking the crate by one of the rope handles at the end he pulled it up the outer ladder runners to the loft. The lid was held by two big knock-away spring clasps at each end. He hit them free and opened the crate. The thing was packed with sawdust. He scraped some away, then groped with his hands inside. It came up with a small brown plastic canister that fitted neatly into the hand. He felt around. There were more of them, all the same. He put one in his pocket, then closed the lid on the others.

In the Edgware Road he caught a taxi and rode it as far as Berkeley Square. From there he walked to the flat.

Belle wasn't in. He knew she wouldn't be. He had passed her on the corner of the street as he had turned down to the garage. She would be in there now with a cloth, polishing, cleaning the interior of the car free of all prints. By now, gloved, she could even be driving it back to the car hire firm which stayed open until midnight on a Saturday—cutting off that section of life, false hire name and address, nothing to trace the car back to them even if some wet afternoon country stroller had happened to notice it in conjunction with the Land-Rover and had memorised the number.

He locked the canister in the safe, then mixed himself a whisky and soda. He sat for half an hour, drinking. Then he went into the bathroom, stripped and lay soaking. The cut on his face had dried up, but the steam and water started the bleeding again.

He heard her come in and move around the room outside.

He called, "Belle?" It was a hell of a name, but he gave it warmth. This was how it had to be. Feel it, not act it. It was a good name, Belle. Beautiful, full of promise.

She said, "Are you all right?"

"Yes. No hitch. Did you get rid of the car?"

"Yes. I suppose you'd like me to get another—tomorrow or Monday?"

Suppose nothing. Stop supposing.

"Monday. Have a drink. I'm two ahead of you." He lay, picturing her at the sideboard. Belle was beautiful. Her body, all of her; the long Burne-Jones face and the stupid hair, the supposes and the nervousness. They were all beautiful, desirable, because he had to have her.

He stepped out of the bath, and began to towel himself. The blood from his face stained the towel. Still half wet he searched the cabinet for sticking plaster and couldn't find any.

He called, "Belle."

She came into the bedroom.

"Yes?"

"Could you find some sticking plaster? I've cut my face."

She didn't answer but he heard her move away and after a moment or two she was back.

"You want it in there?"

"Please. You can fix it for me."

The door opened and she came in.

He sat on the bath stool, the towel draped across his thighs.

She stood there, in her black dress, the pearls she had worn the first time he saw her tight about her throat, immobile, one hand holding up a tin of Band-Aid as though it were a cross, a holy, unbreakable guard between her and evil.

He cocked his head sideways so that she could see the cut.

"Be an angel and fix it for me."

She came over and avoided his eyes as she opened the tin

68

and selected a plaster. She put the tin down on the side of the bath.

He saw the little over-frown of concentration as she half-peeled the protective cover from the plaster strip.

He said, knowing that she would know that he was not telling the truth, but that it was conventional and would be what she would expect of a man like him, "I got it on the side of the loft dragging the case up."

She nodded, and bent, beginning to fix the plaster on his cheek, her long fingers, firm, expert in the woman's work. As she did so, he put his hands forward and up under the hem of her dress and held her thighs, his hands sliding over the top of her stockings on to the warm, bare flesh. He felt a slow, involuntary tremble of her body, a slender birch taking the first pulse of a rising breeze. She said nothing, her breath against his ear, her fingers smoothing the plaster home.

Standing away from him she said throatily, "That all right?"

"Yes, fine. Thank you."

She looked down at his knees and made a mouth, twisting the dark red bow. "What about your knee?"

His right knee was heavily bruised from Gilpin's kick. "I must have knocked that, too. I bruise easily."

He stood up and began to finish towelling himself as he would had she been his wife and seen him naked a thousand times. She watched him for a moment and then went back into the bedroom.

When he came out of his bedroom, dressed, she was sitting, drink at her side, reading an *Evening Standard*.

He said, "Do you think we could have some home cooking tonight? I'd rather not go out with this." He touched the plaster.

"There's steak—and a cauliflower."

"Fine. What did old Fu Manchu provide in the way of wine?" He bent and opened the sideboard door and over his shoulder said, "By the way, you can tell him that it all went off all right."

"He's in Malta until Monday."

"When he comes back."

He began to whistle gently as he looked over the bottles of wine.

She lay in bed, Raikes sleeping at her side.

From the moment that she had gone into the bathroom with the plaster, seeing him naked, feeling his hands on her thighs, she had known that she was helpless. What he wanted, she had wanted, despite herself. (You say to yourself that you won't—and then you do. What bloody sense was there in that?) If it had just been him, naked, the sex and their two bodies and nothing beyond that, then she would have felt neither helpless nor afraid. (She knew damned well that he was setting out to use her . . . and she didn't want to be used. With her body, yes . . . but not this other thing which was coming. And yet . . . did it matter so much? Being Sarling's creature wasn't all that good. Being his would at least give her a different kind of hope.) She turned over on her back, wondering why she was struggling with herself.

They'd spent the evening comfortably, pleasantly, and not once by accident or design had he touched her; the memory of his hands on her thighs lasting, and he knowing that it would last. Two hours ago he had come to her, through the bathroom into the dark bedroom, she hearing him from the moment his door had clicked open.

He'd moved in beside her, no words spoken and his hands had touched her again, sliding under the silk of her nightdress, lingering, the slow movement of browsing animals drifting over the smooth pastures of her body.

His mouth had been warm, generous, full of wanting and giving and there was no power in her which could hold back the response of her own lips and tongue . . . only a faint, receding cry of warning somewhere miles behind her. He'd taken her, hard, thrusting into her, thrusting his will into her, claiming her,

70

possessing her and she had met it all with an instinctive, matching brutality, tearing at the muscular sweep of his back, rising
to meet him, spreading herself for him, feeling herself ridden,
swept away, not caring, dying into darkness, spent and not
spent because from that darkness he had brought her back
again and spurred her on to another death, and another, until
body, mind and all time were spent and she lay empty. Then,
knowing she had no power to be anything but what he wanted,
he had filled her with himself, his passion of possession, and the
knowledge that whatever he would ask she would do, whatever
he wanted her to be she would be ... Knowing it, she had
drifted into sleep only to wake now to feel the warmth of him
still alongside her, one arm and hand limp across the nakedness
of her breasts, fingers cupped even in sleep with a mild,
possessive firmness over her flesh, the dry heat of his palm
moving into her hard nipple, into her, claiming a union that
she needed and welcomed.

The hand on her breast moved down, found the placid,
gentle roundness of her stomach, fingers spread and drifted
lower and she knew that he was now awake and knew that she,
too, was awake. He turned, pulling her gently to him, the
possessive hand and arm moving, the hand taking her right
knee, sliding her leg across him. The need he had for her
matched her movements of the need she had for him, and then
magically, unheralded, he was in her, proud now, but gentle,
and it was nothing like the other had been. She felt herself
blossom to a warm, wet-petalled flowering, like nothing before
and, drifting away into the long hungry spasm of abandon, she
felt him come with her, following her, loving her. . . .

He had been going down to Devon the next day, Sunday, but
he stayed with her. He slept with her again that night and
there was tenderness and hardness in him and she gave herself
to both, wanting both, and knew that she was in love with him,
knew that it could lead nowhere but was content to crest with it

from moment to moment. Limp and lazy with their fill of
passion, she waited for him to speak, but he said nothing,
turning to her, cradling her to him and slept.

CHAPTER FIVE

IN THE TRAIN he had with him the morning papers. There had been nothing in the Sunday papers of the raid on the depot. But all the morning papers had, tucked away somewhere as an unimportant item of news, a report on the break-in at an Army depot in Kent, nothing of importance stolen. Raikes had the impression that the authorities had decided to play down the incident. He settled with *The Times* and forgot the depot, putting everything that was London behind him. Everything that was Belle Vickers he had already put behind him the moment the flat door had closed on her.

As he was taking his first drink before dinner, the telephone rang. It was Belle. Sarling was back and she had seen him, reporting that the depot affair had been successful. Sarling had said that he would not want to see Raikes for a week or two, but that she, Belle, was to stay on at the flat. Once she had given the message, he sensed that she wanted to go on talking, wanted to keep this tenuous thread with him unbroken for as long as possible. Relying on her understanding, he said that he had people in for drinks and couldn't stay on the phone any longer. He went back to his drink. Whatever part he had to play with her in London, he didn't want even an echo of it to follow him down here. But as he began to push her out of his mind he had a memory of her face as he had made love to her the morning of their second night. Her eyes had been shut, the lips a little parted, hardly breathing, the life in her as fragile and muted as that of a sleeping child, a stranger's face below him, wiped clear of all lines, all strains, bathed with fresh innocence. For about five seconds he had been oddly moved, stripped of possessiveness, sensing the slow urge to protect and shield whatever it was that spoke to him from the face below his. Remembering it now, he thought he must look at Mary's face the next time. Maybe this was some transcendental dew that bathed them all as they dropped away into warm, unthinking bliss. Transcendental dew, for Christ's sake—that was a new line for him. All he wanted from her was that she should commit herself, be on his side against Sarling—and he knew that when he went back to London he would get it. She would be falling over herself to help.

The next morning, after telephoning Mary, he went up to Alverton Manor to talk with the outgoing owner. Before going in, he sat in the car, halfway up the drive, looking at the greystone, gabled and mullioned-windowed house. Every window, every ledge, every chimney and roof space he knew, had climbed them, fallen from some, knew the holes in the masonry where the daws nested, and the exact crotch in the climbing virginia creeper where the fly-catchers raised two broods each year. He knew the outside and the inside as he knew himself, the one his skin and the other his guts. The present bastard had added a low, glass-roofed, modern loggia affair at one end. The first thing he would do when he took possession would be to pull it down because it stood on the site of his mother's small herb garden. The herb garden should come back, just as it had been, for Mary. He spent an hour going round making an inventory of the furniture he would like to keep, accepting nothing but the furniture which had belonged to his father and had gone at auction. In his present house he had some of the rest, and what he still lacked, a dealer in Exeter was tracing and buying for him.

Driving over to Mary's house in the afternoon, he had, packed in his overnight case, the small canister he had taken from the Z/93 crate. He was taking her out to dinner, then on to a dance at one of their friends' houses and staying the night with her. He made a long detour, knowing exactly where he wanted to go, time on his hands.

74

He drove up Dunkery Beacon from the south side on the Porlock road. Right on top of the moor was a small side road that led from the summit down to a deep valley which had been high-dammed to form a reservoir. He pulled off the road just before the turning. It was an overcast day and the cloud was low, an even, wind-drifted veil of thin mist that left furze and heather and wortleberry growth dewed with leaden water drops. The world existed for fifty yards, and then vanished.

Sitting in the car, he took the canister out of his case and examined it. It fitted the hand, not as a grenade would, but as though its shape had been based on a fat, eight inch roll of clay, held and squeezed gently by fingers and thumb to give a natural, moulded grip. The only markings on it, in raised bakelite, read Z/93. Series GF1. The body of the canister had been moulded into raised rhomboids, much as the body of a grenade was moulded for fragmentation on explosion. The base was slightly concave. At the top, set flush with the flat surface, was a thin strip of light metal, a narrow tongue, the tip of which was held down in a small bridge. A steel pin ran through the top of the side supports to hold the tongue down. Holding the tongue in place with a finger, Raikes tried to pull the pin out. He couldn't move it. Then he saw that one end of the pin was flattened out into a small disc shape, the edges knurled. He turned the disc and the pin revolved and moved out a fraction. He screwed it back into place and got out of the car.

He went down the side road fifty yards to a small sheep track that wound across the hillside. The wind was blowing into his back. After a while he stopped and listened. From somewhere ahead of him and up to the right there came the rough, bronchial fluke-cough of a sheep. He left the path and moved up towards the sound, going slowly through the knee-high heather. The ground dipped to a hollow ahead of him. Cropping on the windward side of a large granite rock were a couple of ewes and three well grown lambs. One of the ewes looked up, saw him, moved nervously for a moment and then went back to her feed. Raikes wetted his finger, held it to check the wind, edged a couple of yards up the hill to bring it on his back, and then holding the metal tongue firmly down began to unscrew the pin. The sheep were forty yards from him and now and again they were lost in a swirl of mist. He freed the pin and tossed the canister underhand twenty yards, hearing the click of the hinged tongue as it sprang free. The container landed on a patch of grass, rolled and came to stop against the stems of a bracken patch. Stepping backwards slowly, he began to count to himself. The sheep fed on undisturbed. At ten there was a soft *phut* and the canister jerked a foot into the air and must have fragmented for he could see no more of it. In fact he could see nothing. There was no obvious escape of gas.

He looked at the sheep. They were still cropping. If there had been anything in the canister, he thought, it must have gone downwind to them by now. Then it happened. Just for a moment the nearest old ewe looked up and then she went down, legs collapsing under her. As though it were some act, some circus trick, done at a signal, timing and coordination beautifully, precisely drilled into them, the other sheep went down. Not sideways, or staggering or protesting, but dropping, surrendering their weight to the pull of gravity. They went down and they stayed down. As he watched, he saw a stonechat come flirting across them four feet from the ground rising to land on the granite rock outthrust. Abruptly from mid-flight, from an eye-catching flicker of red, black and white-flecked wing and throat, airborne, wind-coquetting, the earth claimed it and it dropped like a stone.

Raikes turned and walked back to the car.

Mary came into his room that night as she always did, even when her parents were at home, and she stayed with him until the first light began to come up. As she lay beneath him, full of his morning love before leaving, he looked at her face. It was Mary's face. The face he knew, the face of the girl who was going to fill Alverton with children. Of transcendental dew there was no trace. Sensing he was looking at her, she opened her eyes and then winked at him.

76

She said, "Love me?"

He nodded.

She reached up, kissed him, and said, "Not one of your first-class performances. You were drinking too much last night."

Driving back he made a detour to Dunkery, parked the car and went down to the place of the sheep. There would be no danger now. Whatever had been in the canister must have long been dissipated by the wind.

There was no mist this morning, only bright sunshine on the bronze bracken.

In the shadow of the granite rock lay one of the old ewes, dead. The bird lay there, too, dead. But with the dead ewe, trotting away as he approached, was one of the lambs, crying and then half turning back, but not for milk for it was long past that need from her. Of the other ewe and lambs there was no sign, and no sign of their removal. Although he searched around for them but could not find them, he was sure that they were all right. Nobody had been up here since yesterday. The nearest point a tractor could make was the road a hundred yards away and there would have been signs of the removal of the other bodies. In the heather and bracken close to where the canister had exploded, he found a few bakelite fragments but he left them there untouched.

He drove back, wondering why the ewe had died and the bird, but not the others. He got back home in time to pick up the phone which was ringing. It was Mary.

She said, "How much did you drink last night?"

"Why?"

"Well, you've gone off without your case. I'll bring it over. I'm coming that way later."

He phoned Berners from Devon and two days later met him at the R.A.C. and told him about the canister.

"What the hell does Sarling think he's going to use them for?"

"God knows. I should think they were part of some riot-control stock, kept handy in that depot for quick distribution to the police or army in Kent and Sussex."

Raikes said, "I shouldn't want to see a crowd of people go down the way those sheep did. Some of them would never get up again. What the hell was it?"

"You'd have to ask the boys at Porton or Fort Detrick, Maryland, about that. Sounds like a G-agent or nerve gas. Most of them in an enclosed space will kill." Berners caressed his bald crescent. "It's a great civilisation and neither you nor I are any credit to it. I'll try and find out what the stuff is."

"We've got to do something about Sarling before he lands us in some wild scheme using the stuff."

"The only thing we need for that is the help of Miss Vickers. She can get us all the information we want."

"And she's going to." Raikes stood up. "I'll speak to her when I get back and phone you tomorrow."

He took Belle out to dinner that night and half-way through the meal he began to talk to her about the canister, telling her what had happened in Devon. It was better to talk to her about it here, surrounded by people so that she couldn't get emotional or make any vigorous protest. He put it to her as though it were a business proposition, an unexceptionable discussion of alternative methods.

"He's going to get us all involved with the use of that stuff. That could mean that a lot of people are going to die. God knows what crazy idea he's nursing. You don't think I can stand by and let that happen? Could you? A lot of people being snuffed out just because of Sarling? The only thing to do is to get rid of him. He's got to go and you've got to help us, Belle. Can't you see that?"

"You don't really know he's going to have you use it."

"Of course I do. He didn't get me to steal it just as a boy scout test. Sarling never wastes time on things like that. Belle, I know it's a hell of a thing to ask you—but you can't escape it. You're either going to have the death of Sarling or the deaths

78

of other people to deal with. One or the other. And what's Sarling matter to you or to me when we can save other people and also free ourselves? Can't you see that?"

"Well, yes, I suppose so. When you put it like that."

"That's the way it is. Anyway, you don't have to do anything positive about Sarling. All we want is information. Just think of it that way. A few facts. You give them to us and then you forget all about it . . ."

She looked down at her wine glass, fingering it, twisting it slowly round. "The whole thing frightens me."

"If you help us nothing can go wrong. Berners and I will see to that. Belle, I need you in this. I need you more than I've ever needed anyone . . . Are you going to help?"

It was a long time before she looked up at him. There were a hundred things she wanted to say but she knew that none of them would do her any good, none of them would stop him having his way. All she had to do was to stand up and walk away, away from him and from Sarling and let events take their course. But she knew there was no power in her to do it. He needed her. She wanted to be with him. She raised her head and nodded.

His hand came out and held hers across the table. "You won't regret it. Now let's forget about it and enjoy ourselves. I'll tell you what we want later."

That night, lying in bed with him, she listened to him talk, the darkness, and his words all fantasy, each sentence from him, unopposed by her, committing her deeper and deeper. He was telling her now what he needed to know. So much about Sarling and his houses, so much detail . . . on and on. For God's sake why did he want to know about clothes? Two nasty grey-black tweeds, the colour of wet granite pavements, two dark grey flannel, smooth, unmarked slate. Taking it all in, she added her own commentary, marking things unlisted as though it were a game, played in the mind, to see who could go on longest . . . What about his bowel movements, regularity or otherwise of and duration? Toothpaste used and colour of

79

brush. Dressing and undressing programme, shoes then trousers and *then* socks, or did socks follow shoes and *then* trousers. And a flipping camera, not to be hidden between her tits or under her girdle . . . you never knew, Belle, when some bastard's hands would stray . . . Nor in any body orifice, the word coming to her memory-shed from some article on natives and diamond smuggling . . . And she going round Meon and Park Street like a five-bob stately homes tourist, snapping and gawking. *Click*, an angled view of bed and sidetable with drinking carafe, sleeping pills and the unopened bible; *click*, a badly focussed shot of the study carpet, a chocolate brown spread with one single white line all the way round, six inches from the sides . . . For Pete's sake, it was a game. It had to be a game, lying here in the dark, right after making a woman of her, and still doing it, his passionless but now possessive hand moving over her, the sliding touch keeping the lines of communication open. A game. All these bloody men played games. No matter how serious it was they made a game of it, a serious game, but a game. *Stamp out Sarling*—colourfully boxed, any number from three upwards can play. Shake dice and collect your clues and rewards and the first one to complete the murder kit got the pleasure of shooting, stabbing, poisoning, strangling or just with fingertip upsetting the man on the parapet so that he went spinning and cart-wheeling down. After the smash on the pavement, a shuffle of chairs and then, "Well, what do we do now? Monopoly or have a drink and just chat?"

Raikes beside her said, "Are you taking all this in?"

"Yes."

It was his cool voice, county to her, cool, sure, and full of that security which she knew she would never have, evenly accented with the right to enter, speak, demand and question, anywhere, anytime and anyone. Right against the grain of all he was saying, she told herself "All I want is to love and be loved." Didn't he know that? Even if he didn't, wasn't there a kind of magic in the wish itself which had to work itself into him?

Love was a habit. She was full of it; surely some of it would rub off on him, grow on him?

He said, "The one thing, Belle, that can't be risked, is to give him any idea that you're doing this. It could lead to hell for both of us."

"I understand." That was her secretary's voice, notebook closing, rising to her feet, one hand sweeping the lapcrease from her skirt, spoken deliberately because his hands had momentarily left her and she knew the deadly seriousness in him.

To the darkness above him, he said, "He's got to go. Clean out of this bloody world with a doctor's certificate as a safe conduct—for us." Then to her, a hand coming back, "Almost everything depends on you."

The hand eased her round to him, her face feeling his face close in the dark. "I'm putting myself in your hands. If you wanted to, you could betray me and still be safe yourself. You know that, don't you?"

"Yes. But I don't like you to say it."

"I never will again."

Then, from some impudent malice in her, she said, "And what happens when it's all over? I mean, to me and to you?"

Without hesitation, without any break in the flow of his hands which were heralding the rise of desire again in her and in him, he said, "We can talk about that when we're out of trouble and free."

And, while she moved to him, ready and longing to be used, she told herself that she had asked for it and got it, got exactly what she knew she would get. The meeting was adjourned *sine die*.

CHAPTER SIX

AFTER A FEW days of being fully committed to Raikes, there was no nervousness in her, no anxiety about making any mistake that would betray her or Raikes to Sarling. She had insisted on two Minox cameras to avoid the necessity of having to travel a single camera between Park Street and Meon Park. All those journeys were usually done in company with Sarling. She knew him well enough to appreciate that had he any suspicion of her he was capable of stopping the car en route and stripping her. The presence of the chauffeur would mean nothing to him.

When she wasn't using the cameras they were kept well hidden. The one at Meon Park was in her room, Scotch-taped to the inside of the marble crosspiece of the never-used fireplace. At Park Street the other was hidden; taped too, to the inside of the detachable cover of her electric Olympia typewriter in the small office she had adjoining Sarling's study.

Over two weeks she photographed, checked the details which Raikes had asked for, drew plans of both houses, and laid out time-tables of the daily routines of servants and also Sarling's routines when at either place. She would wait until she was in Mount Street before she committed anything to paper and then it was no more than was absolutely necessary. In addition to her own natural competence and caution, she had now, to reinforce it, her desire to do this job immaculately in order to gain Raikes' pleasure and esteem. Committed to him, she was drawn even closer to him and began to imagine something of the same response in him. Quite apart from their love-making,

he seemed to have admitted her into a more intimate relationship ... serious always about the job in hand, but affectionate,
reaching to small vulgarities and jokes, the casual signals of a
new understanding. Standing at his side sometimes while he
sat in a chair, going over some detail with him, he would slide
his hand up her leg and caress her with the absent-minded,
habit-born, naturalness of—so she felt—a couple perfectly
integrated and content with one another. In these weeks she
enjoyed a form of happiness unknown before.

One evening in the Mount Street flat, Raikes said to her,
"Describe for me again Sarling's study at Park Street." He
leaned back in his chair, staring at the ceiling, listening to her.
She'd done it before more than once and as she did it again, he
could see the room. Up the stairs to the first floor landing, study
door on the right, Sarling's bedroom door to the left. Study
door, panelled oak, brass fittings highly polished. Inside, the
study panelled in the same wood, brown carpet with a running
white line round it. Windows in the far wall overlooking a small
yard and garden, each window alarmed and burglar proof.
Sarling's desk in the window—a Chippendale period mahogany
desk with cock-beaded drawers and carved gilt handles (this
from Berners after he had studied one of Belle's photographs)—
and on the right hand wall a mahogany breakfront bookcase.
Then the door into Belle's office. He could have walked around
it in the dark. ... The tall, walnut-cased grandfather clock in
the left corner from the main door, a walnut bureau over against
the left-hand wall and the centre table, the armchair and two
occasional chairs, the two pictures on the wall spaces, one a
Stubbs of a groom holding a black mare, the other a portrait
in oils of Sarling by Graham Sutherland and, dead centre
in the left-hand wall, the oak door that led to the strong
room.

Raikes said, "All right. Give me the routine when Sarling
wants to go into the strong room."

"I've done this before."

"Do it again." His voice was almost sharp. "Shut your eyes

and go over it and try to remember everything he does . . . normally, that is."

"Well, he tells me he wants to go into the strong room. That means he wants me to go into my office until he has the door open."

"The ordinary oak door?"

"No. The door behind that, the strong-room door."

"The oak door is locked?"

"No."

"So, you go into your office. Do you shut the door?"

"I used to at first. But often now I leave it half open."

"You've seen him go up to the strong-room door?"

"Once or twice. And don't ask me what the door looks like. You've got the photograph."

That was the trouble. They had photographs of the door, the one in Mount Street and the one at Meon, and they were both the same. There was no combination dial, no handles, no locks, nothing except the great rectangle of steel and three-quarters of the way up on the left outer edge a brass square plate, a six-inch square of metal.

"His back's to you but can you see what he does?"

"Well, he doesn't fiddle with keys or anything like that. He just puts up his hand and slides that brass square back."

"Which hand?"

"Well, the right, I suppose."

"Don't suppose. Shut your eyes and see it. Which hand?"

"The right."

"And then what?"

"The door opens."

"But you know it doesn't. You've slid the brass plate back yourself and nothing happens."

It was true, she had, on his instructions only a week before. Behind the brass plate in the six-inch recess there was nothing except a plain facing of metal, not steel, but some kind of chromium, highly polished. The pressure of her fingers had also slid this back to reveal the unmarked steel of the door behind. After a few seconds this inner plate had returned to its original position, probably activated by some hidden spring, she thought.

"Well, he must slide the inner plate over, too. But I did that, you know. Then it just came back."

"I know. Go up to the wall, pretend it's the door and go through the motions. His motions. Just let yourself be him, be what you've seen."

Obediently, she did as he said; moving up to the wall, imagining Sarling as she had once or twice seen him from behind.

Raikes said, "When he walks up, does he feel in his pockets for anything . . . keys, anything?"

"No. He just puts up a hand like this." She immersed herself in Sarling, was him, translating herself into the memory of the man's movements, and she went right through the performance. . . . Slide the brass plate over, and then the chromium one. She finished the mime.

From behind her, he said, "Do it again."

She went through the performance again.

"All right."

She turned, to find him looking pleased and she knew something had happened.

"What did I do?" she asked.

"Don't you know?"

"No. Well, just what he did, I suppose. But I've gone through all this—"

"Not before you haven't. Not this way. You made yourself into Sarling. That was good. And you put up your right hand to slide over the brass plate. But when you pretended to slide over the plate beneath, do you know what you did?"

"Just slid it over."

"You slid it over with your left hand."

"Did I?"

"Yes."

"Is that important?"

85

"God knows. But it's something to work on. Why not just slide it over with your right hand? It's raised, ready for action. But he puts up his left hand."

He moved over to get a drink, his face thoughtful. Over his shoulder, he said, "Try and watch him the next time he opens the door. Watch his left hand. It should be in your view. I want to know exactly what he does. Okay?"

"Yes, but—" she laughed, glad that he was pleased, glad that somehow she had produced something he wanted "—you could ask him yourself. He's coming to see you tomorrow. He asked me to tell you today. Just before lunch tomorrow. Here."

To her surprise, he ignored her joke, saying, "Now, tell me the sequence right through from when he pushes that second plate over. The steel door slides back into the right-hand wall, right?"

"Yes."

"When he comes out, what happens? How does he close it?"

"I've told you. There's a kind of bell-push thing in the wall outside the door. He just pushes it and the door comes sliding back into place. And don't ask me if I've tried pushing the thing when the door's shut. I have. And nothing happens. What about a drink for me?" This was the familiar, intimate, gentle bullying she could claim now.

He began to mix her a drink and said, "The procedure at Meon is the same?"

"Exactly. Only his study is different. But he opens the strong-room door just the same." She took her drink from him. "Personally I don't see how you're ever going to get into either strong room. Why don't you just play along with him until you've done whatever it is he wants? He'll never bother you again. He's given his word."

He said, angrily, "The bastard's got to go! He's got to go if either of us is ever going to have any peace. Can't you understand? Sarling isn't going to let go. Do one thing for him and then there'll be another and another. Oh, he may give you a break in between, but not for long. He likes owning people and using them. Well, he's not bloody well using me!"

86

He came over and put an arm around her shoulder, the fingers tightening and crooking against her flesh. She had the feeling of everything in her of love and longing being drawn out, drained from her to him. She moved hard against him, seeking him, wanting to rouse him. He kissed her between the top of her jaw and her ear, then turned from her and said, "Two other points. If he were at Park Street or Meon, late at night, would it be unusual for him to make a change of mind suddenly and decide to motor up to or down from London? Out of the blue?"

"No. He's like all rich men are. Changeable. Suddenly wanting something quite different. Not caring a damn what trouble it puts people to. He'd leave London at midnight . . . sometimes without telephoning ahead to Meon. I've known him even start to make a late journey like that and then change his mind halfway."

"Would he always be chauffeur-driven?"

"Not always. It wouldn't be unusual for me to drive him. Either in the Rolls, or my car, or one of the others."

Later, in bed, satisfied, Raikes sleeping heavily alongside her, as she stared into the darkness she could hear him saying, his voice bitter and angry, "He likes owning people and using them." But it was true of him, too. Whatever he had thought of her originally, no matter how much their present relationship had been forced on him, he was now at the point when he liked owning and using her. She belonged to him now in a way that Sarling had never possessed her. He and Berners were going to murder Sarling. They were going to set themselves free. That would be freeing her, too. When she had freedom? What then? Would he still want to own her? She had enough common sense to realise that he would never marry her. He had a life down in Devon. There had to be—or would be eventually— someone down there who would become his wife. Well, so what? He wasn't the kind of man a wife would satisfy completely, surely? She could have him still. He would want her, want some part of his life to be hers. Like Sarling, he wouldn't give anything he owned away. He might not use it for weeks, months, but he would never give it away.

Sarling sat in an armchair by the window, his legs wide apart, his body thrust forward, hands resting on the top of his walking stick. Sometimes he lowered his square, blunt, ugly head until his chin rested on the knuckles of one hand, a gargoyle pose, fixing Raikes with his brown eyes, the lemon sunlight through the window rinsing through the grey fluff of his hair.

Raikes, after a few minutes, had seen that Sarling was in a completely different mood from any he had known before. He was easy, confidential, talking as though they were boon companions.

Sarling said, "I was the seventh son of a seventh son. Maybe that should mean something."

"In Devon it means that such a man has the power to charm fish, but if he ever kills one then the power is lost."

"Interesting. Four of the other sons died before they were twenty. I left home when I was sixteen and I've never been back. It was a small village in Huntingdonshire. This—" he let one hand flow contemptuously down the stubby length of his body "—I got from a runt of a father and a scarecrow of a mother who'd had all the juice sucked out of her by my six brothers. And this—" he touched his face "—happened when I was twenty-one. I'd made my first fifty thousand. I celebrated with drink and a beautiful titled woman I wanted—who cost me five hundred pounds before she would even go through the bedroom door. She left a cigarette burning on top of a box of matches on the dressing table, and the room caught fire. I woke up thinking I was in hell, literally in a bed of flames. Since that time I've never touched alcohol or tobacco. Surgeons played about with my face for years. They produced a grotesque. I've been living with him ever since, grown fond of him, and wanted to do everything I could for him. You know why I tell you this?"

88

"You wouldn't be trying to get sympathy, would you?"

"From you?" Sarling laughed.

"Perhaps you're trying to justify yourself with me. That also would be a waste of time."

"Would it? A psychoanalyst would assure you that the rest of my life since this—" he put his fingers against his face "—has been no more than a compensation for being small of body and ugly to look at. Frankly that is all nonsense. The only thing that happened to me at twenty-one was that my face got mucked up and I learned that life was better without drink or smoke. If we could change bodies, I would be sitting here still, telling you about myself, the truth about myself."

"Which is?"

"That any ordinary way of living bores me and leaves me dissatisfied. I'm a gambler. I have to put myself and my ideas at risk in order to feel that I am alive. After you've made your first fifty thousand you have to be an idiot not to have a million in ten years and all without stepping outside the law. I did that and it wasn't enough. So, every so often, I began to step out-side the law. I put myself at risk in all sorts of ways and I got satisfaction and I got money. In a way I'm like a man who has a compulsion he doesn't understand to expose himself in public every so often. With me—well, each time I want to take bigger risks. This time it's going to be an audacious risk. That's why I need you. One which in years to come—when we are both dead—will make us both legends—if the truth is ever known."

"Dead or alive I don't want to be part of any bloody legend!"

"You don't have any choice. But as compensation you'll make a lot of money." He raised his stick and pointed it at Raikes. "I can guarantee you and Berners at least half a million between you."

"We don't want any more money."

"You don't know what you need. You've never faced it."

"I know exactly what I need. I need your files and photo-stats in my hands and you dead and then I can go back where I belong."

Sarling chuckled and rubbed the knob of his cane against the underside of his chin. "Haven't you really learned about yourself yet? What do you think made you do what you did? To revenge your father, to get back the old family home, to have the roots of a family called Raikes dig still deeper in the ground? You really believe that?"

"What I believe is my damn business!"

"And mine. If you were free now you'd last two years at the most. Then you would take to the high seas again. You're a plunderer, an adventurer—not a settler. And at heart you know it so well that you hate it. When the truth comes into your mind you overshout it with words like Alverton Manor, Mary Warburton, Devon and family. Even if you got rid of me there would be no escape for you. That's why I picked you from all the men in my files. Because you're like me . . . the big gamble, the big risk is the only thing that keeps you really alive."

"You're mad."

"But of course. We both are. It's only another way of saying that we're not like ninety-five per cent of other men. We have different dreams. We belong not to life but to the legends it creates."

Raikes shrugged his shoulders. "All right. When do we start making this dream a reality?"

"In a few months."

"And what is it to be?"

Sarling stood up. "You'll be told in time."

Sarcastically Raikes said, "It seems to me that all this talk of your love of risk really boils down to the fact that Berners and I will be taking it."

"Most of the physical part, yes. But you know as well as I do that risks are not just physical. There are risks a man can take in his mind, take by just talking over a telephone. To risk oneself, one's soul, one's destiny, one's spirit—that is the real joy."

Raikes, suddenly bored at the dramatics, said, "You need treatment—and I know what mine would be, given a chance."

Sarling beamed, an ugly contortion of face muscles, and said, delighted, "That too. That is part of my risk which makes me more alive than most men can be—knowing that I only have to make one mistake and you will kill me. I'm grateful to you for it."

"Don't bother with the gratitude. Just make the mistake and I promise you that the day I murder you I will feel more alive than most men ever can be."

Sarling gave a little nod of his head and went, and Raikes sat there thinking about his words. For Christ's sake, an adventurer, not a settler. Putting oneself at high risk in order to get an adrenalin kick. The man was crazy. But denying Sarling in his mind, he was conscious of having to do so more vigorously than should have been necessary. To forget about Sarling's words, he concentrated on the problem of getting rid of Sarling. Earlier that day he had met Berners in the R.A.C. where they had had a long discussion over the preliminary details they now held and had sketched between them a rough outline of a plan. No final plan could be made until they had solved the problem of the locks to the two strong rooms.

Just before Berners had left, Raikes had said, "Did you find out about the gas in those canisters?"

Berners nodded.

"Yes. You'd be surprised how much information there is in the public domain—if you know where to look for it."

He went on to tell Raikes about the gas. In the past year there had been a conference on Chemical and Biological Warfare, held in the Bonnington Hotel, London, sponsored by the J. D. Bernal Peace Library—this was an educational trust set up to collect material and provide information of assistance in the struggle to ensure the realisation of the fullest potentialities of science in building a world prosperous and without war. The aim of the conference had been to assess the present level of development of chemical and biological weapons and to discuss the ethical responsibility of scientists in relation to their development and use. All the papers read at the discussion had been published in book form.

"I just took a chance," said Berners. "I rang them and asked what they knew about a gas called Z/93. GF1. They said it was a nerve gas. What the Americans call a V- or G-agent, known as CMPF, or in full—cyclohexyl methylphosphonofluoridate. Used in the open it's for riot control, knocking a man out in a few seconds . . . colourless, odourless. It dissipates very quickly. Used in a confined space, where it could persist for more than a few minutes, it's lethal. Any doctor, not knowing the gas had been used, would ascribe death to heart failure. In fact that's what it would be. Some nice scientists around, aren't there?"

And they had a crate of it! He remembered how the sheep had gone down. And the old ewe. She'd caught the full sweep of it.

He got up and fixed himself a drink. Suddenly, he felt tired, played out. When Belle returned, she saw at once that he was surly and a little tight; an ashtray full of stubs on the floor by his side, one hand balancing the whisky glass on the arm of his chair. He looked up at her and said, "Tell me something good. Say he's fallen down the stairs and broken his neck."

"It wouldn't help if he had. There's still the files and the photostats." She came over and kissed him lightly on the forehead. "What's the trouble?"

"Nothing. I'm just waiting to wake up."

"I know." She went into her bedroom, took off her coat, and repaired the lipstick on her mouth.

Reflected in the mirror through the open bedroom door she could see him sitting in his chair, one hand coming up, scrubbing for a moment at the back of his head, a movement of exasperation, indicating the frustration in him. She knew how he felt. There was an anticipation growing in her now of his moods. She knew his gestures and movements and frequently knew what they shadowed in his mind. That was something which had never happened between her and any other man before.

She went back to him, sitting on the arm of a chair, knowing she looked good, noticing how even in his absorption his eyes followed the crossing of her long legs and then came up to notice, but not to comment on, her new orange-coloured dress. She wrinkled her nose at him and he gave her a slow wink.

She said, "I've got something for you."

"I knew you had."

"Clever dick."

"You've found out something about the safe."

"Mind reader." She was pleased, liked to feel that there were these intimate currents of understanding between them. "Yes. He was at home most of the day. He used it twice and I managed to watch him and get a good view. He slides the top plate across with his right hand, just using two or three fingers on it. But for the plate underneath he raises his left hand and puts his thumb on it. Like this." She imitated the movement. "He keeps it firmly there for a few seconds and then slides the plate across with the tips of his fingers against the edge of the plate. After about five seconds the door swings open. It's clearly something to do with the way he puts his thumb on it."

"Did you try it yourself that way?"

"Yes. After he'd gone. But nothing happened for me. I put my left thumb on the plate and pushed it over and waited. But after about five seconds it just came back into position again. Don't you think that's odd?"

He sat forward. "Yes, I do. But that's just what it's meant to be."

"I did something else, too. He's had Meon Park for a long time, but we've only been in Mount Street for four years. He had a lot of work done on the place before he went in. Having that strong room put in was one of the things. All the bills for the work on the house, like everything at Meon Park, household accounts, fuel bills and all that . . . well, they're kept. That's part of my job. So I went right back over them—and guess what I found?"

He smiled, reached out and drew the tip of a forefinger down the front of her right leg. The touch was like a small electric current going through her.

"You found the bill for the installation of the strong room."

93

"Yes. It was put in by a London firm. Finch and Lyle, Lock and Safe Company. They're in Fitzroy Square. The account said to installing etcetera and etcetera as per specification of existing strong room at Meon Park. The same firm did them both."

"No details of the lock mechanism?"

"No. Something else too. Finch and Lyle are a subsidiary of one of his bigger companies. I don't know whether that means anything, but I thought you'd like to know. It was quite odd to watch, you know. All this time with him and I'd never really taken all that much notice. He just put his left thumb on it, pushed it over and it opened. What kind of lock is that?"

"I don't know. But I'm going to find out." He stood up, drew her to him, kissed her and said, "What would I do without you?"

"Find someone else?"

He raised his right hand and touched her cheek with his knuckles, an affectionate kneading of his skin against hers, sensation moving deep down into her.

"You know why you say that, don't you?"

"Do I?"

"Yes. We both want to get out. To get out I'd do anything. Use anyone. I'll be honest. Right at the beginning I did decide to use you. Be nice to you and get you on my side . . . But no matter how it started—that's not the way it is now. And you know it. You know it when I put my arms around you, when I'm in bed with you, or when we're both sitting quietly in our chairs reading, don't you?"

"Well, yes, I suppose so—"

"Don't suppose any longer."

He pulled her to him and kissed her. He felt her cling to him, her body trembling with pathetic, undisguisable need for him. He strained her to him as though the same need existed in himself. But in the cold, remote laboratory of his mind he knew that a stage had been reached when she could be counted on as a constant factor, unshakably on his side, a modulus that would

94

be utterly reliable in his and Berners' calculations until Sarling was gone—and then she would have to go. Against his cheek he felt the warm touch of a happy tear from her, as he considered the best way to tackle this Finch and Lyle thing. It wasn't something he need bother Berners with yet.

Raikes, under another name, booked a room at Brown's Hotel in Dover Street. From there he rang Finch and Lyle and spoke to the sales manager. He explained that he was a partner in a firm of architects in the north of England who were the designers of a new factory to be put up by a nationally-known firm of carpet manufacturers in Northern Ireland. He, Raikes, was approaching various firms about the supply of certain hardware for the proposed factory. Chiefly he was interested in door fittings, locks, handles, and safes. It was a contract that would run into thousands of pounds . . . The sales manager rose hungrily. He had the feeling he got on the river when a winter grayling came hard up from four feet below, grabbed the fly and turned down with it.

The following morning he spent two hours at the offices of Finch and Lyle going over their catalogues and inspecting samples of their products and then took the sales manager out to lunch, preparing him with three large pink gins and easing him into a state of goodwill and bonhomie with a bottle of burgundy and two brandies with their coffee. Raikes let slip that he was lunching the next day with a representative from another firm—"Naturally, old man, one has to survey the field, but your stuff looks just the job for me"—knowing that a touch of anxiety made a ready victim readier. He lunched the man again and this time spoke without much enthusiasm of the other firm he had seen, and hinted that if Finch and Lyle got the contract—strictly on a competitive basis, old man, you know, with a wink—then there wasn't any reason why a little something on the side mightn't be managed if things went well. Two days later—spent ostensibly in a trip to the Midlands—he

95

had the sales manager out to dinner. He cemented their friendship with food and drink and then commented that the chairman
of the carpet company wanted a small strong room off his office.
"Colourful type, always after something new, like to find
something that would really please him, something he could
boast about. . . ." Spent, played out, belly turning as he was
drawn nearer the net, the fish let itself be landed.

"You know, we might have just the thing. Not in production
yet, but we have made a few prototypes. Damned ingenious.
Really on our secret list. Fact, tell you who's got a couple.
Chairman of our Group. Trouble is getting costs down . . .
you know, for a general market."

Into Raikes' lap was poured all he wanted. At midnight he
put the man in a taxi, the parting of true friends—Raikes to
return up North. Two days later, with Belle playing the secretary first, Raikes came on, sadness and anger alternating,
saying that the whole bloody project had hit a snag, trouble with
the Northern Ireland authorities over the site and finance, not
definitely off but the look of it not liked. "I'll give you a call the
moment anything breaks. . . ." The call, of course, never to
come.

Settling back with his drink, Belle busy in the small kitchen,
he knew that it was the information which they needed to send
Sarling neatly and cleanly out of this world and put the photostats at Meon and the files at Mount Street safely into his hands.
A thumbprint lock. Provisional patents already approved, but
the thing itself—while no dead secret—still not ready for
general production. You put your thumb on the shiny metal
plate, making a nice clear print. You slid the plate into its recess
and somewhere in there a little photo-electric eye scanned the
whorls and convolutions, matching the new thumbprint with the
master one already installed. If the match were right, then other
impulses slid back the great locking bars and rods and the door
swung open. Put an alien thumbprint on the plate and the
inhuman eye within the recess rejected it at once and pushed the
plate back, wiping it clean automatically, and the door

remained shut. Berners had been fascinated when he had told him. It was the kind of device Berners loved, no matter how much he preferred the eighteenth to the twentieth century. From now on the rest was routine. Sarling would die. He and Berners would be free and, when they were, they would have the comparatively minor problem of Belle, fussing now in the kitchen, humming to herself, content, as though they had been married years.

In the kitchen, preparing to cook, Belle leaned over the small table on which the cookery book lay open, humming gently to herself, two lines of thought running clear in her mind. The book below her said, "Simmer the scallops in white wine for ten minutes, then cut them in quarters. . . ." He had said, "It opens with his thumbprint. I don't entirely understand the technical side of it. But that's how it works." And the book, "Toss them in butter with shallots, mushrooms and parsley. Stir in a little flour and enough of the cooking liquid to make a thick sauce." God, why didn't she have the knack of cooking like other women? What did toss them in butter really mean, swirl them round? He was changing. No doubt about it. And it had been honest of him to say what he had. Use her. She'd known it. But not now. Something was happening. "Cook all together for a few minutes." And let's hope to God it all turns out right, the scallops and this thing between us. White wine? What kind of white wine did they mean? Sweet or dry? She straightened up, pushing her hair back from one eye. She had both. Better mix it, half and half.

Berners sat at the window, papers and photographs, notes and plans spread before him on the small Queen Anne table. The midday was hazy with the old gold light of a low winter sun. Tomorrow, thought Berners, he would go to Meon Park, to see on the ground what lay before him now in the photographs and plans. Park Street he already knew, could shut his eyes and move through it with the sureness of a cat in the dark, could have

97

gone into the dining room and without a glimmer from the out-side street light have reached out to the sideboard and picked out the sherry decanter from the port unerringly. Meon Park already was coming to life for him, but until he had actually seen it from the outside with his own eyes he knew that he would not possess it completely. He sipped at his hock, full of a mild pleasure, a pleasure curiously that he had not known since he had retired from business with Frampton.

Methodically, he went over the broad plan which he had built up since he had been told of the thumbprint lock. The operation would have to start at Meon Park. (This, simply because there were fewer servants at Park Street than at Meon, and the fewer servants in the place the less risk of observation or disturbance would there be for the final phase of the opera-tion.) Sarling had to be at Meon, surprised and taken, the strong room opened with the print of his left thumb. . . . Sarling gagged or unconscious, Sarling knowing exactly what lay before him, seeing in a flash their plan and his own help-lessness. He was glad that there were so many complexities in this. There would have been no pleasure, only tedium, in a task which could have been easily achieved. The strong room at Meon opened and the photostats in their hands Sarling would have to make a change of plan, call for a car and announce that he was going to London. Eccentric, self-willed, stumping down the great oak stairway, out to a waiting car with Miss Vickers to drive, the rear lights moving down the elm-lined drive, a wisp of exhaust fume like floating hoar frost wreathing for a moment behind it . . . Only it wouldn't, couldn't be Sarling. It must be him. Height and build were much the same . . . There was no fear or apprehension in him at this thought.

Somewhere the car must stop for the real Sarling and Raikes to be picked up. He let his mind run on, seeing it all, teasing now and then at some point of procedure, the inevitable dove-tailing and search for flaws. The gas canisters made no great noise when they exploded, but the fragmentation would have to be contained. Dead or alive Sarling's thumbprint would work at Mount Street ... Ingenious the thumbprint lock, but it carried its own dangers. Every lock did. There was no lock that man could not break or cajole. Memory slipping into his deliberations brought back the picture of a lock he had once seen in the Victoria and Albert Museum. He searched for the maker's name. An antique detector lock ... Yes, Johannes Wilkes de Birmingham ... He'd always liked the *de Birmingham* ... *Johannes Wilkes de Birmingham Fecit.* Well, the death of Sarling could soon be under-written *Aubrey Catwell Fecit*; Sarling dead, mortality mixing with sleep, the raw, red, blotched and ugly face a stiff mask to the dawn as a man-servant drew the curtains, stared down at the counterpaned lump that had once been life and felt shock but no pity, no sorrow, for men like Sarling had no way to the hearts of other men.

He sat there planning the detail because this was the division between himself and Frampton. Frampton stood out in front, bringing confidence and assurance, and the right word and manner to all their dealings with the public, the two of them dovetailing to a combination which had only once shown the smallest fleck of bad workmanship. Although it had been Frampton's fault, he had no condemnation, anger or regret. It was, in a way, welcome. It gave him this problem to absorb him. Perhaps, after all, he had been getting a little bored with his brief days in Brighton.

The following morning at ten Sarling arrived at the Mount Street flat. Only Raikes was there. For fifteen minutes he sat in the armchair by the window and talked with very little interruption from Raikes. He sat there, a small bunched up crow of a man, his voice precise, authoritative, the chairman reviewing a situation, decision already made, the programme of work now being delegated and the few interruptions swiftly dealt with. There was no momentary softening of his persona-lity, no touch of friendliness or acknowledgment of the basic antagonism between them. Raikes was given an exposition and then his orders.

When he rose to go, Raikes said, "And where is all this stuff coming from?"

"That you will know later."

"And it'll be my job to get it?"

"Of course."

"I don't see why you can't tell me the details now."

"There's no need for you to know yet. First, we must arrange the market. You've got all the facts you need for that."

"And I'm to appear as the principal in this?"

"Yes."

"But this man will know I'm not if he's got any sense."

"Of course he will. He's not a principal himself. In this kind of business the principals never appear. In fact they're seldom known. All you have to do is to make your introduction to him and talk business."

"He might want to know where the stuff is coming from."

"If he asks you that question you get up and leave."

At the door Raikes said sharply, "You know, sometimes I feel like telling you to go to hell. Do your worst. I'm walking out."

"Naturally, but that's only an emotional phase. You know you can't do that."

Sarling gone, Raikes went to the telephone and dialled a number. A man's voice at the other end said, "Yes?"

Raikes said, "Tony's back and wants an appointment."

"Which Tony?" There was no lift, no curiosity in the voice.

"The Applegate one."

Raikes heard the phone put down firmly on to the receiver rests and the line went dead. He put back his own receiver, walked to the window and lit a cigarette. It was all a cold, bare dream, and he was in it, a principal in it.

Five minutes later his telephone rang.

The same voice on the other end said, "Tony?"

"Yes."

"Four o'clock today. The Ritz. Room 97. Go straight up. Don't knock. Just walk in."

"Thank you."

The line at the other end went dead.

At four o'clock Raikes walked into the Ritz Hotel. A wedding reception was just breaking up in the main hall; men in morning suits studded with carnations, high-heeled girls in silk suits and dresses and a bizarre movement of wedding hats ... this was how it would be when he married Mary ... grey and black toppers, the pop of flash bulbs and champagne corks ... half the county and the same high chatter and laughter ... Raikes taking his bride back to Alverton ... Raikes now, he thought, going up in the lift to fix up a deal ... gold bullion that still had to be stolen by him. *Tony's back and wants an appointment.* What world was he being pushed into?

He opened the door of number 97 and walked through a small hall to the open door of the sitting room. It was furnished in green: green carpet, green settee and chairs and green and white curtains. A bowl of chrysanthemums on the table exploded great puffs of yellow, bronze and red in the air. A man was sitting at a small desk writing. He turned, gave Raikes a smile and a nod and waved a hand at a chair, a movement that flashed a frost-white cuff and a gleam of gold cuff-link. He was about thirty, tanned skin, dark hair and everything about him very clean, fresh-pressed and laundered. His teeth shone and the whites of his eyes were healthy, the eyes smiling and friendly. He was full of warmth of the Mediterranean sun; the smallest of his movements sleek and assured, knowing where he came from, certain of where he was going, content with his secret world; poised, with a smooth air of knowing the arcane rituals demanded of him as though he had been born fully equipped, adult from a boy to fill his destined niche in a luxurious twilight underworld where gold ruled.

"Cigarettes in the box there, if you use them. Excuse me a minute." He turned back to the desk and went on writing.

It was a psychological pause, full of friendly understanding, to give Raikes a moment or two to get settled.

With surprise Raikes recognised that he was nervous and unready. He took a cigarette from his own case and lit it. The man turned at the snap of the lighter and then swung his chair right round to face Raikes.

"Like to get right down to it? No polite preliminary chat?"

"Yes." His voice shadowed the resentment inside him. The man was being nice to him because he knew he was nervous.

"Good. What's the offer?"

"I want a price, chiefly for 'good delivery bars'. Four hundred ounces. There might be also some kilo bars."

"How many of each?"

"It's not certain yet. But anything from fifty up to a hundred of the big bars. The kilo bars . . . I don't know. But that doesn't stop a price being fixed."

The man smiled. "Nothing stops a price being fixed when there's good will on both sides. At thirty-five dollars an ounce— which is the U.S.A. Treasury price—the four-hundred-ounce jobs are worth somewhere around fourteen thousand dollars a piece. The kilos, say, a thousand one hundred and twenty. That's not our price, of course. On the free market the price runs from well over forty dollars an ounce upwards. The big boys would have to be smelted. For our trade we like the kilos or the real babies like this."

He put his hand in his pocket and tossed something across to Raikes who caught it. It was a piece of gold in the shape of a large chocolate.

"Ten-tola bar. There are millions of them being hoarded in places like India . . . all the countries of the East. They don't have much faith in paper currencies. Gold is gold. It never changes. Your stuff would be from London?"

"Probably."

"Delivery date?"

"Sometime next April."

"Where? It affects the price."

"I'd like a price for England, and another for the Continent."

"You'd drop a lot on an English delivery. We'll give you one, but we'd prefer the Continent. That'll put up your operating cost but not as much as the price difference. What about payment?"

"Dollars?"

"Anything you say." He smiled. "Vietnamese piastres or Cambodian riels, if you like."

"Dollars. Deposited abroad."

"When a price is fixed, you give me the details. Any bank you like, Switzerland, Beirut . . . but watch where you choose because if our price is in dollars you'll have to watch the exchange rates. You don't mind me saying that, do you?"

"Should I?"

"Well, I get the impression that this is the first time you've handled this type of merchandise. It can be a tricky business. But you don't have to worry about trusting us. We fix a price, you deliver and we pay. In this business if you cheat someone once you don't get any more business. The word goes round. Sometimes the small boys, the agents and carriers try it . . . well, then they just go right out of business for life. We find them and fix them wherever they go. So, for your peace of mind I'm telling you that within its own framework it's strictly honest. We're just business men operating a market which governments have created by their regulations, gold price fixing, and some of them by refusing their citizens the right to buy or hold gold. Thirty-five dollars an ounce is the official price. You can get anything from forty to sixty dollars and upwards on the black market, but out of the difference we've got all our expenses and losses to meet. I've known a Dubai dhow captain on the Persian Gulf–India run dump his whole shipment overboard in an emergency and never recover it. We stood the loss—a hundred and thirty thousand dollars' worth. But the captain did what he had to and he still works for us. Sorry if I'm chatting too much, but I didn't want you to have any wrong ideas about us. You can trust us."

103

"And you can trust me?"

The white teeth flashed. "Somebody gave us your phone number, and you the word 'Applegate' and a phone number. That's where the trust is." He stood up. "Ring the number you've got in a couple of weeks, we'll have something for you by then."

"Thank you." Raikes rose and held out the ten-tola bar to him. He shook his head. "Keep it. Give it to your girl friend. As a citizen of the United Kingdom you're not allowed to hold gold, but I doubt whether that will worry you." He moved to the door with Raikes, held out his hand and added, "Don't bother to check when you get down below. I'm registered in the name of Benson. Very English, no?"

For the first time in his life Raikes felt himself inadequate, humbled almost. He felt like a new, raw employee, moving to a master's orders and not fully comprehending them. For him this was novel and immediately resented. He was used to being his own boss and to navigating waters that he understood fully. Nothing about this was real. It was a game of make believe where he had to pretend that one day he would be fully engaged in some operation already conceived in Sarling's brain. But he wasn't going to be engaged in anything. Sarling was going to be killed, and he was going to go back to Devon. He couldn't take any real interest in the gold smuggling world because he knew he was never going to be involved in it. Fifty "good delivery bars", 400 ounces each at fourteen thousand dollars . . . seven hundred thousand dollars . . . one hundred such bars would be one million four hundred thousand dollars . . . that was getting on for nearly three-quarters of a million pounds. What craziness had Sarling in mind? The man had to be put down. He stopped halfway up Bond Street and, unbothered by the pavement crowds and traffic, dropped the ten-tola bar down a gutter drain. So much for Sarling and Benson.

Berners when they met in the R.A.C. said, "He couldn't be stupid enough to think a bank could be tackled? One of the bullion dealers perhaps? Or something in transit?"

At ease now, smoothed by Berners' presence, himself again, knowing exactly where he was going, Raikes said, "I don't know what he's got in his mind. I'm just not having any part of it. You've been to Meon—how soon could you be ready?"

"I'm ready now. All we want is a few hours' warning that Sarling is going to Meon Park for the night. Enough time for us to get there before him."

"He goes abroad tomorrow. For three weeks, according to Miss Vickers."

"That's good. It gives us time for a final meeting and I'll let you have all the details. Then you can brief her."

Raikes shook his head. "All this gold business. This chap Benson just sat there as though we were agreeing the delivery of carpets . . . everything square and above board."

Berners smiled, pushing a hand over his pale hair. "You did the same only on a smaller scale and with different goods. Sarling obviously got you in there. That wasn't difficult for him. Most of these millionaire international types hold gold in some vault or other abroad. No matter how respectable he is he'd have contacts, probably some oil tycoon or a Greek shipping magnate who would only have to give him a phone number and a few code phrases and then forget all about it. For all you know Sarling may have an interest in gold smuggling to the East. He'd be so far back from the real operations he could never be traced. I must say I'd like to know what his project is before we finish with him."

"Why?"

Berners rolled a few cake crumbs under his finger on the table. "We might begin thinking it over and decide to take it on—by ourselves."

"Not me! I just want him out of the way so that I can go back where I came from. Don't you?"

"Yes . . . I suppose so."

"Then let's get him out of the way."

"And the girl?"

"Her, too. But we won't be able to rush that, and it'll have to look like an accident. And I'm not asking you to have anything to do with that. I'll do it."

Berners shook his head. "I'll do it with you. Everything in this affair we do together." He looked at his watch. "I must get my train."

CHAPTER SEVEN

RAIKES WENT DOWN to Devon for Christmas and stayed over well into the New Year. While in London he had kept in touch with Mary through letters and a few phone calls from his club. He had plenty to do while he was at home. He would be taking over Alverton soon. There were builders' estimates to be approved for the alterations he wanted made before he moved in and lists of furniture still to be bought for him by his Exeter dealer for the moment of his re-entry. In addition there were a lot of new furnishings which had to be provided for the house. He spent a good deal of time with Mary discussing this and arranging with her for the various purchases. Although they were not officially engaged, it was understood that they would be as soon as the house was his. He wanted the engagement to be made from the house.

Mary stayed two days with him at his present house, rumpling the bed in the spare room for Mrs. Hamilton to make in the morning, a courtesy which Mrs. Hamilton appreciated but which did not deceive her, nor was intended to. They went shopping, paid visits together, and took long walks either along the river or up on the moors. Sarling, Mount Street and all the fantasy that London held receded from him. This was his country and his place and he had only to be back for a few hours and it claimed him absolutely as it had always done. But this time there was a difference which he could not help but notice. There was a change in his relationship with Mary and it was impossible for him to tell whether it came from her or from him. To satisfy himself, he explained it by the unseen presence

107

of Belle. No matter how contrived and forced by circumstances, nor how genuine he had had to make it seem for Belle, the aura of their relationship persisted with him down here. He felt that something of this made itself known to Mary. There were moments when he would turn to find that she was looking at him reflectively. He pretended not to notice and she, as though in willing conspiracy, threw off her mood, effervescing into gaiety and talk to convince him, utterly if she could, that there had not been anything.

But there were moments when this pretence betrayed itself. Lying by her side one night, waking and feeling her near him, he reached out in the dark and his hand found her face, smoothing the line of her cheek. To his surprise he felt the wetness of tears. In the dark he pulled her face gently to his and kissed her eyes.

"Why?" he asked.

After a moment for time and darkness to raise a defence for her she said, "Why not? Because I'm happy. Because you're here and there's so much ahead of us. When a girl's happy she gets the choice of smiles or tears. Sometimes I like to cry because I'm happy—only I'm not too keen about your seeing the tears. Men always think tears are for unhappiness."

He said, "You'd tell me if anything was wrong, wouldn't you?"

"If it was something you had to know, yes."

The moon, dying from its full, laid a great sword blade of cold light from the window across the far wall. Outside there was hard frost and the long grass would be white, crisp meringue to the feet in the morning.

"Anything that was wrong between us I would have to know." His hand moved, sliding over the curve of a breast, fingertips softly acknowledging the nipple, hovering, barely touching until it rose in hardness to him.

"I've got everything I want. No troubles. So let me have my sloppy tears, too."

He pulled her to him, made love to her, a rare gentleness guiding and possessing him and her. Afterwards, while she slept, he lay watching the blade of moonlight on the wall thicken from rapier thinness to a blunt Roman sword, and he knew that he had, not everything he wanted, but nearly everything. The things he lacked would come. . . .

Another day, coming back from a country house sale near Minehead where he had been buying some old silver with Mary, they stopped for an evening drink at the Anchor Inn at Dulverton. Sitting together in the bar, fox masks over the fireplace, a stuffed monster trout in a case behind them, Mary from out of the blue had suddenly said, "If you had to list the things that mean most to you in order of preference what would you put at the top?"

"You, of course."

"Because you love me? Oh, I know we have our own ideas about what love means exactly. But me, because you really love me, no matter what?"

"Yes, you. But what's the 'no matter what' bit about?"

"I don't know really. Well, yes, I suppose I mean real love for me. Not just wanting me as part of a picture you've got in your mind. You know, us, Alverton, you retiring, children, the good life."

"Well, of course, I want all that. But over and above that I want you. What's got into you?"

She laughed. "Two dry martinis, I should think."

He smiled. "Have another drink. That'll take you clear out on the other side."

But driving back, the question kept coming to him—What is she trying to say? Always before she'd accepted, as he did, the fact of their love. She couldn't be jealous of other women. She knew perfectly well that he had them occasionally. And she knew equally well that when they were married he wouldn't have any other woman but her . . . wouldn't want any other. Then the thought came to him, perhaps she isn't trying to say anything to me, perhaps she's waiting for me to say something. Perhaps something of all this Sarling business shows and she wants reassurance that I am what I've always been.

In the headlights something moved across the country road. Mary said, "Fox?"

"No. Otter. Travelling. Probably coming up from the Barle and over into the Exe."

He carried the lumping hindquarter movement of the animal in his mind. Down on the river at home when the snows came there was a bank which the otters turned into a slide. At the age of eight he had stood, screened by the snow-mantled bulk of a holly tree, hand in his father's and first seen the play, until finally, unable to hold back half shout half laugh as the old dog otter had gone down on his back, paws waving and tail thumping, the noise had ended the exhibition. Eight years old . . . in eight years' time he wanted to stand there, a small hand in his.

He went back to London, arriving late on a Wednesday evening. Although she was disappointed that he did not make love to her that night Belle showed him no sign of it. He came from one world into another. There had to be time for readjustment.

On the Thursday he met Berners at the R.A.C. and they completed their detailed arrangements for dealing with Sarling the moment he gave them a chance after his return.

After the meeting at the club, Raikes went back to Mount Street and briefed Belle with the details of their plan. From this moment they waited on Sarling's return and his first visit to Meon Park.

That night Raikes made love to Belle and as far as he was concerned it was no different from many another night. He needed her; they needed her, she had to be kept as their creature until they had no more use for her.

He would have gone back to Devon for the weekend but Belle had a call from Sarling in Paris saying that he was probably returning on the Saturday and she could drive him down later that day to spend the weekend at Meon.

The next morning at eight o'clock the telephone in the Mount Street flat rang. Belle answered it. It was Sarling from

Paris. When Sarling had finished talking to her, she went into the bedroom where Raikes was half-dressed in shirt and trousers. He turned from brushing his hair, an untied tie hanging loose over his shirt and smiled at her. He stood there big and solid, the man she knew she loved, all question of doubt gone from her. He came to her, put up his hands and cradled her face, looking at her, and then, sliding the hands up and into her hair, tilted her face to his.

"Who was it?"

"Sarling. He's definitely coming back."

"When?"

"Tomorrow, about lunchtime. I've got to be at Park Street to meet him. Then I'm to drive him down to Meon. He'll be there over the weekend."

He stood there close to her, yet entirely remote from her. Then, without a word, he went into the sitting room. She stayed in the bedroom, heard him dialling and knew that he was calling Berners. She heard the careful words, masquerading his true meaning yet clearly understood by the man at the other end. She moved into the room as he put the receiver down.

She said, "You're really going through with it?"

He turned, bulkily silhouetted against the window, his hands going up, taking the loose tie and beginning to knot it, and said without emotion or emphasis, "In two days' time the bastard will be dead."

Goaded by his coldness, she said, "I could tell him."

In the same even voice, he said, "Tell him then. Spoil it all. But I'll find some other way. I am not living as his creature one day longer than I have to."

He came over to her, put his arm around her shoulder, holding her to him, and she knew that he was not beginning to cajole her, to win her round again. He knew he had her, knew that she would never tell Sarling. He kissed her and stepped away from her and said, "I know how you feel. It's the hour before dawn. It's always the coldest of the night. I prescribe hot coffee."

"I'm sorry. I suppose it was just . . . well, a bit of a shock. Him phoning like that and suddenly it all being right on top of us."

"Coffee—and stop worrying," he said briskly, touched her cheek and turned back into his bedroom. She went through to the kitchen to make coffee, all the doors open behind her and heard him whistling. She realised that for the first time since she had known him he was really happy. Sarling's call was the beginning of his release . . . he was thundering down the stairs, rushing out of school, out of prison, whistling like a bloody bird because the days ahead were full of freedom.

Sarling arrived at London Airport just after midday. A car and chauffeur from the Overseas Mercantile Bank waited for him. Forty minutes later he walked into the Mount Street flat. Raikes was sitting in a chair by the window reading a newspaper.

Sarling said, "Belle is at Park Street?"

"Yes."

"I haven't had lunch. Could I have a glass of milk?"

For a moment Raikes was tempted to tell him to help himself. Then, seeing him as dead already, he decided that it would be polite to offer him some last service, the first coin placed on the dead eyelid. He fetched milk from the kitchen.

Sarling sat and drank. He said, "I know you have commitments in Devon. I thought I'd come and have a talk and get things cleared up so that you could feel free for a while. Free to do what you want—and also to think about what I want."

"Your famous operation?"

"Precisely." Sarling drained the glass and put it on a table, the milk film staining the inside of the tumbler in a grey wash. "What happened about the gold?"

"I'm getting a price and delivery details soon."

"Good. There's one point I'd like to make clear. Half of the profit we make on this goes to yourself and Berners."

"You're only really interested in the kicks. The big risk?"

"Yes."

"Aren't they going to fall flat? Berners and I have to plan and execute it. You'll just be riding on our backs, waving a little flag."

"You've got it wrong. All I want from you is the execution. The plan is mine."

"It's a comfortable division for you, isn't it? If anything goes wrong—and don't tell me you haven't thought of this one—nothing will be traced to you. You will be so far back being an eminent international financier that nobody would be able to touch you even if they for one moment suspected that you should be touched. However . . . just give me my holiday task and I'll go away and get on with it."

"Very well. We're going to steal gold bullion."

"I'd gathered that."

"Not from a bank, not from any City gold dealer's vaults or from any security van. We're going to take it on the high seas from a ship. Does that appeal to you?"

"No. But to some of my ancestors it might have. One of them was a captain with Drake. Which ship?"

"From the newest and most beautiful in the world, the latest of a famous line."

Sarling opened the brief case on his lap and pulled out a large brochure. He handed it over to Raikes. It was a large quarto-sized brochure, thickish, the white cover of glossy paper. Red lettering at the top ran—THE NEW CUNARDER QUEEN ELIZABETH 2.

Raikes opened the brochure at random. Below him was a two-page spread showing three men, half length, in the uniform of the Cunard line; the Captain, the Chief Engineer and the Hotel Manager of the *Queen Elizabeth 2* . . . white-topped caps, on their peaks scrambled egg and the crown-crested emblem of the Cunard Line, a lion holding up the world, white shirts, black ties, medal ribbons on their shoulders, eight brass buttons gleaming against the dark blue jackets, four gold rings on the captain's sleeves, and the captain's face, sea- and sun-tanned, bearded, weathered and character-creased and looking something like Sir Francis Drake, or maybe that was just the beard. His eye caught the blurbs of print against each man ... Captain William Eldon Warwick. "What do I like about this job?" And the printed answer, seeming almost an answer from Raikes' own ego. "Well, I suppose it's one of the last ways of life where you are on your own and your own boss." Your own boss. Numbness thawed. Raikes looked at Sarling. Sarling said nothing.

Still held by the magnitude of the other man's fantasy, his fingers turned the publicity-packed pages ... images flicking up at him. A blonde girl in a red dress sprawled across a bed in a de-luxe cabin ... a bronzed, old-gold shot of a propeller, the six flanged blades in silhouette like the thrusting head of some heavily armoured prehistoric animal.

"You're mad," said Raikes.

"On the contrary I am a practical man."

Another two-page spread, the new ship itself, an artist's impression; Caribbean palm fronds, amethyst sea, and the long lovely length of the ship, dark hull sheering from the bows, the brilliant red waterline mark, dazzling white upper decks and superstructure, and lifeboats festooned along her boat deck like cocoons below the stark, wind-cheating line of the funnel.

Raikes tossed the brochure back to Sarling. He was himself now, complete, his secret revolt already successful because by the next day Sarling would be dead, but even this knowledge was not enough to edge with the thinnest aura of pretence the genuineness of his protest. "It's the maddest bloody thing I've ever heard!"

"On the contrary, it's a practical proposition."

"For Christ's sake, Sarling!" He was angry now. "What is this? Captain Blood and the Crown Jewels, The Man Who Broke the Bank at Monte Carlo, The Great Mail Train Robbery? You've gone round the bend."

"We're going to do it. My plan and your execution." He took other papers from the brief case, clipped them inside the brochure and put the brochure on the side table. "There's some stuff there you can read through. Some of it just normal press handouts and publicity matter. Some of it notes I've made from information which has come to me through my business life. None of it is secret. Anyone could have got it. Read it."

"Why should I? I can tell you now that you'd need an army. More men than you've got on your files. Forget it. Why not ask me to get the Crown Jewels? That, now, I might just manage for you."

Sarling shook his head. "It can be done. At the moment, as you've probably read in the press, she's not in service yet. She's at Southampton and there's been trouble over her turbines so that the Cunard people have had to cancel all her schedules. That means we can't fix any dates at the moment—but what we're going to do is to take the gold off her on her first regular westbound run across the North Atlantic to New York."

"Then you'd better hire a battleship to hold her up. Sarling, be sensible. All right, maybe you had a bad childhood, maybe your face got mucked about—but this is overcompensating. Just keep it for your dreams."

"The gold comes out of her Specie Room on her maiden outward run. We don't need a battleship or an army of men. It can be done by having just two people aboard, and done without violence and without fuss. She carries three thousand passengers and crew. Not more than a couple of dozen, most of them just curious, unsuspecting onlookers, will ever see it happen. You've got plenty of time. Go away and then come back and tell me how it is to be done. I know. It amuses me to speculate whether you can match my plan. Two people, no violence and the gold vanishes." He chuckled, his ugly face contorting, his glee childish in sound, hands rubbing together, dry-skinned, rasping, the happy master of ceremonies who had set the party an apparently impossible conundrum . . . three men on a river bank, one boat, how do they all get to the other side and yet leave the boat on the bank where they had found it?

"Well, nothing about this amuses me. Nothing." In fact, there was an element of sacrilege about it. He was a Devon man, the sea and its ships were part of the heritage of every Devon man. Men of his family long before him had been with Raleigh, Hawkins and Drake, with Fisher and Beatty; his two brothers had been submariners, a ship their coffin, the sea their grave. The memory of a picture book of his childhood flashed back into his mind like the sudden, sun-brightened leap of a salmon, each detail etched vivid and clear for a second, a picture of a red-stacked, paddle-wheeled boat, the *Britannia*, the first Cunarder, which had bucketted across the North Atlantic for the first time in 1840 to Halifax, Nova Scotia, her passageways lit by candles and a cow on deck to provide fresh milk for the passengers. Turn the pages of memory and they were all there . . . the *Mauretania*, holding for 22 years the Atlantic record, and then the Queens, *Queen Mary, Queen Elizabeth*. . . . War could ravage them all, destroy them, but to steal from them would be an act of desecration like the taking of silver candlesticks and salvers from an altar.

Raikes said angrily, "You're not taking me with you on this."

Sarling stood up. "I am. You'll get used to the idea. You'll fall in love with it. I know you. You'll come back to me in a month, and you'll have a plan. It might even be as good as my own. Walk round to Cunard House in Regent Street sometime. There's a model of the ship in their window. I often go and look at it. A new ship, the best that was ever built. And we're going to take the golden heart out of her on her first truly maiden run across the Atlantic."

He went to the door, paused, looked back, and waited for Raikes to speak. Raikes, back to him, moved to the sideboard. Two sparrows suddenly alighted in fight on the windowsill, their cries high and chattering. A car braked in the road outside, tyres screeching in agony at their brief and violent meld against the road. Raikes picked up the brandy bottle, tipped liquid amber, swirling, sun-pierced colour, into a glass. He

116

turned and raised the glass to Sarling, smiled over it, skin creasing mouth and cheeks in a slow act of defiance. He tipped the glass and drank, emptying it in one gesture that could have been greeting or farewell.

For a moment coldness struck through the euphoria of Sarling's mood, then he turned and left the flat. But going down the stairs the warmth of his dream closed in on him. Raikes was his.

Two minutes after Sarling had gone Raikes called the Park Street house. Belle answered.

"He's been here. Now he's on his way round to you. Everything's clear in your mind?"

"Yes, darling . . . yes, yes."

She was nervous, but he knew that it had to be like that with her until things actually started.

Because so much depended on her he gave generously. "Don't worry, love. There's nothing we can't do between us. I'm leaving now and picking up Berners. We'll be watching the place, we'll know when you've arrived. When it's dark and he's in his study—the very first time—just show yourself at the window. Just stand there and turn your back to us. We'll be watching. All right?"

"Yes."

"That's my girl."

"Andy . . . Andy, just suppose—"

"Suppose nothing. It will all go just as we've planned. Just relax and remember I'll be thinking of you every minute. Bye, darling . . ."

He put the phone down. Andy. She'd started to call him that recently and something rusty and unoiled seemed to turn in him every time he heard it.

He went to the safe and took out one of the canisters of Z/93, GF1. In the kitchen he pulled out of a cupboard a small wicker picnic basket, opened it and checked the contents, a thirty-foot coil of climbing rope, a large bandana handkerchief, two

117

six-foot lengths of soft manilla cord, two pairs of thin, black cotton gloves, and a pair of gauntletted leather gloves.

Going about the flat, changing his clothes quickly, gathering his things, Raikes thought, Why did I waste my breath in protest against him? From artifice to keep him unsuspecting? *We're going to take the golden heart out of her.* No, from real impulse. Gold bars piled on the floor of a specie room, deep below decks. Two people and no violence ... and Berners waiting for him now in Wiltshire, already wearing a Sarling moustache and a Sarling topcoat, silk scarf and black Homburg hat ... waiting to play his brief part as Sarling.

The Cunarder brochure on the table caught his eye. He picked it up and ripped it in half, dropping the two sections into the wastepaper basket.

Carrying the cane basket he went out, flagged a taxi and was driven to his lock-up garage and his car. Ten minutes later he was going westwards across London on his way to Wiltshire, avoiding the route which he knew Belle would be taking with Sarling. Even the coincidence of a quick overtaking on the road had to be insured against. Sarling had to go.

He switched on the car radio and a man's voice, precise, neat, technical, was saying, ". . . well, it cost somewhere around one hundred thousand pounds and is based on the Ferranti Argus 400 computer. Its principal functions will be to record data connected with the main engine and print the engine-room log, and then there's an alarm scanning system for detecting undue temperatures and pressures in the machinery. All in all, there's no question that the QE2's computer is the most sophisticated on any merchant ship. Another interesting point is—"

Raikes swore and turned the radio off.

CHAPTER EIGHT

HE WAS LEANING back in his chair, a small, puppet figure, made smaller by the wide spread of desk before him; polished red morocco leather, gold-tooled in a running design around the edges, the desk lamp throwing black shadows from the inkstand and the hand-carved alabaster paperweight. He had his eyes fixed on some point beyond her head as he dictated from his notes the details of a Paris conference.

On the pages of her notebook, couched on her lap, white against the folds of her green dress, the Pitman hieroglyphics flowed from her pencil. He stopped now and then, teasing at his scrubby moustache, seeking for some phrase, forming it in his mind before moving on, the skin under his raised chin red and contorted like the face, his other hand outstretched to his glass of milk, finger and thumb, like some claw, sliding slowly up and down the long length of engraved crystal.

She knew quite well that the Paris conference held only part of his thoughts. From the moment they had got into the car, all the way down and all through dinner, up to this moment here, she had known that something else was in his mind. At dinner, over his spinach and poached eggs, he had had something of the air of a small boy who knows something and debates whether to tell. He never drank wine but he had insisted that she have a half bottle of Chablis with her grilled sole. He had been kind, considerate, almost abnormally polite, and when they had risen to go into his sitting room for coffee, his hand had taken her upper arm, guiding her, his fingers sliding up the inside of her arm, close into her armpit with an even pressure that could have been a caress or the confident hold of a friendly warder. Yes, something was in his mind and she knew that when it came out it might be followed by blow or embrace.

He dictated, "I spoke to Monsieur Lacouvre about the delay in the Nantes installation. It was his opinion that the earliest we could expect it to go on stream would be next March, but that full production would depend on the dependability of bulk supply of components from the main accessory contractors in . . ."

Outside, Belle, she told herself, are two men waiting to come in. Sarling would never see next March. They were out there in the darkness of the park, in some shrubbery, cloud above, mist moving around them with damp fingers. Two men who were absolutely sure of themselves, their plan and their own ability. But until she went to the window, showed herself and slipped the catch they must remain in the darkness. If she never went to the window, they would wait and then go away and this man would go on living for another term . . . but it would only be a term for the two outside would return again and again. From a school run by nuns, from a pub at Headington, from sliding slowly down the aisles of Marks and Spencers to lift a cheap tin of talcum powder, from brief love-making at a West-End hotel, weekends at Brighton, submission to Sarling, and complete possession by the one outside, how had she come to this? Sitting here, waiting to let death in. Not death. Murder. A hundred newspaper headlines and paragraphs from the past flocked over her like a cloud of birds, and the same query from the past kept running in her mind—'How do they ever do it? How do they ever get themselves to that point?" And now she was at the point herself and still didn't know.

"That's all." Sarling finished dictating. He came forward in his chair and propped his elbows on the desk, face resting between his fingertips, the tortured skin pushed upwards, narrowing the eyes.

"You'd like me to type it now?"

"No. When we get back to London tomorrow."

"Tomorrow?"

"You don't like working on a Sunday?"

"You know I don't mind. I just thought we were staying down here."

"We're going back tonight."

"I see."

"Do you, Belle?"

"You want me to order the car?"

"In a moment. You can drive me up. We shall be going to the City first."

"Very good." There was an unexpected relief in her but she did not show it in her voice. How long would relief last? The two men outside would go away. But they would come back.

Sarling looked at her in silence, holding her with his skin-creased eyes, embarrassing her, preparing her perhaps to be unsettled into truth by swift attack.

"Belle, how far have Raikes and Berners got with their plan to murder me?"

"I don't know what you're talking about." The name Raikes was the key to the easy, immediate response. Not from her must come anything that would hurt Raikes. In a fraction of time, like the swift wheel of a mirror reflected distantly by the sun, her mind and heart were glass-bright with images of him; his fingers through her hair, his body covering hers in possession, her arms around him in protection he might never know he wanted or had even had; Raikes in her with all his passion of ownership, yet owning nothing because she was closed around him, hiding him, cherishing him and shielding him, knowing that protection too was ownership.

"Belle, I said how far have they got?"

"Would he be likely to tell me?"

"If he wanted your help, yes."

"Well, he hasn't asked for it—and he wouldn't get it if he did!"

Sarling smiled. "I wonder—anyway it doesn't matter. Raikes wants me dead, but he can't touch me so long as I have his file and photostat."

121

He tipped back in the chair suddenly, holding himself with big hair-backed hands on the arms, and talked over her head, ignoring her, dismissing her, his dialogue with an absent man ... the man who waited outside unknown to him, but who was for him in this room now, real and a threat, but more than that a beloved antagonist, the challenge between them a strange joy to him. "I have to die. But first the file and the photostats must be in his hands. Given that, death follows. But I need Raikes and I am not letting him go until he has helped me to what I want."

Sarling let his chair drop back, and shook his head at her. "You can't deceive me, Belle. You're helping him—because you're in love with him. That's why I'm taking the photostats from here tonight. They'll go into the City office safe until Monday morning and then into a bank vault. The files must be kept handy at Park Street because Raikes will soon need them."

Do that, she thought. Yes, do that, and close the door against murder. Not even Raikes and Berners could tackle a bank vault, though, God knew, Raikes would try and find some way ... some faked authority from Sarling. But that was so far ahead she could give it only passing lodging in her mind.

Sarling stood up. "Did you tell him how the safe here and at Park Street worked?"

"Even if he asked how could I? I don't know." Anger spurted in her, covering her deceit, as she watched him move across the room, the back of his velvet smoking jacket marked in shadowed creases from the chair.

He half turned to her, smiling, the monkey grimace showing uneven teeth. "You're an intelligent girl. You would only have to watch me and detail my actions to him. He would work it out. Has worked it out, hasn't he?"

"I know nothing about what he's done."

"Liar. You know everything about him. He owns you and you are glad to be owned, glad to give him your love though he doesn't care a tuppenny-damn about it. You've become a stupid woman, Belle. You've let yourself fall in love with a man who, give him cause, would think no more of killing you than he does of killing me. So—" warmth, almost paternalism, rounded out the syllable, "—I must protect you. Next week I'm sending you to America. To the New York office. You'll be there for six months. You'll enjoy that, won't you? You've always liked New York when we've been there before."

"I don't care where you send me. That's your privilege. But I'm hurt at your thinking that I . . . well, that I'd have anything to do with a thing like this."

"Like what, Belle?"

"Like helping any man to murder you. For God's sake, what do you think I am?"

Calmly, turning from her, moving to the oak door that hid the strong-room door, he said, "Exactly what you are. A woman willing to give her love to the first man who offers her the chance of freedom. You should thank me, Belle. He'd have given you nothing in return. Except perhaps death. Oh, yes, I'm sure that he's thought of killing you once he gets rid of me. He would have to. He's that kind of man. He wouldn't be content with anything less than complete security in the life he's planning for himself in Devon. Haven't you ever thought of that, Belle?"

She stood up. "No, I haven't."

Back to her, opening the oak door, Sarling said, "Just ring down and have the car brought round. You can drive. And you'd better let Baines know at Park Street that we're coming back. Tell him we'll be late. He needn't stay up for us."

The oak door was open now. Belle walked away, around the desk, towards the house telephone on a small table by the wall. She watched him put up his right hand and slide the protecting plate aside on the strong-room door. Then he put up his left hand and pressed his thumb on the polished surface of the inner plate. Before he pushed it into the door recess which contained the photo-electric cell, the little eye all too ready to call *Stranger in the house*, he turned to her and held up his left thumb, smiling.

"Tell him when you see him on Monday that I'm no longer a walking key for him to steal. In another four hours he'll have to break into a bank vault. Watch his face when you tell him. You won't see any of his thoughts touch it. But I know what he'll be thinking. How is it to be done? How? That's the kind of man he is. That's the kind of man I want."

He turned back and pushed the inner plate over. A few seconds later, the strong-room door slid back into the right-hand wall with a sound like the long, slow sigh of a tired old man.

Belle stood there and watched him go into the strong room. Two feet from her was the curtained window of the study. All she had to do was to move, pull aside the curtains briefly, slip the window catch, stand two seconds with her back to the world aside, and then walk to the telephone and order the car.

I can't do it, she thought. Not now when Sarling was so near the truth, so much on guard. Don't, Belle, don't. He'll understand, agree the risk was too great. Another time, another place or perhaps, because that was what she really wanted, no other time, no other place. Never. Never to move away from design and desire into action. Two small steps to the window. That was all he asked of her. No, she couldn't do it. Knew now that she had never been going to do it. No, no, no, no! The silent protest was vehement in her as she moved towards the window.

In the darkness they were so still, rooted in watchfulness with the long probing sureness of their intent like a great tap running down through them into the wet earth, that they could hear behind them in the shrubbery the stir of uneasy, night-roosting birds, starlings bunched for comfort, pheasants with sleep-bound muscles holding claw and toe rigid on rough bark. Now and then came a slow shake of wings and breast feathers against the silent loading of mist drops. High overhead a jet streamed unseen through the clouds, planing down for some distant field, whistling on a low note with relief at a journey near done. The clock that was his brain told Raikes that it must be nine. Confirming, from across the park and the fields, the sound of a church clock bell began to come through the moisture-laden air.

For an hour they had stood there without speaking. No need for words between them. All the speaking had long been done. They inhabited this house, this park and this night with the familiarity of a given birthright. On the darkness thickened darkness which was the long stretch of the house, a hundred yards away, no shape or detail visible, he could paint from memory every feature of mullioned window, weathered cornice, pilastered and pierced parapet, the lead veins of heavy, Edwardian water pipes, the twisted, ancient ropes of autumn-pruned wistaria like a boarding net over the walls to take him to the run of the first floor balcony. Main bedroom, bathroom, guest bedroom, bathroom, big hall window light, study. . . . Just one broad signal of light from the study and they would be moving, Berners alongside him, homburged, top-coated, white silk scarf untidy around coat collar and neck, shadowed face, scrubby moustache, the Sarling familiar.

Away to the right in the darkness which was the house, near the roof, a window light went up and a silhouette stepped forward and drew curtains. Servants' quarters, some maid sitting on her bed now, pulling off her shoes, flopping back, idle hand reaching out for transistor and Radio Luxembourg, for cigarettes and lighter, to lie and dream open-eyed of some pop star where, fifty years before, in the Alverton servants' quarters Mrs. Hamilton, then Jennie Jago, had dreamed of Mr. Right and where, twenty years later, catching him and one of the maids had boxed first her ears and then his and then, no doubt, in the privacy of her bed with Hamilton had shook her head with slow laughter and said "Little bastard, only thirteen and already wanting to be at it. You men."

Then, through the darkness, the signal was made. The curtains were pulled in the study, a shaft of light, rigid-sided, then suffusing and dying into the mist, held the movement of a figure he knew, the movement of a hand and then the turn of a back, silhouette unmoving momentarily and then the

125

curtain falling back. The light died, leaving a grey shadow on his retina.

He reached into his pocket and drew out the cotton gloves. Touching Berners, no word passing between them, he began to move, pulling on the gloves, keeping to the lawns, avoiding the gravel paths until the last four-yard stretch across to the house. He was near enough now to make out the bulge of the bow of the great mullioned ground floor window. Beyond the window lay the dining room. He could have listed every item of furniture, silver, painting and glass within.

He moved to the right hand side of the window, gravel right up to the wall, no soft, winter-turned flower bed to take footprints. The main stem of the wistaria was a foot in diameter, twisted taut in growth like a rope, and the thick lateral runners made easy footholds for the climb. He went upwards feeling the arthritic-shaped fingers of the pruned spurs brush against his face. Stepping over the low balustrade at the top of the window, he stood on the balcony roof and waited for Berners to follow him. Berners came up, the slow movements of white gloved hands faint ectoplasm in the darkness. They stood together for a moment unmoving, letting the darkness and the night move round them, sensing it for danger and then, satisfied, they moved along the roof run. Main bedroom windows, bathroom, guest room, hall window, and now the barest sliver of light at the edge of one of the study windows. The centre pair were two feet six inches wide, four feet high. One of them, bronze catch free, was open half an inch.

Raikes put his finger under the metal frame and pulled the window open, stepping through with the movement, brushing the curtain aside, moving on into the familiarity of the room, dazzled for a moment by the soft lights, recovering, and seeing it all in tableau.

Belle was standing by the telephone, half turned to him, one hand raised holding the receiver, her face white, frozen with anxiety, her dark painted lips half open. The far door to the upper landing was shut, paper with handwritten notes lay on

126

the desk blotter, the spherical, milky-grey alabaster paper-weight floated on the red leather like a dead planet. A great pot of flame-coloured azaleas stood on a mahogany torchère near the strong-room oak door.

Behind him he heard Berners enter and felt the brush of his sleeve as he passed him, moving straight across the room to lock the main door; Sarling in shape and appearance already beginning to supplant the real Sarling.

Belle put the receiver back on its rest and nodded to the strong room. Raikes crossed to it and met Sarling coming out, a green file box under one arm. Raikes slid his arm round the man's shoulders, taking advantage of his surprise, and eased him clear of the door and into the room.

Raikes said, "If you shout no one will hear you."

Almost without concern, Sarling said, "No doubt you know the room is soundproof."

Berners, coming back from the door, said, "I could tell you what firm did the work and how much you paid." He took the box from Sarling and put it on the table.

Belle said, "The photostats are in the box. He was taking them to London tonight—to the office safe. I've just rung for the car. I'm driving him."

Sarling, rump against the edge of the desk, calm, trapped, showing no fear, though fear he had, looked at Belle and said, "While we talked ... all the time, you knew they were outside?"

"Yes."

He shrugged his shoulders, faced Raikes and said with his grotesque of a smile, "She served you well. I hope you suitably reward her."

Raikes reached into his raincoat pocket and pulled out the gauntletted driving gloves, handing them to Sarling.

"Put them on."

"You have another strong room to open?"

"You know we have. With any sharp edge you could mutilate your left thumbprint."

"I'd already thought of it."

127

Sarling drew on the gloves and Raikes tied his hands together in front of him, wrapping the soft manilla length tight but not constricting over the leather. When Sarling died there must be no bruise on him, no chafed skin.

At the desk, the green box in his hands, Berners said, "It's locked."

"The key is in my right pocket."

Raikes reached into the smoking-jacket pocket for the key and handed it to Berners.

"Check yours and check mine."

Berners opened the box and began to check through a pile of small envelopes, each one labelled with a name.

Belle said, "There's mine, too."

Sarling laughed. "They'll keep it. You're only changing masters, Belle. There's no escape for you."

Berners pulled an envelope from the pack and, without looking at Belle, handed it to her.

Sarling said, "They'll still have your file."

Belle, fingers teasing at the envelope in her hands, said, "Can't it be done differently? Andy . . . surely you can make some arrangement now?"

Raikes choked down a sudden desire for anger at the use of his name. What a stupid bitch she was.

"All the arrangements have been made."

He moved Sarling from the desk, unwound the long length of climbing rope from his waist and began to knot a harness for Sarling's body, a cradle to lower him into the darkness.

Berners said, "They're here."

"Take the lot. Put them in his brief case. Leave the box here." Then to Belle, he said, "How long ago did you order the car?"

"Just."

"His hat and coat?"

"In his room."

"Go and get it."

He watched her, over Sarling's shoulder, cross the room with

128

Berners to unlock and lock the door for her, and she had nothing for him. No one in this room had any compassionate meaning for him. He was moving, as he had always known he would move, susceptible only to the design and the plan, no scrap of personality ever to show. Perhaps that was why the *Andy* stung him so ... Berners would understand. Berners and he had moved like this before. So, no doubt, had Sarling and Wurther.

He pulled the bandana handkerchief from his pocket as Berners came back from the door. He held it up in front of Sarling. "This is only until we get to the car."

Sarling nodded, and then almost sadly said, "You came a little sooner than I expected."

Raikes wadded soft tissues on the inside of the handkerchief, folded it and put the pad on Sarling's mouth.

There was a tap on the room door. Berners opened it. Belle came in with Sarling's hat and coat. She gave them to Berners and then went over and threw the switch for the strong-room door to close.

Raikes said, "I'm going. Give me a hand on the roof."

Raikes went through the window first and then he and Berners helped Sarling through. They took Sarling up to the end of the roof run. Raikes went down the wistaria and stood below as Berners lowered Sarling over. The moment the man's legs were swinging free, Raikes reached up and prisoned the ankles. He did not want Sarling kicking sideways and trying to break any of the window glass.

Sarling came to the ground, swayed, and was firmed by Raikes. Berners dropped the trailing length of rope to the ground. Sarling's hat and coat were tossed down. Raikes draped the coat over Sarling's shoulders and put the hat on him. He wound the rope in loops over his arm, took Sarling by the elbow and moved off into the darkness.

They went across the park, retracing a route already followed by Raikes, under a tall clump of Douglas pines, dead needles slipping under their feet, by the smooth darkness of still lake water, across a cropped length of sward where the darkness momentarily thudded with the panic of a handful of sheep, and then through a copse, rank with the smell of wet leaves, to a small gate that gave on to a side road. Raikes stood well back inside the gate and unfastened the rope harness from Sarling.

They waited, mist settling on branch and twig above them, the slow drip of water weeping to the ground. A car went swiftly down the road, its headlights silvering the lichen patches on the old gate in front of them. Marking time in the darkness the distant church clock struck ten. They would be in London well by one o'clock. It was the right time, not too much traffic, no huddle of cars at the lights where idle eyes swept sideways to appraise other cars and their occupants.

Sarling coughed suddenly against his gag, shoulders kicking forward in the spasm. Raikes held him up, steadied him and thought, Tomorrow . . . tomorrow.

A car came down the road, headlights dipped, slowed and stopped. The headlights died, twin points of sidelights holding small cones of drifting mist.

He took Sarling through the gate. Berners got out from the back of the car and they put Sarling in. Belle sat at the wheel, looking straight ahead of her.

Raikes said to Berners, "You get the other car."

Without a word, Berners turned back up the road.

Belle driving. The windscreen wipers moving slowly against mist which had thickened to a drizzle. Behind her, seen in the over-head driving mirror, Sarling, mouth no longer gagged, slumped back into the corner of his seat staring straight ahead of him. At his side sat Raikes, raincoat unbuttoned, lying back, easy, relaxed, a cigarette in his hand. All the sprawled length of him was instant with alertness, all his consciousness occupied with the man at his side. Why had she gone to the window, pulled the curtain and slipped the catch? Some other Belle had inhabited her, another woman, less than familiar, to whom she had protested but who had moved on, hearing, but unheeding.

For an hour she had driven and neither of the two in the back had spoken after the first few seconds of entering the car when Raikes had told Sarling that if he made any move to attract attention he would be pushed down below the seats and covered with the car rug. Winchester was far behind them and the Saturday night traffic had thinned away. For long stretches of road they had the night to themselves.

From behind her Sarling said quietly, "Belle."

She flicked a glance at him in the mirror then turned her eyes back to the road ahead, cat's eyes gleaming around a curve, the tyres bumping rhythmically over them.

"Yes."

"I'd left you fifty thousand pounds in my will."

"So?"

"No man likes to die. I know it's no good making any plea to Raikes. But with you it could be different."

Raikes said, "I wondered how long it would take him to get to this point."

"With you, Belle, it should be different. I need your help. Perhaps in a little way you owe it to me. If you'd gone on the way you were you would have ended in prison."

"Maybe."

In the mirror, fleetingly, she saw Sarling put up a gloved hand and rub his moustache, his face lost in deep shadows under the Homburg.

"All you have to do, Belle, is so simple. For your own good, and for mine. You don't want to be mixed up in murder, do you?"

Of course she didn't, but she was. What answer could she give sitting here not wanting to be where she was, not knowing where she was going . . . wanting only this rotten night to be over. She tightened her lips, concentrating on the road, not wanting to think, not wanting any part of the two men behind her, fixing her attention on the night details skimming up from darkness into the blaze of the beams, the hump of a railway bridge, the smooth black slabs of the iron parapet, rivet heads half silvered in the light, a long length of white line eating away into the dark future.

Raikes said quietly, "Of course she doesn't want to be mixed up in murder. Nor do I. But we both are—and you mixed us up, Sarling. You and Wurther long ago when you started to collect men and women. You should have made it old masters, anything . . . but not men and women." He gave a dry grunt of contempt. "You want me to tell her your proposition? He'll give you a hundred thousand, Belle. First thing on Monday morning. All you have to do is to drive this car off the road into the ditch. Break a traffic regulation the moment we hit the suburbs. Skid it. Wreck it. Ram it into a stationary van. Anything like that—and he's free." His voice went on, no anger, no rise in tone, just a one-level, even-keeled voice with no emotion in it. "And first thing Monday morning, Belle, you'll be rich. He'll give you your freedom. First thing Monday morning, you get your file to add to your photostat. If you wanted to you could make better terms. Two hundred thousand, Meon Park . . . the world, Belle. He'll offer you everything you've ever dreamt of—on Monday morning. But when Monday morning comes, you know exactly where you'll be, don't you? Sitting at a typewriter banging away at one of his company reports. And Monday evening, to put gilt on the gingerbread, he'll come into your room and, even if you don't feel like it, he'll make you spread your legs for him. However, if that's what you want who can stop you?"

She cried, "Stop it! Do you hear—I don't want any more about me."

Behind her they were silent.

Then, so long afterwards that she had to search for the link with the recent past, Sarling gave a little laugh and said, "You're right, of course, Raikes. I'd have offered the world and trimmed the bargain afterwards—but not as much as you imagined."

"Just sit tight and leave her alone. It's bad for Belle's driving."

From then on she was an automaton, following the rules long established between them of this dark game of murder. Now and again she heard them talking, but she heard without listening. Deliberately she shut her mind to all thought of what lay ahead. She was driving Sarling back to London. Just that. They would drive into the garage at the back of the house and Sarling would go up the stairs, up to his bedroom, and in the morning he would have died in his sleep. That was how it must be always to her, and since it had to be so, she was already making it a truth in her mind. Sarling was going to die in his sleep.

It was twenty to one when the car pulled up in front of the garage doors. Their drive across London had been smooth and uninterrupted. Belle got out, unlocked the doors, opened them and then drove in.

As she went back to close the garage doors, Berners, hatted and coated as Sarling still, came from the shadows and moved into the garage, carrying in his hand Raikes' cane basket. Without a word he took Sarling's brief case from Raikes and handed him the cane basket.

Berners and Belle went through into the house. A blue, dim pilot light burned over the door which they shut behind them. Raikes turned to Sarling, pulling the bandana handkerchief from his pocket. Before he could begin to tie it Sarling said, "There's nothing I can offer you?"

"Nothing."

"Any other man would have said 'I'm sorry. Nothing.' "

"Any other man would have made some attempt to shout or escape."

"So I would with anyone but you. All right, I'm resigned. Not to death. But to your ruthlessness and my rightness about you. That's why you must let me speak before you put that thing on. You're taking my life. That puts you in my debt. You know how it must be repaid, don't you?"

"No."

"Two ways. The first, perhaps of little importance to me. A matter of sentiment. If you can do it, find some way of sparing Belle. Without her you wouldn't be here. Be kind to

133

her if you can. People like you, like me, owe one kindness in life. Let her go and do it for both of us."

"And the second?" There was no real curiosity in his voice, just plain, near-impatient enquiry.

"You know it. I don't even demand it, couldn't. But you will do it. I know you will do it."

Raikes didn't answer. He put the folded bandana against Sarling's mouth, knowing that at the last moment Sarling would have shouted, knowing that against every wayward moment there had to be a safeguard. He knotted it and eased the edge of it down from the man's nose so that he could breathe.

He got out, wound up the driving window, checked that all the others were up and then came back to the rear door. He reached in, opened the cane basket and pulled out a canister of Z/93, GF1. He unscrewed the armature release and held the spring down with his finger, watching Sarling, knowing he might try to kick out, but not seeing Sarling as Sarling, not thinking of him in any terms but as someone, something, of no consequence to him except the last bar between him and freedom. His eyes met Sarling's eyes shadowed under the Homburg. He saw the man's body move, bound hands straining against the cord that held them to his body, saw the wild shake of his head that threw the Homburg suddenly, comically, low across his brow. He released the armature and dropped the canister into the cane basket. He closed the lid, quickly flicking its centre catch home. He shut the rear door just before the canister softly exploded.

Turning, he went towards the inner door, walking in the thin blue light with a sureness and deliberation that he would have had were the place in darkness. Without looking back he reached up and pressed a wall switch by the door. A ventilation fan over the garage doors began to whine and then dropped to a steady purr. He went through the door into the darkness of a small back hall—darkness that was a set of photographs taken by Belle, lines and symbols on white paper by Berners, and in

134

the nothingness of the darkness he took two steps on hard coir matting and then sat, fingertips momentarily checking its position, on a chair.

He sat and waited. And because there was no curiosity in him about what was happening either above him with Belle and Berners or in the garage with Sarling, because he had sat many times before and seen it all clearly, he let his mind spin clear of the place, leaving only his body and its attendant, armouring senses to sit out the vigil, the hour long wait for the toxic gas to deteriorate and decompose, to lose stability and persistence. And while his body waited, his mind was back at Alverton, calmly planning the restoration of the abandoned greenhouse.

An hour later Berners came through the darkness and put a hand on his shoulder.

"Well?" His word held no more sound than a breath.

"Baines came out to see if there was anything I wanted. He only saw my back. Miss Vickers sent him back."

They went into the garage and moved down the car, one on each side, and without hurry they reached out and opened the two front doors. They moved back into the hall, closed the door and waited another fifteen minutes, side by side in the darkness, unmoving, backed by the detailed knowledge Berners had acquired of GFI, yet trusting only themselves to decide the limits of risk in this enterprise.

When they went back the garage held the scent only of oil and petrol. Sarling was slumped in the back seat. They lifted him out. Raikes hoisted him across his shoulders and Berners moved ahead of him, carrying the loose Homburg hat, wearing his own still.

They went through the darkness of the hall, into the darkness of a passage, and across the main hall lit by one small light. Their feet cushioned and muted by the carpet on the main flight of stairs, they climbed to the first floor. The servants' quarters were right at the top of the house. Up the stairs, the first door on the right, into the study, curtains drawn, Berners opening and shutting the door and then switching on the light, the oak door to the strong room already open.

Easing Sarling from his shoulder like a sack of corn before the steel strong-room door, Raikes hauled him upright, holding him from behind with his hands under his armpits. Berners slid aside the protecting plate and then took Sarling's left hand, drew off the glove, raised the arm and carefully pressed the left thumb against the master plate.

Raikes drew Sarling back, the man's head dropping over one shoulder, the weight of the small body easily sustained by his hands. Berners slid the master plate into its recess. There was no anxiety in Raikes as he waited the few seconds for the scanning device to accept its data and work on it. From the moment of stepping through the window at Meon all action had become routine, mechanical, passing from one small operation to another without flaw.

The door slid back.

"Help me with him. Then collect the files."

Berners went to the room door and opened it. They took Sarling, comradely supported between them, across the narrow strip of landing and into his bedroom and dropped him on his bed. Berners went out.

Belle came forward from the shadows beyond the bed-table lamp on the other side of the bed, went to the bedroom door and locked it. As she turned back she saw that Raikes was already leaning over Sarling, beginning to undress him.

Raikes half turned his head and said, "Give me a hand with him."

"I can't. I couldn't touch him."

Already she had banished Sarling from her mind. Even when she had laid out his pyjamas, dressing gown, the bedsocks he always wore, she had laid them out for something without a name.

Quietly Raikes said, "Come here." He reached back and drew her to the bed. "Look at him. He's nothing. Not a man. Just something we have to arrange." His right hand slid up

136

and held her chin, the fingers firm against her flesh and he gave her a little shake. "You can do anything I say. Get his shoes off."

He released her and she bent down by the bed and began to take off Sarling's shoes. A wet oak leaf was stuck to one of the shoes. Absently she plucked it from the leather and put it in her dress pocket where she would find it a week later dried to brittle fragments, substance peeled from the leaf to leave part of the veining skeletal.

They undressed him, put on his pyjamas and bedsocks and slid him into the bed, Raikes making him comfortable, rumpling the pillow and sheets, Sarling's body still pliable under his hands, a memory flashing back of talk with Berners in the Royal Automobile Club about body cooling and rigor mortis, a clothed body losing heat at the rate of about two and a half degrees an hour for the first six hours . . . Sarling's body still warm to the touch, the sensation of its warmth still on his shoulder where he had carried him. Rigor mortis would be just setting in by the time Baines came to call him. Dead in his sleep, time of death around one o'clock. Everything natural, except the death itself, and perhaps even that natural for a man like this who had wanted to manipulate him and others as though they were puppets. Man tries to own others at his peril.

He turned to Belle. She was tidying and putting away Sarling's clothes as he would have done had he come in late on his own.

He said, "Get finished quickly. Go to bed and take three sleeping pills." He went to her where she was standing, holding Sarling's shirt, absently taking out the cufflinks, and he put his arms around her and kissed her, dry lips against dry lips, pulled back, slid a hand up and caressed her cheek, then turned and was gone.

He went out and down to the garage. Berners, moustache gone, was waiting for him, holding under one arm a pile of pink, foolscap-sized files a foot high. Raikes pulled the cane basket from the car, opened it, saw the fragments of the

137

canister on the canvas bottom, and then glanced round the back of the car to check that nothing was being left. Gloved, he took the ashtray container and tipped into his handkerchief the stubs and ashes of the three cigarettes he had smoked on the way up.

They put the files in the cane basket. Berners went out of the garage, and Raikes stayed close up against the shut door. It was a quarter to three. Any man walking through back mews, along side streets, carrying a cane basket might be stopped by the police. Berners alone, walking to his parked car, would cause no comment, offer no hold for suspicion even if he were stopped. Ten minutes later Raikes heard the car go by. He went out, pulling the self-locking door behind him gently, and walked fifty yards to the car, stepped in, and they drove away. On the seat by Raikes lay the brief case with the photostats from Meon.

A few minutes later they were at Mount Street. Berners went in carrying the cane basket and the brief case and with Raikes' key let himself into the flat. Raikes drove the car to his lock-up and caught a late roving taxi back. Sarling's gloves, the rope and the bindings were left in the car in the lock-up.

Berners was sitting in a chair, a drink in his hand. Raikes poured himself a whisky, neat, a half tumblerful, and sat opposite him. He raised the glass to Berners, nodded and then drank. They sat silently, the union of their interests, the thick cord of their unspoken communion firm. They just sat, the knowledge of each other's presence all they needed, until after a long while Berners said, "I don't know what he paid for that desk at Meon. From the photographs I thought it was Chippendale. But it's a fake. Good, but a fake."

Back at Park Street in her bed, Belle was staring wide-eyed into the darkness, knowing that the sleeping pills were not going to work.

138

CHAPTER NINE

SUNDAY MORNING, eight o'clock, and Berners sitting in an easy chair, his feet up on a stool, fully dressed, wanting no bed for the night that was past, content, insisting on just sitting, waiting for the time of an early train back to Brighton. Outside, the noises of a London Sunday morning . . . high and thick heels tapping the pavement with a slower rhythm, people coming back from early mass and service, a man whistling, the sudden hoot of a ship in the Pool carrying clean across the crowded acres, a woman calling to a dog, the clear rattle of an electric milk float and the clank of bottles jostled up steps in a wire basket, the sharp ringing of a bicycle bell . . . drowned all week, but coming into their own today.

From the bathroom came the sound of Raikes moving and dressing. He came into the room fresh-bathed, clean-shaved, alert, strong, all confidence, no elation from pride or vanity, four hours' sleep washed over him like a tide to recede and leave no mark of the past day. Raikes, standing for a moment looking down at him, fresh-laundered sports shirt and a white foulard, dark blue flannel trousers, brogues with a polish that was like old mahogany, blue eyes lustred with health, the fair brown hair darkened over his ears with damp from his bath; Raikes knowing and he knowing that no matter their appearance, the difference in wombs, they were brothers, knowing that between them there was an accord stronger than love and void of all petty demands.

"Coffee?"

"If there's some going."

"You've got time?"

139

"My train doesn't go for an hour, and anyway there's always another."

Raikes went into the kitchen, leaving the door open and began to set things going for the coffee.

Through the open door Raikes said, "Coming up in the car, he told Belle that he was leaving her fifty thousand pounds. Think he has?"

"No. What are we going to do about her?"

"Nothing yet. There's got to be a decent interval. Employer and then secretary in a short space of time might raise questions. Also, there's a certain amount of clearing up here and elsewhere for which I shall need her."

"Well, when the time comes let me know."

"I can handle it."

"No. We've always done things together."

"You wouldn't have liked what Sarling wanted us to do together."

"I might have five years ago."

Raikes came to the door and looked at him, surprised. Berners nodded at the table beside him. The two halves of the Cunard brochure lay on it.

"I found it in the wastepaper basket last night. Some of his notes are very interesting."

"I never read them. He wanted us to take over a million in gold bullion from her. Just two people, he said, could do it with the minimum of fuss. Don't tell me you really would have gone for that?"

"I said five years ago. I was thinking about it while you slept. I'd have bought myself an estate like his—only in France. A great wall all around the park, one of those châteaux with slate roofs, full of the right furniture, a room of my own with leather-covered walls, velvety brown with gold tooling. I've always wanted that since I saw one somewhere." He smiled. "I'd have walled myself up with all I wanted."

Raikes grinned and went back into the kitchen, saying, "With you, it's things, isn't it?"

"Yes. Good things."

"What's the answer to human beings?"

"We all have a private madness. Happy the man who can afford his own luxuriously appointed asylum."

"You'd better have some coffee."

Raikes came in with the tray, everything set out neatly, cream, sugar, silver spoons, coffee jug and cups and saucers in matching china.

Berners said, "You'd have done it, too."

"Not me, not even five years, ten years ago. Not my line."

"I think you would have done. The trouble is it came from him. With you, it would have had to have been your idea, your challenge. You don't like things second-hand. With Frampton, it has to spring unique from within."

"It's Raikes, not Frampton."

"Frampton and Berners. Those are the real people. This is the first time you've ever made coffee for me."

"I hope it's good."

"Not as good as Angers makes. However . . ." He reached out and picked up the two halves of the brochure. "You want this?"

"No."

Berners dropped the halves into the wastepaper basket.

Half an hour later Berners left. At the door, he said, "Get in touch with me about Miss Vickers."

Belle arrived at half-past six that evening. He took her hat and coat, fixed her a drink and lit a cigarette for her, handling her with a gentle fuss, each move deliberately designed because he knew the nervousness in her and was physician to her needless fears.

"I didn't like to phone or anything. . . . You know, it mightn't have been wise. Actually, of course —" she gave a quick laugh "—it wasn't anything like as bad as I thought it would be. You know, when you know what's happened, you kind of expect that it must be there for everyone to see. Even in your face. But they don't, do they?"

141

"If the label on the bottle says gin, you don't ask to taste it in the shop. Just relax and tell me."

He sat down opposite her, close, putting out a hand and holding her knee. She bent forward, wanting more contact, hair falling across the side of her face, the rough graining of her eyebrow make-up clumsy and crude at close quarters as though he saw it through a magnifying glass. He kissed her, knowing that this was the peak of her twenty-four-hour strain, that by tomorrow morning she would have begun to absorb and make commonplace what had been routine for him and Berners from the moment they had stepped through the window at Meon.

She pulled back from him and said, "Thank you, Andy."

"Just tell me."

"Well, Baines found him. He came to me. I hadn't slept, you know. Well, I suppose I did, but not properly, and I was a bit doped with the pills. Anyway, I called his doctor. That was awful, waiting for him, and then waiting while he was in the room. He came out and I had coffee ready for him and—God, I can hear him now—he just said it was heart failure. Not unexpected. He'd had trouble with his heart a few years ago. I told him about his changing his mind and coming back late and he just nodded. . . . He said he'd look after all the arrangements, and would I get in touch with Sarling's solicitor and let him know and some of his co-directors."

"No talk about a post mortem or anything like that?"

"No. He just sat down and wrote out a certificate of death and told me to let the solicitors have it. He didn't even ask about relatives or anything. In a way I could have been angry. He's had hundreds out of Sarling, but he just didn't care, and it was almost as though he took it for granted that I didn't care either."

"You'd probably mucked up his morning round of golf at Wentworth."

"Perhaps that's why he felt my bottom as he went out. Some kind of compensation. Yes, he did. Just stared straight ahead of him at the door and then put his hand behind me and had a good feel. Christ!"

She began to laugh and he let her.

She stopped, took some of her drink and said, "I'm sorry. It's just that I can let go with you. But I haven't let you down anywhere else, I swear. I did it all all right, didn't I? Even in the car when he started to offer me things?"

"You did everything beautifully."

"That's good."

He got up and gave her another drink. Standing beside her, he said, "Forget Sarling. Just think of him as a nothing. A great zero mark. You'll be out of that place soon. In the meantime we've got things to do, things to clear up. First of all, forget you even heard of Berners." He dropped her pink file into her lap. "Take that and get rid of it with your photostat. I haven't read it and I don't want to."

"There's nothing in there about me. Not the me I am now. Not the me you know, Andy."

It was hard to take but he showed no sign of his distaste. Waiting for her to come he had known that their shared experience over Sarling would give her a feeling of closer, warmer identification with him. The last thing he had to do was to let her feel or see that he wanted her far from him as soon as possible, obliterated from his thoughts and his life.

"How much longer has the lease got to run on this flat?"

"It's paid up until the end of May."

"There's no need to do anything about that yet. I'll stay up here until after the funeral. Then I've just got to go back to Devon. But I'll be up again. I've got to find a way of getting rid of those canisters. I can't just dump them, they're too dangerous. But I don't want them in that garage a moment longer than is necessary. Still, that's my problem. What about you being here, sleeping here I mean?"

"Well, not tonight or for a few nights. Not until I see what's happening around at Park Street. But, of course, I can always come and see you, Andy."

143

"You'd better." He gave her a smile, his hand reaching for the nape of her neck below him, caressing her. "Then there's the car. We'd better hang on to that until I've got rid of the canisters. Then we can pack it in with the garage. Pack in everything that has any connection with him. God, am I glad to be free of him."

He went to the sideboard for a drink. Turning he saw her watching him and he knew it was coming, the thing which from the first cold light of this morning when she had wakened from drugged half-sleep would have been stranded in her mind only shallowly submerged among her fears and now, the fears abating, would have surfaced, demanding attention. Knowing it had to be dealt with, he invited it.

"What's the matter?"

"You know what's the matter."

"Do I?" He was offering no help now that it had started.

"Yes. You're free of him. Glad to be free of him. But what about me, Andy? Are you going to be free of me, and glad of it?"

He shook his head, smiling, his understanding and sympathy big, broad and warming, embracing her, and then, an amalgam of memories of other soft sells kaleidoscoping through his mind, he said quietly, moving to her, "Two people don't go through this kind of thing together and then just politely say goodbye. No matter what our individual circumstances . . . no matter what obligations we may have to other people, no matter how difficult it may be in the future, you and I can't escape what we feel for one another, what we've done together. We don't even have to use words about it—" But he was, stringing them like beads and amulets, charms against all her fears, bestowing them on her like a cheap trading gift, taking from her in return the rich bounty, valued exactly, weighed in his favour on the rigged scales. "—We know what we are to one another. For the moment that's all that matters."

He pulled her up to him, giving her now no chance to speak, moving himself genuinely beyond words, because the trade

144

between man and woman must finish with the silent ritual love ceremony of touch and caress. He kissed her, held her, her weight dropping in his arms and he carried her to the bedroom, undressed her without a word, stripped himself and loved her; so much part of his own deceit that he himself was deceived while it lasted, and when she lay spent in his arms, cradled to him, he still went on following his deceit, enchanted by it, out of a sudden wonder in him that love could—though for ever out of his reach—come to some men and women without thought, without design.

The Times on the following Tuesday carried a half-page, two-column obituary of Joseph Sarling. It was the day on which Raikes went to his lock-up garage and transferred the canisters from the crate into a large cardboard carton. There were thirty-eight of them. He wrapped the crate in a blanket and drove to Epping Forest and dumped it behind some bushes where it was found four days later by two boys who took it home and made a rabbit hutch from it. It was the day that Belle came to the flat while he was out and tidied up for him, putting clean sheets on his bed and stocking up the larder with fresh supplies. In the half-full wastepaper basket she found the torn Cunard brochure. Pulling it out she found two pages of Sarling's notes torn in half inside. Because Sarling now was beginning to become a comfortable nothing in her mind, his death accepted at Park Street, in the City and the Press, his cremation only two days away, there was a sudden genuine curiosity in her about this brochure. She repaired the torn brochure and Sarling's notes with transparent tape and put them by her bedside, under some magazines, to read later. Half an hour later, when Raikes came in, she had forgotten them. It was the day, the first day since Sarling's death, when she stayed the full night in the flat with Raikes.

The next morning Raikes caught an early train down to Taunton, picked up his car and drove back to London, arriving in the late evening. The following day was Sarling's funeral and Belle went to it. He stayed in the flat all day, phoned Berners with the little news he had and told him that for the next couple of weeks he could always get in touch with him through Belle at the flat. He packed a suitcase with his stuff, and another with Sarling's files and photostats. The central heating in Devon was run from an old-fashioned coke boiler and he would burn them in it.

Belle came back at six. She was wearing a black costume and a small white and black hat, her lipstick, out of some shadowy respect for the dead, pale against her pale face. Her hair was drawn back, caught up behind her head with a severity that changed her and made almost a stranger of her, and he found that he liked it. Cut out all her "supposes", "I thinks", and "sort ofs", refashion her like this and in a few weeks she would pass easily with Mary's crowd. She had something, the trouble was that she seldom showed it. He kissed her and gave her a hug. On the drive down tomorrow he would have to think about her. She knew far too much about him. Making a plan for her would be less difficult than for Sarling. But the actual moment of execution would be harder. Sarling he had hated. This girl discovered moments in him when he liked her . . . almost needed her.

She said, "One of the executors spoke to me afterwards. About the will, I mean. What do you think?"

"I think that in the car Sarling exaggerated."

"Not by much. Twenty thousand, he left me. But, you know, I was thinking. I didn't really ought to take it."

"Don't be a fool. It wasn't a gift. You've earned every penny of it from him."

"They want me to stay on for a month or two to clear things up . . . apparently it's going to take ages. There was some family there. I met one of the brothers. He wasn't a bit like him, a big, healthy-looking sort of farmery type."

"He would be. That was Sarling's beef. He was just the pitman."

"Pitman?"

146

He laughed, holding her, one hand on her breast. "The weakest piglet in the litter. Always getting kicked to the end of the row where the milk was in short supply."

He went to the sideboard to get drinks and from behind him, out of the blue, she said, "Funerals do things to you, don't they? It's funny, I keep thinking I ought to feel guilty about it . . . kind of shocked just at the thought of what we did. I did do for a bit that first night. But not now. I just can't feel anything."

He turned. "You don't have to feel anything. Sarling is just a handful of ashes."

He drove down to Devon the next day. Before he got to Salisbury, he had worked out, except for a few small details, a way to get rid of Belle. The details could wait. It would have to be some weeks before anything could be done. At his house he put the carton of canisters in his wine cellar and locked the door. Nobody but himself ever went in there. After dinner, when Mrs. Hamilton had gone, he got out the pink files and went through them. Once or twice while reading he was tempted to keep them, put them away in his safe against some vague, future moment of need. But in the end he carried them down to the boiler house and burnt them, raking about in the flames with a draw iron until they were all cinders and ash. All he had to do now was to get rid of the canisters. That meant a trip up on the moors to find a place which was safe.

The next day he put six of the canisters in his coat pockets and drove up on to the moors. He was not going to risk having the full carton of canisters in his car. Other people make accidents . . . canisters spilled all over the road . . . no matter how many in a thousand the chance was he was not taking it. Any more than he was going to take the chance of going to the same place each time to explode the canisters. Farm labourers, shepherds, river bailiffs, hunt people returning late from a meet, they all had sharp eyes, and many of them knew him, and any of them would be curious for this was January and the moors were empty of tourists. Over the weeks he would find different places and get rid of the canisters in batches. He picked a wide stretch of empty hillside, checked the country around through his glasses, and then exploded the six canisters, backing up into the wind fifty yards between each one. It was late afternoon, the light just beginning to go from a high, cloudless sky, the strong profile of the moors rounded against the pomegranate red and yellow flush of the western horizon. A sparrowhawk came low down the hillside, rose, and hovered, shrew-observing, between him and his last canister. He waited, canister in hand, watching the pulse of its wings, head swinging low until it tipped sideways and slid away across the wind. He threw the canister, walked away, and heard the soft explosion, a gentle *plock* faint against the wind over the heather.

At that moment as Raikes turned his face to the wind and began to walk up the heather and tufted moor grass slopes to his car, Mary Warburton was sitting in her bedroom, a few minutes after returning from a shopping expedition in Exeter, holding in her hand a letter which had been in the afternoon post for her. The contents of the letter had set for her a problem which she had suspected for some time had existed. She left her room and went downstairs to the telephone.

And at that moment a man was sitting in a room in Paris having just read the obituary notice of Sarling in *The Times*. He was long past middle-age, a fair-haired man, the hair white above the ears, his face long, forbidding, the nose hooked to give him something of a Wellington look. He put the obituary down and stared through the uncurtained window at the Seine far below. Daylight had almost drained from the sky and yellow beads of light were strung along the river. A skein of barges went downstream towards the Pont de l'Alma. He flicked the black tongue of his intercom.

A woman's voice said, "Monsieur?"

"Have you a file on Applegate?"

"It's a London file, monsieur. But we have a copy."

"Let me have it. Also I want a call to Benson."

He flicked off the intercom before she could answer and turned to the rest of the papers on his desk.

Raikes and Mary had had dinner together. Mrs. Hamilton was gone and Mary was staying the night. The birch logs in the fire burst now and then into thick yellow and blue flame, tiny eruptions of creamy smoke spurting from the peeling silver bark.

Raikes tossed aside that week's copy of *The Field* and settled back in his chair, relaxed and at home. Almost unaware of Mary, he was remembering a chalk stream in Hampshire and the gentle take of a trout to an upstream nymph.

Mary said, "A penny for them."

He came back to her and smiled. "You won't like it."

"Try me."

"I was thinking of a fish."

"Oh, Andy." She laughed.

He laughed too, and in the ease between them wondered why the *Andy* from her was so different. She was lying back in her chair, red trousered legs perched on a small tapestried footstool, wearing an angora wool jumper dyed a sulphury yellow-green. Just, he thought, the colour of a blue tit's breast. She ran her hands backwards from the sides of her neck, through the loose fall of her hair and gave her head a little shake. It was a movement he knew so well, had seen her make here in this chair, and upstairs in bed when their lovemaking was finished and he dropped away from her; that familiar run of her hands and then the naked flexing of arms and shoulders. He reached for the cigarette box, held it to her questioningly and, when she shook her head, took a cigarette for himself.

She watched him light it, the brown hand steady on the lighter, the flame unwavering in the room's still air. Not to tell him, she thought, would be a cheat.

And, because she was forthright, not the kind to try and work a conversation round to a point which would serve for an easy entry into the unpleasant, she had decided—even before she

149

had gone down from her room to telephone and say she was coming over for dinner and to spend the night—that the right moment would be after dinner, after his brandy, when bed was near, and to go bluntly into her admission, knowing that her love for him was of a different nature from his love for her, his love made up of so many things, peripheral things like Alverton, a wife and family, a Raikes tradition, and hers just him, wanting him, wanting to give him the things he wanted.

So, bluntly, she launched into it, thinking, God I hope it doesn't go badly, and above all no crying, no tears, they just make a man give on-the-spot promises which he regrets the next morning.

"Andy, there's something I've got to tell you."

"Oh?"

The lazy, unsuspecting smile was hard to take.

"Yes. For the last six months I haven't been wearing a loop or taking the pill." Which was what she had been doing before, insuring one against the other.

He sat forward. "Hell, wasn't that risky?"

"Would you have minded if anything had happened? We could always have married and waited for Alverton."

"I suppose we could. But it wasn't the way I saw it. Anyway, why?"

"Because I wanted to know if I could have a baby." She rushed on. "Do you know how many times we've been together in these six months? Of course, you don't, but I do—exactly. Thirty-seven. And nothing's happened."

"That doesn't prove anything. The Bostocks went five years and then they adopted a kid and two months later she was pregnant."

"I'm not interested in the Bostocks, or anybody else's peculiarities. I'm thinking about us. Perhaps more about you, because I know how much it means to you to have children. And the plain fact is that it's highly unlikely that I ever will. There, I've said it."

She tightened her mouth, schooling herself. For God's sake

150

don't get emotional. Just facts. She reached into her trouser pocket, seeing his eyes follow every movement, and pulled out the letter.

"Read this."

He took the letter, unfolded it, turned it over and looked at the blank back first almost as though any delay in reading was welcome.

He turned it over. He heard Mary say, "He's a gynaecologist in Plymouth. He's known us for years . . ."

The typed script came up at him:

With reference to your attendance last week at my surgery for a screening examination with regard to your forthcoming marriage . . . You will remember that we had quite an anxious time over your appendicitis six years ago. As I explained to your parents then you had a considerable pelvic abscess which had to be drained. At the time of the operation the appendix was removed as well as the right ovary and a large part of the right Fallopian tube. The left Fallopian tube was also involved . . .

I am afraid that this was an extreme measure which had to be carried out for the safety of your own life. Although I regret having to say this to you, I must since you have asked me the direct question. It is my considered opinion that your chances of becoming pregnant by normal conception are remote . . .

He lowered the letter to his knees, looking at her. He could see that she was near to tears but fighting them. He felt himself swamped with sympathy for her, sympathy perhaps that partly included himself, and with admiration for her honesty and he said to himself, a commentator remote from the room, if only I knew what it was to love and really loved her it wouldn't matter a damn.

He said, "Your people never told you about this?"

"Only vaguely. I was hardly out of school. Somehow it didn't register. Or maybe they didn't want it to register."

151

He handed the letter back to her. "It's not absolutely positive."

"Does it have to be absolutely?"

"What are you getting at?"

"Andy, you know and I know how we feel about one another. Let's be honest—the big thing in your mind is Alverton and the Raikes family. You want a woman who can fill that house with children for you. I may not be able to do that."

"Well, that's a chance we'll have to take, isn't it?"

He got up, went over to her and knelt down, holding her hands.

"Is it? I know how much children mean to you. I don't think it's a chance I can ask you to gamble on."

"What kind of a man do you think I am? A blood stock dealer who's just gone around and picked himself the best mare he can for breeding? You think that first time up on the moors there was any thought like that in my mind?"

"No, I don't. You weren't thinking that far ahead. But it's there now, large and clear. Alverton, children, a couple of boys going off to Blundell's where all the Raikes men have gone . . . Don't you think I see that? Don't you think I know your thoughts when you're down on the river . . . seeing yourself with a boy, teaching him all the things about the river and the country that your father taught you?"

"Well, if there isn't going to be a boy, there isn't, and that's that. I've asked you to marry me and you've said yes. What do you think I'm going to say because you show me that?" He flipped the letter which lay in her lap. "That I'm sorry, but I must buy another mare? For Christ's sake!"

"No, I don't expect you to say it. Not now. But it's what you're going to feel like later. You won't be able to avoid it. That's why I want you to know that I'm not holding you to anything, Andy. Not to anything."

"Don't be bloody silly!" He stood and pulled her up to him, holding her. "You think I care what some bloody doctor says? Doctors, lawyers, all these professional types, they don't know their own jobs."

152

He held her to him, kissing her eyes, knowing how much this had cost her, knowing her fears and knowing he had to banish them, but knowing also that she was right, that the one thing he wanted was children, his own children, children with the Raikes' blood in them.

She pulled her face back from him, his arms still round her, and looked up at him.

"You're being nice, Andy. But I mean it. You know I mean it—and what's more I don't want you to make any quick promise now."

"I don't want to hear any more about it. Not another word. You're going to put it right out of your mind and so am I."

Much later, in bed, in the darkness, their love-making over, he lay and knew that there was no question of putting it out of his mind. Talk could be controlled, but not his thoughts, and in the blackness, with Mary warm alongside him, it was hard to keep from his mind a bitter protest. For years he'd worked, taken a hundred risks, to be able to come back and buy Alverton and take a wife there. But it seemed now, in the silent disorder of night thoughts, that there was something down here that rejected him, wanted to bar his coming back, wanted to break the cherished continuity of family that meant so much to him. He had come back once, only to be summoned by Sarling. He had freed himself from that and was back again. And now there was this. Sarling he had been able to deal with, but Mary was different. Against her straightforward honesty, knowing the agony in her of offering him release, he had—for the moment, at least—no weapons that he was willing to use. It would have been a hundred times better if she had been less honest, kept her doubts to herself, never gone to the Plymouth man ... that way no onus would have been put upon him to make a decision. They would have gone on through the years until the thing slowly became apparent ... and then? What would he have done then? God alone knew. All he knew was that if he couldn't go back to Alverton on his own terms then he didn't want to go back ... Why did he want Alverton and children so much? Was it because he was afraid of something? Knew that at Alverton he could hide from it, forget it? Was it true that he really was Frampton not Raikes, that he had done what he had done with Berners not to pay a debt owed by life to his father, not to settle at Alverton and re-establish the name of Raikes, but had done it because it was in his nature to do it? That all the time he had been crying out and working for a secure pastoral life he had been denying his real impulse ... masking that terrible challenge that lives inside some men to defy convention and venture themselves and their intelligence against society because society held no true place of contentment for them?

CHAPTER TEN

BEFORE SHE HAD taken her bath Belle had washed out some underclothes, girdles and stockings and strung them up on a nylon line cross the bathroom. Bathed now, she powdered herself and slipped into her nightdress. From her bedroom came the sound of the radio which she kept on at night for company when she was alone here. She took her dressing gown down from behind the door and went into the bedroom, throwing the gown across the foot of the bed. She was crossing the room to switch off the main bedroom light when the door opened.

It was a smooth, even movement, but nevertheless she jumped, shocked, her heart thumping violently, and gave a little cry.

The woman standing in the doorway said gently, "I'm sorry. I didn't mean to frighten you."

Belle said nothing, standing there, fighting to get her breath back.

The woman said, "Don't worry. No one's going to harm you. Just put on your dressing gown and come out."

"Who are you? What are you doing here? How did you get in?"

The woman smiled. "A lot of questions, but you'll get the answers. Just put something on and come out."

Keeping her eyes on the woman, Belle reached for her dressing gown. I should have screamed, she thought. Why didn't I scream and then perhaps someone would have come? The woman watched her, a pleasant smile on her face. She was short, very slim, wearing a black and white checked suit and she had blue framed glasses that went up at the corners like little ears, a small, dark, pleasant woman of about thirty-odd. She said, "I was for ringing the bell, but he said no you might not answer. So we came in and I'm sorry to have frightened you. I'd have screamed myself. By the way, my name's Saunders. Ethel. And his is Benson. John Benson."

She came forward and, as though they had been friends for years, took the cord of the dressing gown and tied it about Belle's waist and then put a hand on her shoulder and moved her into the sitting room.

A man was standing looking at the picture of the Camargue horses. He turned from the picture and smiled at Belle, giving a half nod to the picture.

He said, "I was down there once and watched a round up of the horses. It's a bad picture though. I hope you don't mind our coming in unannounced, Miss Vickers?"

Recovering now, Belle said, "I do indeed. It's no way to go on at all. And anyway, what do you want?"

"Questions," said Ethel Saunders. "We'll have to try to be fair and answer some of yours and then you can answer some of ours. But it will all be easier if we sit." Her hand came out and moved Belle to a chair, gently pressing her down.

The man said, "I'm Benson and that's Miss Saunders—my secretary. We wouldn't wish to say any more about ourselves at the moment. We opened the door with this." He held up a bunch of keys. There was a flash of immaculate white cuff, of a gold link and a smile just shadowed the tanned skin of his face. He was a big, clean, unhurried, confident man . . . foreign, somewhere, Belle thought, a little too much dressing on the dark hair for her fancy . . . Oh, God, what had that got to do with anything right now? What were they doing here . . .? Suddenly, the shock they had caused her, the quick upsurge of fright at the woman's appearance faded and another fear took over. Oh Christ, what was it all about?

Maybe the man knew this for he said to Miss Saunders, "Give her a brandy. Good for the nerves."

156

"No thank you," said Belle. Drink at this moment would make her sick.

"Just as you like. Let's talk."

Stupidly Belle said, "You're not going to steal anything, are you? I mean there's nothing here."

They both laughed.

"Just questions," said Benson. "Ordinary, simple questions. You're Miss Belle Vickers, aren't you?"

"Yes, but—"

"No, no—your turn will come. Miss Belle Vickers. But the door outside says Mr. and Mrs. Vickers."

"So what?" Although it wasn't diminishing her fear, spirit was coming back. At least they weren't going to steal anything or be violent.

"So we understand perfectly. Mr. and Mrs. Vickers but not in the eyes of the Law. So who cares? Where's Mr. Vickers?"

"He's away."

"Where?"

"I don't know. Travelling. That's what he does—travels. For a firm, I mean."

"I see." Benson nodded. Then he turned to Miss Saunders. "Ethel, take a look around. A good look. Begin with Mr. Vickers' bedroom."

Belle said, "I don't care for that."

Miss Saunders said, "Don't worry, I'm not going to take anything. And I won't be untidy." She moved towards the far bedroom door.

Benson said to Belle, "How old is Mr. Vickers?"

There was no question now in Belle's mind that his real interest was in Raikes, and there was no question in her mind of how she had to deal with this.

"About fifty."

"What's he like? To look at, I mean."

"Well ... I don't know. I suppose you'd say he was kind of shortish and plump, going a little bald. Look, why don't you tell me what all this is about?"

157

"Why don't you tell me why, without knowing what it's all about, you feel it necessary to lie about Mr. Vickers? I've met him, you know. He's not short, or plump, or going bald. However, don't let us bother with that. You were Mr. Sarling's secretary, weren't you?"

"So what?"

"Did he know you lived here with Mr. Vickers?"

"I worked for Mr. Sarling. He had no interest in my private life."

"That sounds reasonable. Were you upset when he died?"

Belle's lips tightened. Hold on, Belle, hold on, she told herself.

"Naturally," she said. "And I really insist that both of you leave this place at once; otherwise I shall ring down for the porter . . . or even the police."

Benson gave a little shrug of his broad shoulders. "All right. We're not leaving just yet so you must do what you will. Personally I would suggest the police." He nodded towards the telephone.

Belle sat unmoving. Why had she said that? It was a damned fool thing to say. She didn't want the porter or the police up here.

Benson smiled. "I give you the chance and you don't choose to take it. I wonder why? Mind, I have my own theory, but we won't bother to go into it. Tell me—who keeps the key of the safe behind the picture?"

"Mr. Vickers and he's got it with him."

"Sensible man. Now tell me, and I do wish you'd do this without much hesitation, what is Mr. Vickers' first name?"

"Bob. That's for Robert."

"Thank you. Bob for Robert. Now, since you're no longer interested in the police or the porter coming here, try and answer a few more questions with, shall we say, the same promptness. All right?"

Belle stood up. "I think I will have that brandy." She went to the sideboard and began to make herself a drink.

Behind her Benson said, "Don't bother to do one for me. I don't drink and I don't smoke. Just like Mr. Sarling. Did you sleep with him often?"

"I have in the past."

"Did he leave you any money?"

"Twenty thousand pounds."

"I'm happy for you. Did he ever come here?"

"No."

Belle came back to the chair with her brandy. As she sat she could hear Miss Saunders in her bedroom.

"But he knew you had this flat?"

"Yes."

"Knew about Mr. Vickers?"

"If he did he never told me."

"And he never met Mr. Vickers?"

"Not that I know."

"You're a loyal girl, aren't you?"

"No. Now that I know you're not going to rob me or beat me up, I'm just anxious to satisfy you and get rid of you."

"You've recovered fast. Tell me—your name is Vickers. But it's inconceivable that his should be Vickers, too. What is his name?"

Belle looked at him over the top of her glass. "You say you've met him. What name did he give you?"

Benson laughed quietly. "The name he gave me was Tony Applegate—but, of course, I knew it wasn't his real name. What is his name?"

"Why do you want to know all this? Why are you so interested?"

"It would take too long to tell. But just as we don't mean you any harm, neither do we wish him any. All we want really is to meet him again and talk some business. Now, what's his name and where—when he's not here—can we find him?"

Stubbornly, Belle said, "I'm not telling you anything. And don't try to make me or I'll scream my head off."

"All right. I'm not going to try to make you be disloyal. In

159

fact, I approve of your loyalty. However, perhaps you'll do something for me."

"What?"

"When Mr. Vickers gets back, or if you know how to get in touch with him—just say I called and I'd like him to get in touch with me. Mr. Benson wants to hear from Tony Applegate. Clear? He'll know how to get hold of me."

"You're going to have to wait. He's gone abroad for six months."

Benson shook his head, smiling. "No, that won't do."

Miss Saunders came back into the room. Belle saw at once that she was carrying the repaired Cunard brochure in her hands.

Ignoring Belle, Miss Saunders handed the brochure to Benson. "There's nothing but this. There's a page of notes inside."

Benson opened the brochure, flipped through a few pages and then coming to the notes began to read them.

Belle watched him. Something had gone wrong. Something had gone very wrong. She was sure of this. Although these two didn't frighten her now, she knew they could and would if they were given cause. But already deep inside her was her own fright. Through it she was telling herself to keep her head, not to do or say anything which Andy wouldn't have wanted her to do. But how could she know, how could she guess what was the right or wrong thing to say or do? She saw Benson's left hand come up and rub his chin, a big, brown hand, manicured, a plain gold ring on it. He suddenly looked up over the brochure and smiled at her.

"You've read these?" His hand flicked brochure and notes.

"Not really."

"Who tore them in half?"

"I don't know."

"Who stuck them together?"

"I did."

"Why?"

160

"Because I did."

"Just because?"

"Yes."

"They're not really important to you?"

"No."

He stood up and began to move towards the door. "In that case I'll take them."

"You can do what you like with them. They mean nothing to me."

Miss Saunders smiled. "Except that you keep them by your bedside."

Benson said, "We're sorry to have bothered you. Please forgive us. And don't forget to let Mr. Vickers have the message. Tell him we've taken the brochure. He'd want to know that."

They went out, leaving her sitting in the chair, and she stayed there knowing that she had done everything wrong, must have done everything wrong. Damn the brochure. Why had she kept it?

She got up suddenly and went to the telephone. She rang Raikes' number in Devon. From the far end the call sign churred away, grinding and boring like some animal noise at the far end of a dark tunnel. She let it ring for half an hour and there was no answer.

That morning Raikes had taken some more of the canisters up on the moors and exploded them. He had left before the morning post had arrived. On his return just before lunch the post had been waiting for him. With it was a letter from Mary Warburton. It read—

Darling Andy,

You must not be upset if I keep this brief and very factual. In the last few days since telling you about the gynaecologist's report I have made up my mind. I know that your loyalty and affection for me will be making you deny in your heart the decision you would really want to make . . . and one day would make. To help you I am making it for you.

161

When you read this I shall be well on my way to Cyprus to stay with friends. I have told my parents the truth and they entirely agree with what I am doing. They have nothing but kindness and understanding for us both. I am setting you free from our unofficial engagement. No matter what you may feel reading this—I insist on it.

Love,
Mary.

For a time he had sat there re-reading the letter. Then he had got up and made himself a drink and stood staring out of the window and slowly there had moved into him a sense of relief. The logic of his true desires had been inescapable. Everything Mary had said was right. He would have fought for a while against breaking away from her, but in the end he would have done it. With the sharp charity of a woman who loved and understood him, she had done it for him. For the way of life he wanted, was determined to have, he had murdered Sarling, was already planning to rid himself of Belle, and would eventually have dispossessed himself of Mary. He faced the truth about himself frankly and accepted it. But where with Sarling —and with Belle when the moment came—he could be devoid of feeling, the break with Mary left him disturbed. Largely, he knew, it was a form of self-pity—and that for him was an unusual emotion. Mary would have been so right for him, for Alverton, for the life he had planned. Now, he had to find someone else.

He had walked out to his car and driven off. It was Mrs. Hamilton's day for shopping in Barnstaple and she had left him to get his own cold lunch. He had driven to Exeter and gone to the cinema. He had got back about seven, had a couple of drinks and a meal and then, unable to stay in the house, had gone for a long walk. Coming back late he had let himself into Alverton Manor with his key, and had wandered round the house. Another woman, not Mary, would now be mistress here. He sat on the window ledge of his old bedroom—which was in process of being repapered, the wallpaper a close match to the one he remembered from thirty years before. Beside him on the seat he had found a crumpled sheet of the *Daily Mail* in which some workman had brought his sandwiches and a head-line had caught his eye. Below was an account of the turbine difficulties which had beset the new Cunarder, *Queen Elizabeth 2*. Angrily he had reached out and crumpled up the sheet. It was almost as though Sarling had suddenly come into the house.

He had walked back late to his own house, his feet loud on the frost-bound road, the hoar hanging in grey plumes from the bare willow and beech branches. From the pine plantations across the river had come the sharp call of a dog fox.

He walked into the hall to hear the telephone ringing in the sitting room. By the time he reached it, it had stopped.

Standing by the telephone he suddenly realised that the last thing he wanted to do for the next few days was to be here, in Devon, near Alverton Manor, near anything that would remind him too openly of Mary. He went upstairs, packed his case and drove through the night to Taunton.

He caught the 2.30 a.m. train, not caring that it was a slow one and was at Paddington by seven o'clock. To the cab driver he gave the name of his club, but half-way there he changed his mind and gave the Mount Street address and he knew exactly why he had changed his mind. There was no point in mooning about and feeling sorry for himself about Mary. Sooner or later he would find another Mary. But the problem of Belle remained, and the best antidote to his present disappointment was work and planning. Before he and Berners could dispose of Belle she had to be out of the flat and all trace of Mr. and Mrs. Vickers wiped clean. His first step was to get her to take another flat, another flat in which he would promise to join her—though he never would—and from which she would one day soon walk out to her death.

He let himself in with his key, put his case in his bedroom and went through the stocking- and underwear-draped bathroom into her bedroom. She woke as he came in and stared at him as though he were some part of a fading dream still with her. Then, as he sat on the edge of the bed, she threw her arms around him, buried her face in his shoulder and began to sob. He knew at once that something had happened. After a little while she calmed down and he began to get the story of Benson's visit from her.

She was sitting opposite him, wrapped in her dressing gown as she had been for Benson. Her hands cradled a mug of coffee which he had made and now, with all her incoherence over, he was beginning to think clearly and sort things out. Mary was gone now, pushed back into the dark fringes of his mind. There was only this. Benson had been in this room. Benson, like Sarling, and like Belle, had to be dealt with. Perhaps, he thought, this was some irony of the gods. He was going to get what he wanted, but they weren't going to let it be easy. Perhaps sometime in all these years he should have recognised their power and poured a libation to them, made some acknowledgment of his luck and success. Perhaps in all these years he and Berners, without knowing it, had been pushing their luck and had become too arrogant of their powers . . . God, now he was thinking as his mother used to. Bad luck to her had been as real as rainfall. Never bring hawthorn in flower into the house. Never put a pair of shoes on the table. Never walk under a ladder. Touch wood. Spilled salt over the left shoulder. A saucer of milk in the dairy for the little men . . . All right, he would acknowledge that in all he and Berners had done there had had to be some luck. But now there was this . . . and clear thinking had to run before luck.

He said, "Now don't get fussed up. The whole thing has a simple explanation."

"Oh, Andy . . . I tried not to say anything . . . Like, well you know, the wrong thing."

"Yes, yes, I know. But let me explain it. All he wanted to do was to get in touch with me. I'd been in touch with him about a delivery of gold bullion. Time and place of delivery and price

164

and so on and I was to get in touch with him again after a few weeks. Well, I never did, because no gold bullion was ever going to be stolen. Now, he wants to know why. Why I haven't got in touch with him. Why he isn't going to make a fat profit out of some robbery I'd planned. He's just a business man not wanting to lose a good deal."

"You really think it's like that?"

"How else?"

"But they know about Sarling?"

"Sarling made the contact for me—but he wouldn't have done more than that, wouldn't have said anything about where the gold was coming from. Damn it, he only told me at the last moment. If he had told anyone else about it, or about forcing Berners and myself to steal it, don't you think he would have said so in the car that night? That would have saved him. I wouldn't have murdered him if anyone else had known about it. No, it's more likely that Benson read about Sarling's death, knew he was connected with me, waited for me to show up and then, when I didn't, came along here to find out why. So, now I tell him that the whole thing is off and that's the end of it."

"Oh, Andy, I do hope so."

He stood up, turning away from her to look out of the window. In her dressing gown, hair loose, bare feet rubbing against one another, her face blotchy from sobbing and emotion, she looked like nothing. And every time she said *Oh, Andy* a sour irritation filled him. In the darkness, as he held her body, making love to her, she was without personality, just woman . . . all the same in the dark, as Benjamin Franklin had said. But in daylight there were times when he ached for her to be gone . . . dead and gone. But until she was he had to be for her what she wanted.

Turning back to her he smiled, moved over and put a hand on the warmth of her thin neck under the sweep of auburn hair.

"There's nothing to worry about." He came round and faced her. "But tell me, why did you keep that brochure and repair it?"

165

"Oh, Andy, you're not cross about that."

He felt the muscles of his jaws tighten but he smiled, put out a hand and touched her knee, reassuring her. "No, but I'm curious to know why. You read it?"

"I skipped through it."

"You knew what Sarling wanted me to do? Rob the *Queen Elizabeth 2*?"

"Yes."

"Then why didn't you get rid of it?"

She hesitated for a moment and then said, "Well, I suppose . . . Well, you really want to know?"

Of course, he wanted to know. What the hell did she think he was asking for?

"Of course I do."

"I mean the really real reason?"

"Yes. The true reason."

"Well, I thought you might have been angry about it. Just torn it up and thrown it away because it came from him. But with him out of the way I thought you might begin to think about it . . . Oh, I know it's stupid, but I wanted you to do it because that way it would mean that maybe I could help and we'd be together longer . . . I didn't want to lose you. I wanted you with me as long as possible . . . There, I've said it."

"Belle . . ." He took her hand and held it, knowing that all she needed was the word and the contact. He stood up, bent and kissed her and said, "You'd better get dressed."

As she went back to the bedroom, Raikes picked up the telephone and dialled a number. It rang for some while before it was answered.

A man's voice said, "Yes?"

Raikes said, "Tony's back and wants an appointment."

"Which Tony?"

"The Applegate one."

"I'll ring you during the morning."

The line went dead.

Raikes went back to his chair, dropped into it and picked

166

up the copy of *The Times* which he had bought at Paddington Station. Opening it, skipping through it, his eye was suddenly caught by a headline. *QE2 Ready for Sea by March. From our Scottish Correspondent—Glasgow, Feb. 5.*

Without any emotion, his mind half moving ahead to the coming Applegate appointment, planning it, knowing exactly what line he would take, he read the report:

The turbine trouble that caused delivery of the *Queen Elizabeth 2* on New Year's Day to be cancelled has been diagnosed by engineers at Clydebank, and they hope to have the ship ready for sea again next month.

Mr. Graham Strachan, managing director of John Brown Engineering (Clydebank) Ltd., said at a press conference in Glasgow today that he expected the turbine rotors to be returned to the ship at Southampton by March 7. The installation and preparations for new sea trials could be completed in a further two weeks.

He said a design fault had been made by Pametrada, the organisation set up to centralize turbine research and design, which was dissolved just over a year ago.

Pametrada had been producing a standard turbine design for about 35,000 h.p. where the QE2 required 55,000 h.p. The turbine as built might have coped with the demand but there were external faults in the arrangement of steam pipes and the fitting of couplings which caused vibration. Six rows of blades on the turbine rotors had been affected, and some blades had broken off.

Mr. Strachan said that the blades at the point of stress were being replaced by others about one-tenth of an inch thicker, and the steam pipes were being rearranged and the couplings realigned.

Pametrada had been excellent turbine designers with over 400 successful sets of machinery at sea. The design fault could happen to others and, no matter what precautions were taken, it could happen again.

167

Mr. Strachan said that he hoped the ship would be given sea trials of about nine or 10 days, although this was a matter for Upper Clyde Shipbuilders. The engineers, he said, would want to open the turbines and inspect the blades after the trials.

An official of Upper Clyde Shipbuilders said tonight that until their experts had completed assessments they were unable to give a date either for trials or delivery.

Cunard, who have cancelled all scheduled sailings and cruises for the liner, said they would make no comment until they had received a full report from Upper Clyde Shipbuilders.[1]

Two hours later the telephone rang.

A man's voice said, "Benson. Room 97. The Ritz. Ten o'clock tomorrow morning."

It was the same room. But the flowers this time, instead of being chrysanthemums, were freesias, their red, purple, white and gold blooms reminding him of the caps the flower fairies wore in some childhood picture book. Benson was alone, a tall, dark-haired, composed man, friendly, moving with the unconscious grace natural to some big men and establishing at once an unoffending permissiveness of speech as though, apart from business, they knew one another well.

He said, "Your Miss Vickers is very loyal—though I should have thought hardly your type."

Deciding to feel his way, to show no edge unless their meeting should call for bluntness, Raikes said, "Well, you can't have everything in a woman. But why didn't you give me a ring? You frightened her, walking into the flat like that."

"Yes, I debated that. But then I thought there are times when an unexpected personal visit can be very rewarding."

"And was it?"

"I think so—from a character point of view. Hers, not yours.

[1] Reproduced from *The Times* by permission.

168

She had no brief for the situation, but even so, she did very well. Given a brief she would have been unshakable."

"She had no need for a brief. Anyway, you and I are not here to talk about her. Your real concern, I guess, is business."

"Naturally. You came to me with a proposition, and then I heard no more from you. I'd be a poor business man if I hadn't followed it up. After all, you might have gone to a rival, thinking you were getting better terms. Or you might have run into snags which you felt you couldn't face—not knowing that from our side we'd always be willing to help. Did something like that happen?"

"No. I just decided to drop my particular business plan for good."

"A pity. May I ask why?"

"The risk was too great, I decided. A man should know his limits and stick within them. If he's desperate—well, that's another matter."

"This particular risk?" Benson's hand went back to the desk behind him and he dropped the Cunard brochure on the table in front of Raikes.

"Yes."

"Too great for you? Yet you'd got to the point of contacting us? You'd have thought of all the risks by then. You had a sudden change of heart?"

Raikes smiled. "I don't have sudden changes of heart. I take my time making a decision. And I've made it. This just wasn't my kind of job."

From behind Raikes a man's voice said, "On the contrary, I think it's just your kind of job."

As Raikes turned, Benson stood up, and said, "This is . . . let us say . . . the Chairman of our Company, Mr. Mandel."

Standing just inside the doorway was a tall, white-haired man with a large beaked nose, shoulders a little hunched, his arms reaching flat down at the sides of his body, the whole, still pose suddenly reminding Raikes of the immobile yet intense alertness of a falcon, pine-perched, eyes hooded against

169

the day glare, yet missing no tremor of movement below.

Angered a little by the smooth stage-managing of this other man's appearance, and the timely interjection, Raikes said, "I disagree. The risks I take or don't take I judge for myself."

Mandel came forward, jerked his head at Benson and said, "Please. . . ."

Benson went across the room and through the door to a bedroom. Mandel sat himself squarely in an armchair across the table from Raikes and put out a hand and moved the bowl of freesias three inches to the side so that they had a clear view of one another. His right hand flowed from the movement toward the Cunard brochure and drew it to him.

He said, "In normal circumstances I would never quarrel with your last statement. But these aren't normal circumstances, as I will explain very soon. However, let us go right to the heart of the matter before we concern ourselves with all the whys and wherefores." His words came without any trace of personality, instruments concerned only with the clear precision work of their meaning. "You are going to do this job."

"I am not."

"You are going to do this job for two reasons. Because you are capable of it. And because I am going to force you."

Raikes was tempted to rise to his feet and walk out of the room. With many other men he might have done it, knowing that he was calling a bluff, but this man, he sensed, had long ago given up bluffing to get his way. What he said he meant, and what he meant had to be backed with reason. Just for a moment a weary wave of memory washed over him . . . Sarling, Belle, Mary and Alverton . . . all fighting against him. Schooling himself against the impulse to go, he lit a cigarette, leaned back in his chair and told himself . . . All right, you're not free yet. So what? You know what you want, you know what you're going to have—so work for it just a little longer, don't let anyone make you impatient. Think. Keep that motto hanging on the wall of your mind.

He said easily, "All right, Mr. Mandel. You've made a very positive statement. Now back it up."

Mandel raised a finger and rubbed the bony bridge of his nose. "I will. Your contact with us was arranged by a Mr. Sarling."

"Was it?"

"Yes. Mr. Sarling had used us many times for some of his unorthodox affairs. He had had the code name Applegate for years, for himself and for his associates. So, you were working for Mr. Sarling."

"Yes."

He tapped the brochure. "Have you read the notes in here?"

"No."

"They are in his handwriting. Which I know because I had contacts with him on a social level and he sometimes wrote to me. He wanted you to rob the *Queen Elizabeth 2*."

"Yes."

"If he wanted you to do that it would only have been because he considered you capable of doing it. There is no secret in some circles about his methods. For his extra-business affairs he only used people in whom he had confidence and over whom he had some hold usually ferretted out for him by the man Wurther, who is now dead."

"As Sarling himself is. All right, I'll grant you that. But when Sarling died I became a free man. No matter my capabilities as assessed by him, I was free. And I have exercised my choice, Mr. Mandel."

"You exercised it too soon. You have no choice."

"Why not?"

"Because if Sarling died a natural death you should be a very worried man. Maybe you are, but that is not the impression you give. Your own words were that you became a free man. Could that be true? Sarling was methodical. He would have records of all the people he used, their misdeeds, their secrets ... all those things which he could use against them. These on his death might—at his own instruction—be destroyed without being opened. But a dead man's wishes are not always obeyed.

171

Some risk would remain—and you are a man who calculates risks. Would you like to make some comment on that?"

"None at all."

"All right. You sit there a free man unworried. A clever man, a determined man, a man clearly who knows what he wants from life. Now, if Sarling's was not a natural death. Let's assume murder for instance, and you the murderer. I'm not saying you are. Frankly, I don't know. But we will assume you are. All right. You would never have murdered him—and let's face it the actual murder would be the simpler part of the operation—without making sure that you could get your hands on your records and the records of anyone else working with you, like Miss Vickers, for instance. Would it surprise you if I knew about his two strong rooms which could only be opened by his own left thumbprint?"

"It not only surprises me, but it's news to me. I knew nothing about his security arrangements."

For the first time Mandel smiled. It was a momentary rictus that showed very even, very white false teeth.

"You may be telling the truth. But I don't think you are. In my business facts are clumsy, obvious things. Most of our work is by inference to begin with. What would be the obvious, the most salient fact to emerge if you *had* murdered Sarling? A fact that you couldn't hide, that would be reported in the press—and, indeed, has been? That Sarling would have been murdered in one or other of his houses so that you could have used his thumbprint to open the strong room either before or after you killed him. But more than that emerges—and this increases my admiration for you and confirms to me that you can do this Cunard job. Sarling died in his London house, but he left his country house, late at night, only a few hours previous to his death. Two strong rooms, would you say? Two occasions on which to use his thumbprint and—by deduction, therefore—two sets of records, one in the country and one in London. My overall conclusion is that you, with Miss Vickers, and a man called Berners between you murdered Sarling."

172

"I don't know anyone called Berners."

"You should have read Sarling's notes." He slid a finger over the glossy cover of the Cunard brochure. "He is mentioned in association with you."

Raikes shrugged. "So, where the hell does all this get us? You have suppositions and draw inferences from them." He spoke easily, giving nothing away, but in his heart he knew that, whether he liked it or not, everything had already been given away. Even so, one didn't despair. There was always a way out. Nothing was impossible if you had a true dream, a true wish which was fire in your guts, and he had that. . . .

"When the inferences are strong enough I am prepared to act on them. I am a business man. You could do the QE2 job and we could make a lot of money from it. It is going to be done."

Raikes shook his head. "Then make me. Nothing you've said so far can make me."

"We come to that, now—Mr. Raikes of Alverton."

"So, you know that?"

"We make it our business to know as much as we can before we form an association. The Mount Street flat was watched for some time before Miss Vickers was visited. At least three times you walked to your club from there. The rest was easy. I have a son-in-law who is a member."

"We get all sorts even in the good clubs these days. However, I still want to know how you're going to make me associate with you."

"You must have thought of it already. All it needs is a word or two to the police. Not difficult to arrange and not coming from me. The death of Sarling is worth investigating. They get your name, Miss Vickers' and Berners'. You and Berners might stand firm. But Miss Vickers would crack. In addition you're a man with some kind of past, even if you have no criminal record. The police would be given that hint, too, and they would follow it up. You said you understood the limits of risk. Would you risk that?"

Raikes stood up. He stubbed out his cigarette in the table

173

ash tray and then picked up the Cunard brochure. He folded it in two and pushed in into his coat pocket.

He said, "I'll consider it."

"You will do it."

"Not if it can't be done."

"Sarling had faith in you. So have I. You can do it."

"And if I do—what guarantee have I of being left in peace afterwards?"

"My word. No more. When a man enters the criminal world he forfeits forever true peace of mind, true security. It is the unavoidable result of an unorthodox way of life. Whatever you did in the past that Sarling knew about, then from that moment you could have no true peace of mind. But in our world there is trust of a kind . . . in many ways a high form of trust. That's all I can offer you. Thousands of men are content with it. I am. You must be."

It was true. Like it or not, Raikes had to acknowledge its truth. No true peace; always an element of fear. Well, a man could learn to live with fear and be happy, just as men learnt to live with want or disability and be happy.

Raikes said, "You think I killed Sarling?"

"I have less doubt about it now."

"I might kill you."

"No. There are too many people behind me. Sarling stood alone. It was his one fault. He had no protection except an arrogant belief—pathetic, really, in a man of his experience—in his own self-sufficiency."

Raikes picked up his hat. Through the window outside he saw the thick, grey flakes of a February snow-flurry mottling the sky.

He said, "Would I be obliged to use Berners?"

"Clearly. Leave him out and when he hears of the robbery he becomes a security risk. Involve him and he is no risk. The same applies to Miss Vickers."

Mandel stood up, the movement like the sudden lengthening of a falcon's body, the slow shake-down of plumage.

174

Raikes said, "Did Sarling mean anything to you personally?"

"Nothing. Occasionally we did business together. Always in gold. I am not interested in anything else. Now you and I are going to do business. That's my only interest in you, and since most of the risk will be on your side, you will take seventy-five per cent and feel free to call on us for any help you want. Just deal, along the lines you already have done, with Benson. Goodbye, Mr. Raikes."

Mandel's arm and hand came out stiffly across the table. Raikes looked down at the man's hand and shook his head. "You're forcing me, Mandel. Forcing me hard. You're making me change my plans, and you may even be destroying something which means everything to me—you expect me to take your hand on that? No, I promise you that if I ever touch you it will be to kill you. This I promise you."

He went out of the room. Mandel sat down. Benson came back into the room.

"Well?"

Mandel looked up at him and his right hand went out absently and pushed the vase of flowers back into its original spot. "He is going to do it. You'll hear from him. Give him every help he wants. Everything. And never forget for one moment the kind of man you're dealing with. We've disturbed his dream. . . ."

Deliberately he walked through the snowfall to Lower Regent Street. He knew exactly what he wanted to do, knew even that it was a form of masochism. There was no escape for him that he could immediately see; perhaps no escape for him ever. If that were so he must begin to learn to live with it, to fashion his life around it. His life here, not his life at Alverton. For the time being that had been removed. Sarling had begun the delay, Mary had lengthened it, and now this man Mandel had postponed it *sine die*. There was no anger in him; just a dull, solid resentment, the brute acceptance of enslavement, and the beginning of a patience which he knew would grow and sustain him for as long as he needed it . . . until the moment, if ever offered, when he would reward himself with the act of violence and revenge that his temperament demanded. The thought of that act, uncomposed, unframed, would for him now, through weeks, months or years if necessary, take the place of hope and feed his strength. One day, Mr. Bloody Mandel . . . one day.

He halted in front of the large right-hand window of the Cunard Building and the world came back. Poised in the middle of the window was a model of the new *Queen Elizabeth 2*. The snow mantling his shoulders, he looked at the model, at the long rake of the dark grey hull, the broad red footing above the water line, looking down on her as though he were seeing her from the air, blue water shining in the lido pools aft, the neatly slung lifeboats, the stubby ears of the wheelhouse wings, the strange, untraditional funnel born of a thousand wind-tunnel tests, wind scoop at its base to throw a current of air upwards to carry away smut and smoke, the mast which was no mast at all but an exhaust pipe for the kitchens and a hatrack for communication devices, aerials, radar scanners, fog horns and a photoelectric cell connected to another in one of the restaurants to adjust the lighting with every variation of the daylight outside, the smooth step down of boatdeck, quarterdeck and foredeck . . . looking at the model, Raikes told himself without emotion that in the past Sarling had stood here, unaware of the people who passed, full of his dream.

He turned away abruptly and signalled a taxi. He caught the 12.28 p.m. train to Brighton from Victoria. In the train he pulled out Sarling's Cunard brochure. Clipped inside were two pieces of quarto notepaper covered in Sarling's handwriting. They had been torn in half and carefully joined together with transparent tape.

SOME NOTES FOR FRAMPTON AND BERNERS
At the moment the first regular run of the QE2 is scheduled as follows—Leave Southampton 1200 hrs. 18th April, 1969.

176

Arrive Le Havre 1900 hrs. Depart Le Havre 2100 hrs. Arrive New York afternoon 23rd April. (At the moment, because of the present turbine troubles of the QE2 and alteration of schedules (this first run is likely to be postponed to a later date).

The intention is to rob the QE2 of the bullion from her Specie Room on this first westwards North Atlantic run from Southampton to New York.

The whole operation is to be carried out with not more than two operators aboard, and should not take more than forty minutes to an hour. Duress will be used, but no violence and no more than a minimum amount of disturbance to passengers. In fact there is no reason why the course of the operation should be known to anyone except certain ship's officers and crew.

The operation will take place during the midnight–0400 hrs watch. In the wheelhouse at that time will be a First and Third Officer, a Quartermaster, and a boy. The Specie Room is on No. 8 Deck. There is a large service lift opposite the Specie Room which runs all the way up to One Deck. The keys to the Specie Room are held in the safe in the Captain's quarters.

Nearer the date the actual shipments of bullion to go aboard can be checked from City sources. With the old Queens it was not unusual to have ten tons aboard—gold and silver. A minimum shipment of two tons could be expected.

Disposal of bullion through the Applegate connection. This connection would, when the time comes, be prepared to give *outside* assistance in the operation. But at no time would more than two operators be aboard.

Think it over and let me have your plan. I shall be interested to see how nearly it matches, or even improves on, my own.

Raikes put the brochure in his pocket and leaned back,

closing his eyes. Just at that moment Sarling was alive again, very much alive in his mind. What on earth had ever put this idea into his head. Had he at some time gone into the shipping world and had his fingers burnt? So much so that there was a need in him to deface the symbol of his failure? Or had it been the idle challenge of a puzzle which in some bored moment had come into his mind? How do you take gold bullion from a ship without any fuss and using only two people aboard—and those two people, obviously, when it was all done, to remain secure and untouchable and untraceable? Physically two people couldn't do it by themselves. They couldn't lift and transport any large weight of gold without taking hours of time—and all this on a ship alive with three thousand souls. Well, the simple answer was that, since they couldn't do it, they had to get others to do it for them—authoritatively, quietly and without fuss. That's what Sarling meant by duress, but no violence. Despite himself, the challenge of the puzzle held him. How did you put under duress, suborn, intimidate and command a ship's company, or certain key individuals of it to do exactly what you wanted and without question? (Quite apart from the problem of getting the stuff off the boat at sea using—he saw this only too clearly —the *outside* assistance Sarling mentioned.) On a ship there was only one man who could command and be unquestioned. That was the captain. A ship at sea was a world of its own and one man ruled it. Christ, he couldn't imagine any captain calmly handing over his bullion cargo. But that was how it would have to be. Then, how the hell did you go about creating that condition, making it impossible for the captain to do anything else? That question stayed with him all the way to Brighton.

At two o'clock he rang the doorbell of Berners' house. Berners, wearing a dark blue blazer with silver buttons, a silver tie, fawn trousers and suede shoes, let him in.

CHAPTER ELEVEN

BERNERS WAS HAPPY. It was not something he would show openly, but after an hour of talking to him Raikes realised that it was there. Any emotion he had himself had now hardened to an easily shouldered burden. They had both agreed that this thing had to be done. All right. Let it be done and finished with. But he sensed now that where he was approaching it as one more task before he could walk into the comparative freedom of the life he wanted, Berners was thinking no farther ahead than the task itself . . . and that not a task, but an operation he welcomed. So, he told himself, if you live long enough and work long enough with a man it is still not possible to come to the end of all discovery about him. Berners, snug in this house, endowed for life, should have been resenting the dictate which had been handed to him. But he was accepting it, calm and subdued outwardly, but eagerly and with relish inwardly.

Raikes stood up. "Well, there it all is. I suggest we think about it separately for a few days and then get in touch and compare notes. From what I've seen in the press the QE2 is not likely to make that April the 18th date, so we've plenty of time."

Berners nodded, and then not getting up, clearly wanting to hold Raikes to this room for a while, he said, "Why don't you say openly that you're surprised at my reaction?"

"You want me to?"

"Why not? We're going to do this. The more we understand one another and ourselves the more efficiently we work together."

"You're talking in riddles."

"No, I'm not. I'm talking freely. Why don't we both look at

the thing squarely? We did some pretty daring things together. Risky. Dangerous. But not outrageous. But we didn't do them just to get money, did we?"

"I did."

"You tell yourself you did. But if you really think about it you'll have to admit—as I do—that there was something else. Some element in us which forces us to behave differently from the majority of men. It's an element we can't ignore. You never had any conscience over murdering Sarling, did you?"

"None."

"Any normal man would have done. It proves my point. He was a bigger challenge than any we'd had before—and we never questioned not killing him. Any more than we were questioning killing Miss Vickers—though that's out of court now. It's as simple as this. When we first met you'd found a groove, a line of country which suited us. But Sarling gave us something different to think about, something that discovered a different potential in us. Look at us now—once we murdered to protect what we have and to ensure freedom from fear. And now? We accept that for the rest of life we must learn to live without complete peace of mind, must learn to live on trust . . . trust that rests in the hands of other people. You know why we make that shift so easily?"

"Because we have no choice. Because I'm determined to restore the status quo as near as possible to what it was before Sarling came along."

Berners shook his head. "No. Any kind of status that spelled contentment, pleasant, well-heeled routine would drive us up the wall. We are what we are, and we shall always be wanting to venture ourselves. Not resenting it even when other people force us to venture ourselves. We're misfits."

"For God's sake, Berners."

"We are. Face it. We don't fit into normal society. We can make the motions and the faces—but we don't belong. So, let's accept it and be happy about it for as long as we can."

Suddenly Raikes laughed. "No, Berners—this is just your

way of adjusting to this situation. Okay, why shouldn't it be true, or seem true to you? I don't question it. But I know how I feel and stand. I know what I want and what waits for me beyond this bloody QE2 thing. And I'm going to have it— come hell or high water. I'm going back to my true place. I'm going to have a wife and kids and the life I've always wanted. And God help anyone who tries to muck it up!"

Berners stood up and shrugged his shoulders.

"All right."

Raikes said, "You want me to leave the brochure and the notes?"

"No. It's a simple problem. The main line is clear. Once we've established the fundamentals it's just a question of details. Whatever Sarling's plan was it must have hinged on those canisters you stole. As you said, that was no boy scout exercise. You've got some left?"

"Quite a few yet."

Raikes went back to London. Berners had surprised him. Misfits. Away from Berners he had begun to grow angry over it, and the angry denial was still with him, and with it an anger against the whole situation.

When he walked into the flat Belle was standing in her bedroom door. She turned and he saw the anxiety on her face. She'd spent hours wondering where he was, wondering what he was doing . . . full of her stupid anxiety . . . He could read it all in her now as she came toward him, arms out . . . *Andy* on her lips . . . and the sight of her roused a silent fury in him.

He lifted her, stopped her silly mouth with a kiss and carried her through into the bedroom. He dropped her on the bed, hearing her giggle, his face smiling, masking his fury, and his hands, lifting her skirt and stripping her pants, were rough and eager, not with a lover's haste for rut, but with an impatience to possess and punish and obliterate her. He took her hard and long, whipping her body with his, spending his rare fury on her, exhausting it and her and himself, and knowing that all the time she was taking for passion what was punishment, taking for love what was anger and a venting of frustration. . . .

Two weeks later, now almost the end of February, Raikes drove down to Southampton and booked in at the Polygon Hotel.

In that two weeks he had seen Berners twice and between them they had arrived at a broad, overall plan of their strategy. But now the time had come to go over the actual ground on which they would be working. There were dozens of small points of detail which had to be checked and minor problems that had to be solved. The only way to do this was to go over the ship itself—and that was not easy because she was still in the hands of the Upper Clyde Shipbuilders and no casual visitors were allowed aboard. One had to be working on the ship or officially connected with it. The only detailed plans of the ship Raikes had were the publicity lay-outs issued by the Cunard people. These ran from the Fifth Deck right up to the Signal Deck, but gave no lay-out of the captain's and officers' quarters, or of the wheelhouse. It was essential that Raikes should familiarise himself with the ship before he went aboard for the real operation because the plan he and Berners had worked out depended on the gold being stolen within sixteen hours of the ship's leaving Southampton. In fact, some three or four hours after she had left Le Havre and when she would still be in the English Channel. When he went aboard on the ship's first west–east passage he had to know his way around with absolute certainty in those areas where he would be operating. The ship was a floating city and it would be the easiest thing in the world to get lost in her.

His first evening at the Polygon, he went into the bar before dinner and sat quietly at a table with his drink and an evening paper. Getting aboard the ship was a problem, but not a big one. In the bar amongst all the talk the sound of more than one Scots accent could be heard. Aboard the ship were scores of Upper Clyde workers and many of them, officials, engineers and the staff of sub-contractors, had been staying at the hotel for some time. Raikes listened, ran his eye over the crowd in the bar and decided to take his time in marking down a man. The long years behind him had taught him that nothing can be forced.

The next morning he got himself a visitor's pass to the docks. He got a taxi to just short of the main dock gate and then walked through, showing his pass to the policeman on duty.

The *Queen Elizabeth 2* was berthed alongside the Ocean Terminal. He walked the quayside, the whole of her length, the great wall of her welded plates rising above him. Midships a gangway went aboard and its entrance was guarded by a policeman and a dock guard, both of them warming themselves at a coke brazier from a cold north-east wind which was whipping down the chasm between the ship and the Ocean Terminal. He walked past and at the far end of the quay turned into the Terminal and went to its upper floor. From here he could look across to the ship's upper decks. Since she was still the property of the Upper Clyde Shipbuilders their house flag was flying at her mast—a purple cross *patée* on a white ground. He stood there looking through the windows, paying particular attention to her foredeck. The main and central part of it was taken up with two big, white painted capstans from which ran the chains for the three anchors, two shipped on the deck and the third housed forward now in the bows. Forward of the two anchors was a small mast about twenty feet high. The sight of this small mast did not please him because he and Berners had decided that the only way to get the gold physically off the ship was to pick it up by helicopter lowering a cargo hoist above this deck. Apart from this mast there was plenty of room for a helicopter to hover, particularly if the ship were brought round into the wind and the speed reduced. In fact the sight of it depressed him. So much in every plan did small, unforeseeable items like this raise big problems.

For the next two evenings Raikes sat in the bar before dinner and let his face become familiar, got on first name terms with the barman and passed the odd word or two with various people. He was in no hurry. It was going to be weeks before the ship was ready for sea and when she was she might do a cruise or two to the Mediterranean or the West Indies before she took her first regular passenger run direct across the North Atlantic to New York. He let it be known that he was from a London property company down here to look over prospective building purchases. It was a field in which he had operated spuriously before and he knew that if with odd bar acquaintances you were guarded about details it was no more than they expected because this was the nature of the business. You never gave away information which might help others to get in ahead of you. Meantime Berners, with some of their old stationery, sent him a steady flow of mail containing on the whole blank sheets of paper. But he knew the value of the legend printed on the envelopes—*London Wall Commercial Properties Limited*. The porters on the main desk came to know him, and the girls in the reception office gave him the bright morning and evening smile, and the restaurant waiters admitted him to their family, and the wine waiter found a first class Gevry Chambertin for him which was not marked on the wine list. He knew them all and they knew and liked him. And unobtrusively he picked their brains about the other permanent guests and marked down his man—Alfred Graham, a young Scot of about thirty from the pay office of the Upper Clyde Shipbuilders who had been sent down to work in the temporary office aboard ship, where he dealt with wage sheets and pay for the workers aboard. Alfred liked his dram and was—justly—proud of the ship his firm had built and angry at the troubles that had beset her, and even angrier at the journalists who had magnified those troubles in the press. For two or three nights Raikes fed Alfred his drams in the bar after dinner and learned that on the Saturday morning he was going to spend the weekend in London. On Friday night he fed Alfred more drams than he could take and at midnight helped him up to his room and put him, snoring before his shoes were off, to bed. When Raikes left the room he had—taken from Alfred's wallet—his pass to board the *Queen Elizabeth 2*.

He went down late the next morning and—solicitous drinking friend—checked with the porter that Alfred had gone off, pale but determined—to London for his weekend. There was no photograph on the pass, just a printed square of pasteboard from the Upper Clyde Shipbuilders authorising A. Graham to go aboard and listing his standing as Pay Clerk.

Within an hour Raikes was at the gangway. From two half hour periods of observation from the Ocean Terminal windows above, he had already seen that only about once in ten times did the gangway guard actually take the profferred pass and examine it. Just the wave of the card was enough.

On this Saturday morning the guard took the pass, looked at the front briefly and then turned it over and examined the blank back as though he expected to find written there some happy message or keen insult and then handed it back.

Raikes went aboard into the maze of alleyways and corridors, public rooms, grill room, coffee room, juke box room, libraries, theatre, stairways, promenade decks, boatdeck, first- and second-class lidos, a vast tunnelled anthill inhabited now by worker ants swarming everywhere to complete the cabins and fittings of the ship. Once aboard there was no further check on passes and he was free to wander without question. That he wandered with no pretence of working made no difference because half the workmen seemed to be doing the same. None of the lifts were working so he had to slog up and down the stairways, checking his way as he went from the guide boards on each deck landing and everywhere he went his memory recorded each lay-out, each twist and turn, angle and corner faithfully. For the most part he stayed forward of midships because he knew that this was the part of the ship which would concern him most and, in this area, he concentrated most on the fore part of the boatdeck. It was here that the blue-painted A Stairway came to an end. He walked the length of this deck along the glassed-in promenade down the port side, then back through the tiered Double Room, along the alleyway of shops, stepping over cables, dodging round stepladders where electricians worked on the light fittings, through the Juke Box Room, with a sideways look through the door of the Theatre, along to the Coffee Shop and then forward through the 736 Room to A Stairway landing. From here forward were the captain's and officers' quarters and the entrance to the wheelhouse beyond them. Forward from here was the brain of the ship. One day he was going to control that brain. A few yards from here he knew that he was going to spend an hour of his life which could lead to disaster unless he were complete and confident master of everything he said and did. And he had to admit to himself as he stood there now that far from the prospect overwhelming him, it was a challenge which for a moment or two he could feel impatient to meet. For an hour at least he was going to be master of this ship. But to be that he must know this part of her as well as he knew his way around Alverton . . . must know everything, every door and every alleyway, every exit and entrance, every detail from the notices saying *Post de Canot de Sauvetage* to the number of glass showcases that lined the starboard side of the landing, know that below him on the next deck was another landing that gave access to the Britannia Restaurant with its coloured figure-head of Britannia dominating the entrance, and forward of it the big Look-Out Room with tall windows looking out to the bows, giving a view over quarterdeck and foredeck to where one day a helicopter would hover at night in the soft glow of the deck lights . . . know all this, and know that one day, too, Belle would stand in that room and—checked half an hour ago—would pull back the canvas blinds (drawn at night to avoid glare being thrown up to confuse the watch in the wheelhouse) a little and watch the gold being lifted from the deck.

And now, Saturday, knowing from bar talk at the Polygon that the Captain and a few officers slept and kept duties aboard, he decided not to go blundering into the officers' quarters, ready with apologies and charm, and no opportunity to be missed to improve on ten seconds' acquaintance, but to keep that for the next day when it would be Sunday and there would probably be even fewer officers there and the Captain, with luck, ashore for lunch or away for the weekend. So, he turned and went back down the blue-carpeted A Stairway and applied himself to the task of selecting a cabin for Belle; a single, first-class cabin for, after the robbery, she would have to go all the way to America, anonymous, unknown, her part in the affair never to be revealed. It had to be a cabin as remote as possible from all others and well forward on the port side so that he could get easily and quickly to A Stairway and so up to the boat-deck. Already he had picked it from the cabin accommodation plans supplied to Belle at Cunard House and learned that every cabin number began with the number of the deck on which it was situated and all those on the port side ended in an even number and all those on the starboard side in an odd number. There were not many single, first-class cabins. When the time came Benson or Mandel would have to use some of his hidden influence to get them Cabin 4004.

He went down now to Four Deck, walked across the landing and swung right into the long alleyway stretching down the inside of the cabins on the port side. He went ten or twelve yards forward to the end of the cabin run. A little side alleyway to the left led first to Cabin 4002 and then to Cabin 4004 beyond it. Hidden by the short turning from the main alleyway there was no one to see him. The door of the cabin was unlocked and he went in. There was a single bed to his left running the length of the wall. On the wall running at an angle to it was the dressing table and a mirror with a blue fabric surround. Under the mirror was a console for lights, radio, and services. Beyond it in the same wall close to the porthole was a wardrobe cupboard and opposite it a partitioned section which held washbasin, toilet and shower. He shut the door and checked the room, knowing that before he came to know it personally he had to know it theoretically because there might be something about it which could in some small way shape the plan which had yet to be perfected. He came out with one important piece of information. There were no bolts on the inside of the main door or the shower room door. They could be locked but not bolted. He would have to check whether passengers carried their own cabin key, but he felt it unlikely. But what was significant was that no passenger could bolt himself in, and a Steward with his pass-key could always get into a cabin if there was ever any question of a cabin search.

Before he left he went up to One Deck and, from the baggage or cargo lift which Sarling had mentioned in his notes, saw that one could move across to the starboard side. Here there was a door to the crew's quarters which was open. He went through. Back to his right a couple of workmen were drinking tea at a long mess table. He turned left and went forward down an alleyway on the starboard side past a door that was marked Stewardesses' Mess and another marked Stewardesses' Recreation Room and then dead ahead of him was an open iron deck door that led straight out on to the foredeck. The route for the gold from the Specie Room—down on Eight Deck with the lift dead opposite it—was a straightforward one out to the foredeck.

Back in his hotel room, lying on his bed, and thinking over the plan, he knew that it could be done. Knew that it had to be done because a few rumours or hints leaked by Mandel to the police would mean the end of him, of Berners and Belle. Knew, too, that Berners was right; that once you entered the world of crime there was no escape, and no freedom from fear. There was only the misshapen form of trust that men like Sarling, Mandel and Benson dealt in . . . but although it was distorted it had its own strength and he knew that it was all he could ever have if he wanted to return to Alverton. Complete peace of mind could only come if he were prepared to abandon his Alverton dreams and disappear—and this he knew he would never do.

The next morning he went aboard again. Work was going on right through the weekend. He wandered around among the workmen, stopping to chat now and then, and finally went up on to the boatdeck landing and down a small alleyway to the left of the 736 Room entrance. He pushed open the door into

188

the Officers' Quarters and walked down a narrow passageway. An open door to his right showed him an officer's cabin, bed unmade, a low table covered with magazines and a bookshelf full of paperbacks. To his left a stairway marked Senior Officers' Quarters ran upwards. Dead ahead of him a glass door gave him a glimpse of what he knew from his study of one of the profile diagrams of the ship given out by Cunard was the Officers' Restaurant and Lounge with big windows looking out forward. An officer with two gold rings on the sleeves of his navy blue jacket came out of the lounge into the corridor and saw him.

Raikes gave him a nod and a smile and said, "My name's Graham. I've just started working aboard in the Upper Clyde pay office. I'm supposed to meet one of our engineers up here, a Mr. Farrar."

"There's no one up here of that name."

"No? He said he knew one of your officers . . . forget his name now . . . He said he'd arranged for me to have a look round . . . see the wheelhouse and all that. I was to meet Farrar outside the 736 Room at half-past ten. Been waiting half an hour so I thought I might have got it wrong and he was in here waiting for me. Here's my card."

Raikes handed the officer his identity card. The officer looked at it briefly and handed it back, saying, "You don't remember the name of the officer, do you?"

"No. I suppose Farrar wouldn't be somewhere around with him? Perhaps in the wheelhouse?"

"We could go and see."

And that was that; everything springing from the simple magic of being aboard, of having an identity card, and of acting and talking with complete confidence, shaking his head and joking over Farrar who was never on time anywhere and had probably forgotten all about his promise. The officer, with hours of Sunday time on his hands and the Captain and Staff Captain ashore, not unwelcoming company and proud of his beautiful ship, offered only too willingly, since basically no security was being broken, to show her off. So, Raikes was

189

taken on a conducted tour, into the splendid Officers' Lounge, then up the stairs to the Senior Officers' quarters. He was given a brief glimpse into the Captain's sitting-room—his eyes sweeping over all details, the mind recording them fast and accurately ... a desk facing the door, a standard lamp with an orange shade at its side, a low, round table away to the left with a silver grey cactus in a bowl on it, a red bloom in flower, settees around the walls and under the forward windows, green covered and strewn with red, yellow and orange cushions, and across on the far left a curtain exit that led up to the wheelhouse and forward of that the door into bedroom and bathroom ... the eyes observing the brain recording ... a jar of sharpened pencils and pens on the desk, telephone, a little pair of book-rests with pocket dictionaries wedged neatly between them ... the whole room photographed and himself knowing that sometime in the future he would be standing in here again, facing the Captain ... balancing himself on the brink of jeopardy but knowing that he would never go over the edge, and knowing that, while he would stand here putting the Captain under duress, the duress had first, so few days ago, been put upon him.

The officer led him up to the wheelhouse, past the Chart Room outside its port entrance, and took him over to the wide run of windows under which spread the long console range of instruments and equipment for controlling the ship ... radar, automatic whistles, bow thrusters, the compass strip and talk back systems to bow, stern, bridge wings and the turbine control room, the engine telegraphs and the table for the log books ... the officer talking, Raikes the wondering tourist, and through the windows all of a Sunday morning Southampton spread out in roof and tower silhouette before them and away to the left the other docks, grey, debris-scummed water, stiff necked cranes and gantries, and the colour-banded funnels of other liners thrusting above sheds and warehouses, and Raikes knowing that he was being lucky, that the gods were moving for him, and seeing himself, too, at some point in the future up here at night when the whole console would give off a soft glow of light. The officer spared him nothing, for he was in love with his ship and he gladly displayed the beauties of his love . . . explaining everything; the central wheel where the quartermaster stood and behind it the true motion radar and the Decca navigator, the huge panelled run at the back of the wheelhouse with its stabiliser panel, watertight doors panel, navigation lights panel, telephone panel and the panel from which would be switched on the foredeck lights when the helicopter came swinging, flying beetle-awkward in over the deck. He was even given a look into the Captain's sea cabin on the starboard side of the bridge and, so far does love and pride go, not spared a glimpse of the officers' bridge toilet and washroom on the left of the port side entrance.

He had a mug of coffee with the officer and they chatted for half an hour, during which time he learnt to his relief that the mast on the foredeck was telescopic and was lowered when the ship put to sea. It was used to carry the anchor ball and lights when the ship was moored. The problem which had worried him so much a few days before had proved no problem at all. He also learned that the door to the Officers' quarters was always kept locked when the ship was in service. He arrived back at the hotel before lunch, sat in the entrance lounge until he saw the head porter leave his desk, then went over and reached across and took Alfred Graham's room key. He went up, put the identity card on Graham's dressing table, where Graham would think that the chambermaid had laid it after finding it on the floor, and then went down to the lounge and handed the key over to the porter saying he had taken it in mistake and claimed his own.

At three o'clock he was on his way back to London.

From the moment that Raikes had come back from his interview with Benson and Mandel and told Belle what he was being forced to do, she had felt sick with nervous apprehension. But the apprehension was not on her own account. Somewhere in the months since she had known Raikes and worked with him she had come to an almost placid resignation about herself. Life, she had told herself, was never going to hand her anything on a plate. Once this thing was over Raikes would be gone for good. All right, she would get used to it, learn to live with it, but it would never alter the fact that he was the only man she truly loved or ever would love. Others would get into bed with her, take her body and give her pleasure, but there would never be anyone to take his real place in her heart.

She lit a cigarette, thinking, poor old Belle, you've got twenty thousand pounds—yes, let's face it, from the murder of your boss—and you'll have more when this thing goes through—but there isn't going to be a damn thing you can buy with it that you really want. Not a thing. One day he's going to walk right out of your life and you won't even get a card at Christmas.

She heard his key in the lock and he came in carrying his case. She sprang up, going to him, crying, "Andy".

He dropped his case, put his arms around her and kissed her and, for the first time in all their relationship, even while she let herself go, sink into the comfort of his nearness, she wondered what lay behind the kiss ... sampled it almost as though somewhere in its passion, somewhere in the feeling of his hands on her she might isolate the strangeness of his hate for her.

He held her away from him at arm's length, smiled and, brown skin crinkling round the blue eyes, said, "I've been lucky. Fix me a large drink while I telephone."

She went to the sideboard and, behind her, heard him dialling and then say, "It's Tony Applegate here. I want an appointment tomorrow. Ring me here."

She turned as he put the receiver down.

He took the glass from her and grinned. "I checked your cabin. 4004. It's small, but comfortable." He sipped his drink and then went on, "You know—if the background were different and this had come up five or ten years ago, I really think I should have thoroughly enjoyed it. Yes, I really think I would."

It was Benson again, but this time not at the Ritz. They met in a suite at the Savoy overlooking the river, and the side table held a great bowl of scarlet and yellow gladioli that had certainly, since this was the beginning of March, not had their roots in English soil. Benson in a well-cut grey silk suit, a neat little butterfly of a striped bow tie and a loose gold chain around his left wrist, looked now far more foreign than he had ever looked to Raikes. And this time because there was Mandel behind Benson and a whole world of people and powers maybe beyond Mandel, Raikes without thought, instinctively promoted himself above this man and was commanding not commanded, undeterred, even though the smile on Benson's lips was ironical, friendly still, marking that he had noticed the change.

Raikes said, "We've got the plan worked out. But not in enough detail yet to give it to you. Before we go further there are certain things I've got to know."

"Like?"

"Only myself and Miss Vickers will be aboard. I don't need a cabin but she does. I want Cabin 4004 for her or one as near to it as possbile. That's on Deck Four forward on the port side."

"In what name?"

"Hers. Belle Vickers. She'll fix all the immigration stuff and visa from the American authorities."

"We shall get the cabin."

"I want the gold taken off the ship three or four hours after she leaves Le Havre. She'll be doing about 27 to 28 knots. That'll put her somewhere north of the Channel islands. I'll let you have exact distances and timings later. But right now I want to know that you can provide a French-based helicopter. I don't care what speed it does but it's got to have a range of around two hundred and fifty miles. It's got to have a winch so that it can hover above the foredeck and drop a net or a cargo hook to bring up the bullion boxes."

"While the ship's doing 28 knots—and maybe in a strong wind?"

"The ship will be slowed down and come up into the wind."
Benson smiled. "On your instructions?"

"On the Captain's."

"I shall be interested to know how you're going to get the
Captain on your side."

"You will in time. I want to know the maximum permissible
wind in which a skilled helicopter pilot could carry out the
manoeuvre. If the wind on the night in question is too strong—
then the operation is off."

"And you'll be left aboard without a cabin. That's presuming
you intend to be taken off by the helicopter."

"Don't worry about that for the moment. I shall be covered.
I just want to know you can provide a helicopter and make
your own security arrangements for take-off from France and
then landing with the bullion."

"It shouldn't be too difficult."

"I want Berners on the helicopter. There's no role for
him aboard. Then there'll be the pilot and another man to
help Berners swing the loaded nets into the helicopter. When
the operation's over I shall go aboard. I want to know the
exact payload that the helicopter can carry with four men
in her. That will govern how much gold we can take on
board."

"If it's the usual kind of shipment, which we can check on
later, the gold will be in small wooden boxes. They're made of
wood fibre and sealed with metal strips. Anything from two to
four 'good delivery' bars to a box. A bar can weigh anything
between 350 to 450 ounces. Usually 400 ounces. That's 25
pounds. Say something like 40 bars to a half ton. Seems to me
with four average-sized men aboard let's say somewhere around
900 pounds the lot, then a helicopter could still reasonably lift
a ton of gold. Maybe more. I will find out. But 80 bars of gold
at around 14,000 dollars minimum a bar gives you . . ." Benson's
head went back, eyes closing briefly against the calculation,
and Raikes watched him, curiously not interested in values,
thinking waywardly of the 25-pound bars and remembering

walking a mile carrying a 20-pound salmon over his shoulder, sensing now in memory the exact feel and weight of it ... remembering the bite of snow flurry and wind against his face. ... "... that's something just over the half a million pound mark. Nice, no? Actually since we'll sell it miles above the official U.S. Treasury rate of 35 dollars an ounce, it will come out nearer three-quarters of a million."

"At the moment I'm more interested in other things. When we've decided on the helicopter I want some trials carried out with it. I want to know how many two- or four-bar boxes at a time can be winched up and handled easily by the two men aboard. And then I want to know the timings to lift half a ton, a ton or two tons. There's a lift aboard the ship that runs right up from opposite the Specie Room. From what I've seen of the top end of the lift it can probably bring a half a ton up easily, but with four seamen, say, working on a ton—and they'll be strong chaps who can easily carry two-bar boxes—it'll mean ten trips for each of them for a ton. I'll give you a layout of the distance they have to go and their timings can be worked out. That's why I want Berners in touch with the helicopter end early on. He'll do all the timings and checks. Can you arrange all this?"

"Naturally. But since this is a business deal, a proportion of the costs will be set off against your share."

"The other thing I want is routeings—separate ones—for Berners and myself once we land in France with this stuff. Berners will tell you where he wants to go—but I want a flight back to England three days later from Nice or somewhere like that and I'll want you to fix a Douane entry stamp in my passport for a week or so prior to my return."

"Simple. When can I tell Mr. Mandel we can expect your complete plan?"

"Let's concentrate on the helicopter first. When I know you can get it and what it's capable of doing ... well, then we can get down to details. Once the balloon goes up on that ship time is the important thing. I'd like to get off within the hour. Two hours is the absolute limit. People get used fast to living in an emergency. They begin to think, they begin to be not quite so afraid and, after that point, they might begin to do something which isn't in the book."

As Benson went to the door of the suite with him, the man said, "Tell me—are you looking forward now to doing this? It stirs something in you?"

"No. I'm doing it because I'm being forced to do it. If I were my own master and the idea had been mine originally I could enjoy it. If that's the word. But not now, Benson. Being somebody else's man gives me a pain in the guts."

Benson shrugged. "Show me someone who isn't somebody else's man. There is no such animal."

From Benson, he took the train down to Brighton and saw Berners. In Berners' elegant sitting room they spent three hours going over their plan, and they worked as they had often worked before, taking the broad plan and then projecting themselves into it, living it, and moving through it small step by small step, each one throwing up objections, possibilities of errors or chance and not moving on to the next step until they had solved or covered all objections. If no solution could be found through lack of information they considered the sources or ways and means of acquiring the information. For instance when Belle went aboard as a passenger Raikes was going to accompany her on a visitor's ticket—which she would get from the shipping authorities—to see her off. But once the robbery had taken place and Raikes had gone off in the helicopter a check would certainly be made to establish how he had come aboard. A check of listed passengers could be made and there would be no one missing. So he would be isolated as a stowaway or a visitor who had stayed aboard. If a list of visitors' passes was kept and the passes were collected as visitors went ashore then the pass issued to Raikes—even though it would be under a false name—would be missed. This—if visitors' passes were linked to the passengers who had requested them—would lead back to Belle and had to be avoided. Berners said that he would find out how the Cunard authorities dealt with the issue of passes and whether they were collected as visitors went off. Each step brought some small problem like this and to Berners it was bread and meat.

He said, "The simplest way is the quickest more often than not. Tomorrow I'll ring the Cunard offices in London and just ask them what their system is. Some girl on the desk will just tell me and forget it within the hour. People have innocent minds. They give information as a cow gives milk."

Raikes knew that this was true. Information was easy to come by. The real problem was taking it and fitting it into a plan which would work. In the past this had been something he enjoyed, and enjoyed more the movement from a plan on paper to the actual execution. Now, he felt suddenly irritated again at the thought that this was not something he was doing of his own choice.

With the impulse of the deep resentment in him, he said, "I wish to God there was some way of avoiding all this. Some way we could get out of it altogether."

Berners looked at him in surprise. "But why do you want to? We can do this between us. Think of the money we shall have. Here, look—" He picked up a copy of that day's *Times* and handed it to Raikes. On the Court page was a photograph of a *famille-rose* dinner service of ninety-six pieces which, the day before at Christie's, had been sold for 21,500 guineas. "Wouldn't you like to be able to afford something like that? I went up to the auction. It's a beautiful service . . . magnificent. Painted in underglaze blue and *famille-rose* enamels and decorated with flowers, birds, squirrels and vines. That's what real money can buy you. Things most other people can never hope to own. That's the kind of thing I want—so I'm prepared to take a risk for it."

"Be forced to take a risk for it, you mean."

"It's unimportant—so long as it means money."

A week later Benson called on him at the flat. He had with him details of the helicopter.

197

He said, "We've decided that the best machine for this job is a Bell 205A. It's an American helicopter, but it's manufactured under patent in Italy and we can get one. Here's a list of the statistics about the machine."

He handed Raikes a typewritten list.

It read:

BELL 205A DATA AND PERFORMANCE

Helicopter

Equipment weight	lb.	5000
Crew (one)	lb.	170
Cargo	lb.	2780
Fuel	lb.	1460
Takeoff		
Gross weight	lb.	9410
Range	miles	320
Cruising speed	m.p.h.	125
Overall length	feet	57
Main rotor, length	feet	48

After Raikes had read it, Benson said, "Those figures only allow for a crew of one. But when she comes there'll be three on board. Berners, the pilot and another man to help him off-load the gold. And when she goes out you'll be aboard. That's three extra people so their weight—call it 510 pounds—must come off the cargo load which will reduce it to 2270 pounds. That's the equivalent of well over a ton of gold. But if you don't want a range of 320 miles then we could make some saving on the fuel weight which would mean we could get more cargo aboard. In any case, by the time they pick you up some of the fuel will be used up."

"We'll need 320 miles. Can you get a machine like this without trouble?"

Benson smiled. "For this job we can get anything—and

when we've finished with it it won't be traced."

"What about the hoist?"

"I've gone into that. We can have an external hoist kit. That's a boom and winch on the top right-hand side of the cabin roof. It can be worked by the pilot or a hoist operator. It sticks out from the top of the cabin and when the load's up it swings it inboard. The cable is 200 feet long and will lift 600 pounds at a rate of 100 feet a minute. If necessary—which it had better not be—there's an emergency cable cutter which the pilot or hoist man can operate."

"You've done your homework, haven't you?"

"I wouldn't come to you if I hadn't."

"Six hundred pounds. In four lifts we could have well over a ton aboard. You're going to have to find a place to hide this machine and also do some dummy lifts so that Berners can work out lifting times."

"We'll do that. But before we do Mr. Mandel is going to have to have the whole plan laid out from your end. How long do you think that will be?"

"Another week or so. I'll let you know."

Benson stood up. "You want to keep those details?"

Raikes shook his head. "No. I've got them in my head." He flicked on his lighter and put the flame to the edge of the sheet and walked with it to the fireplace, dropping it and watching it burn on the tiles in front of the electric fire. When it was ash, he turned and said, "What about the pilot and this extra man?"

"They'll be safe. Men who've worked for us for a long time. They won't know your name or Berners'. But even if they did you'd still be safe. In our world nobody breaks the code and gets away with it. So, nobody breaks the code. There ought to be something like it in ordinary life."

Benson gone, Belle still out of the flat, he fixed himself a drink and sat by the window and picked up the daily paper which he hadn't opened that morning. Almost the first thing he saw was the headline:

MAY 2 FOR MAIDEN VOYAGE OF QE2.

The liner *Queen Elizabeth 2* will make her maiden voyage from Southampton to New York on May 2, a few days after trials of her modified turbines are completed in the second half of April, Sir Basil Smallpeice, chairman of Cunard, announced in New York yesterday.

Cunard hope that she will make 29 Atlantic crossings from May to November, followed by four Caribbean cruises from New York. . . .

Cunard would put the QE2 through a final proving voyage to the Cape Verde Islands in early April before taking final delivery. When she goes to sea again there will be no cause for anxiety. . . .

He sipped his drink. They didn't know it but there would be. Berners would come flying in on the Bell 205A.

She will more than fulfil the promises made to her prospective passengers as to her performance. She will be the most superb example of the shipbuilders' craft the world has yet seen.

Well, as long as she fulfilled the promise he was making to himself, a prospective passenger, though without a ticket, he would be content. He wanted the whole thing over and finished. They were now into March. Two months to go. It was going to be a long wait. Normally a patient man, he knew that they were going to be two long, hard months for him.

The door opened and Belle came in, her arms full of parcels. She dumped them in an armchair and said, "Andy, I suddenly realised that I was a rich woman. Twenty thousand pounds from Sarling. It hadn't sunk home. Then, while I was out, it did, so I went on a shopping spree. And do you know something odd—at the perfume counter in Harrods I suddenly had that old feeling that I wanted to lift something. I had my hand on a bottle of bath essence and . . . well, I damned near slipped it into my bag. Isn't that strange after all these years?"

He stood up, suddenly angry.

"It's not only strange but it's bloody dangerous. You do something like that and get caught and it might lead anywhere.'

"But I didn't do it."

"Don't even think about doing it. Do you hear?" He gripped her arm fiercely.

"Oh, Andy, don't be so cross. Of course I wouldn't do it. I promise you." She kissed him, then turned to the sideboard. "God, I need a drink. I'm exhausted."

He watched her back, watched her movements, and thought —two months. Two months to go before he could walk out and be rid of her, rid of the whole set-up.

He went across to her, running his hand over her bottom and kissing the back of her neck. For two months more the part had to be played.

He said, "Sorry. I didn't mean to let fly. But you know how important all this is." He turned her round and kissed her and felt at once her response to his kindness and affection, and he was thinking to himself, Here I am kissing her, keeping her sweet, and I could just as easily be killing her.

CHAPTER TWELVE

IT WAS THE same suite at the Savoy. The flowers on the side table were carnations, great crimson blooms, their pompom heads held high on wired stems. Mandel sat on a straight-backed chair, hands crossed in his lap, shoulders hunched, like a brooding falcon, his eyes on Raikes who stood near the window. Benson had dropped back into an armchair and was fiddling with one of the gold rings on his finger. Berners in dove-grey trousers, suede shoes, brown jacket sat demurely at a table. Behind Raikes, through the window, there was sunshine on the river.

He was saying, "You'll have questions, but for the moment it will be better if you just make a note of them and ask them afterwards. What I want to do first is to run through the whole operation so that you get the complete picture. Is that all right?"

Mandel nodded. "You tell the story. We'll listen."

"Very well. So far as we know at the moment, the QE2 makes her first westward Atlantic run on May 2nd. She arrives in New York on May 7th. She will be carrying gold bullion in her Specie Room." He looked across at Mandel. "I understand that these days most bullion shipments out of London are by air."

Mandel said, "A certain amount always goes by sea. And this time—since it's a maiden voyage—most City bullion merchants will be shipping bullion as a prestige affair."

"How much do you think?"

"She will have more than you can lift." Mandel smiled briefly. "Some of it will be ours—under a suitable cover—so we shall make a double profit after collecting the insurance money."

"Of which we shall take seventy-five per cent?"

"Yes."

As the man answered Raikes saw Berners' shoulders stir gently.

"All right. At the moment the intention is to lift at least a ton of bullion. The helicopter will hoist six hundred pounds at a time, that's twenty-four good delivery bars. My rough calculation to do that comfortably from Specie Room to helicopter is an hour and a half. Berners can make a more accurate timing later with the helicopter pilot on dummy lifts. I suggest we content ourselves with four lifts. In fact, I insist. I shall have the Captain under duress and various of his officers and crew will be involved. If the period runs too long somebody might be tempted to do something stupid. Agreed?"

Mandel said, "We shall be happy with four lifts."

"Right. The ship leaves Southampton around mid-day. She goes across to Le Havre. The latest time for embarkation there is at eight-thirty on the same day. She leaves around nine o'clock at night. Once she's in the Channel she will begin to work up speed. Giving her an average speed of 25 miles an hour over the four-hour period from nine until one o'clock at night she'll be a hundred miles westwards. There's a chart on the table there. I've marked her position for speeds of twenty, twenty-five and thirty miles an hour. Berners and the helicopter pilot shouldn't have any difficulty in picking her up. Keeping to the broad outline for the moment, I shall be on one of the open afterdecks of the ship from twelve o'clock onwards. Berners will locate the ship from the air and at any time from twelve on he will fire a Very signal from the helicopter. When I see this I shall go into action. Shortly after I have the Captain under duress a Very light signal will be fired from the ship to show Berners that everything is going to plan. Then, the moment the first load of bullion is up on the foredeck another signal—two Very lights—will be fired from the ship for the helicopter to come in and begin off-loading."

203

"Who fires these signals from the ship?" asked Benson.

"I said I'd answer questions afterwards. However, one of the ship's company will. Though I shall provide the pistol and cartridges. The moment the last of the bullion is aboard the helicopter I shall be taken up off the foredeck and the helicopter will return to its base. So far as the security is concerned in France, I'm leaving that to Berners who will be working with your people. You're going to have no trouble coming out to the ship. But from the moment we leave she will be in radio communication with the shore alerting the French authorities. The helicopter does a hundred and twenty-five miles an hour unloaded. I suggest you work within a hard limit of two hours at the most to get clear from the French base." He looked across at Mandel. "If Berners isn't completely satisfied with the arrangements—then the operation is off."

Mandel said, "He will be satisfied. Go on with the details of the operation on board the ship."

"A passage has already been booked for Miss Vickers, in her own name, in Cabin 4004. I shall go aboard with her at Southampton on a visitor's pass and stay aboard when the ship sails. No list is kept of visitors' passes issued and the passes are not collected by anyone as visitors go ashore so there is no way of tracing one who may have stayed aboard, and in any case the pass will be made out in a false name to me. I shall stay in Miss Vickers' cabin until after we leave Le Havre. But at Le Havre I shall want a weather check. It's almost impossible for a helicopter to lift a load from the deck in a wind of fifty miles an hour, and difficult enough at forty miles an hour. On the Beaufort scale a wind of Force 8 to 9 is listed as a gale. That's between 38 to 55 miles an hour. If the scale reading is more than 6 to 7—that's listed as a strong wind—then the operation is off. All I do then is declare myself to the ship's authorities, say I got left aboard at Southampton and go ashore and Miss Vickers goes on to New York—"

"And we try again another time," said Mandel.

"Do we?"

"Yes. At least once more. I'm not being unreasonable. But there must be at least one more try. If that fails—well, we'll be philosophical and forget all about it and all about one another. However, go on with your plan, assuming the weather is good."

"According to my information on the first night out passengers tend to go to bed reasonably early, and the Captain doesn't entertain. The Captain won't be in the wheelhouse during the midnight to four o'clock watch. He'll be going to bed somewhere around midnight. I shall go to his cabin as soon as I get the Very light signal from the helicopter. We shall have a talk and he will do exactly as I want him to do. We'll go up to the wheelhouse and he'll order the ship to be brought up into the wind and slacken speed. One of his officers will fire the Very light signal from the wheelhouse wing to show Berners everything is working to plan. Then the bullion will be ordered up by the Captain and the double Very light signal will be fired when it's ready for off-loading. We shall take off the four loads and then I shall go off myself. And that's it."

"That's it in very broad detail." Mandel stood up and gave himself a little shake, reminding Raikes again of a falcon shivering down its plumage. "Explain how you are going to put the Captain under duress."

Raikes went to the sideboard where drinks stood on a silver tray and began to help himself to a brandy and soda. With his back to them, he said, "Sarling made me steal some gas canisters from an Army depot. They're riot control supplies. I won't go into the chemical details but, in an open space, they cause instant paralysis and unconsciousness. In a confined space they are lethal. I've tested them. When I go aboard I shall be wearing an overcoat and I shall have six of them with me. When I go to see the Captain, Miss Vickers—on one of the afterdecks—will have them in a large handbag. I shall explain to the captain that I have an accomplice aboard with these canisters. If he doesn't do what I order then Miss Vickers will walk through the public rooms on the boatdeck—that includes the big Double

205

Room at the stern, the Juke Box, the Coffee Shop and the 736 Night Club, all of which will have people in them—and leave a canister in each one. The canisters have a ten to fifteen second fuse. In ten seconds a person can walk sixteen to eighteen paces so Miss Vickers will be well clear of the explosion area each time—but a lot of people will be caught—"

"And die. Pretty horrible," said Benson. "But necessary, I can see."

"Nobody's going to die. Apart from the ship itself, the first duty of the Captain is the safety of the passengers. He won't take any risks."

"But—if he refuses to do what you say—will Miss Vickers fire the canisters?" asked Mandel.

"If a Very signal is not fired from the ship within half an hour of my leaving her and going to the Captain—yes, she will. I shall have no way of recalling her."

"She's prepared to do it?" Benson moved to the sideboard and poured himself a glass of water. Berners sat at the table still, head down examining the palms of his hands.

"Yes. But she won't have to do it. This is the crux of the whole plan. If there was any doubt in my mind that the Captain would refuse I wouldn't be going into all this. It's something he's got to do. You've put me under duress and I'm doing this. I don't want to do it, but I'm doing it—and you knew I would. He'll be in the same position. He's got to do it. No man in his position is going to risk the lives of twenty or fifty passengers for the sake of saving part of a cargo of bullion. Human lives against gold? He'd be condemned for life."

Mandel ran a finger down the long beak of his nose and said, "There's no doubt in my mind that you are right. It's not even a gamble. However, there are one or two other points. Will Miss Vickers be able to see the Very light signal from the wheelhouse?"

"Yes. She'll be on one of the afterdecks in the open. When she sees the signal she'll drop the canisters over the side, go up to the boatdeck and walk right forward to the big Look-

Out Room. It's a public room and she'll be able to watch the whole lifting operation from there."

"How are you going to get into the Captain's quarters?"

"Walk in. There's an entrance to the Officers' quarters on the boatdeck. There's no guard. At that time of night there shouldn't be anyone much about. If there is and I'm stopped then I shall have to knock the man out."

"Are you going to be armed?" asked Benson.

"Yes. I shall have an automatic."

"Six canisters, a Very pistol and cartridges, and an automatic—a lot to carry aboard."

"In an overcoat with big pockets and folded over my arm? There's no problem there."

Mandel said, "Have you considered something going wrong after the Captain's agreed to bring up the bullion? Somebody out of his control might make a stupid bid to stop the bullion lift. Say something like that happens? Miss Vickers will have thrown away the cannisters. She'll be all right, untraceable, unknown, indeed. But you could be left aboard, a fugitive, the whole plan gone wrong around your ears."

"If I hadn't considered it I'd be a fool," said Raikes sharply. "Yes, indeed, I might be left holding the baby, and there's not much I can do about it. When I go aboard I shall have my own passport with me, and I shall have a United States entry visa. My only chance will be to run for it, hide from time to time in Miss Vickers' cabin and hope to get ashore in New York. After all, my papers will be in order. If you think it's a possibility and you're worried about it . . . well, all you have to do is to be considerate enough to call the whole thing off. I'd be delighted. Is your concern for me enough to make you do that?"

Mandel shrugged his shoulders. "No. Anyway I was only considering a very remote possibility."

"Were you?"

"What else?"

"If things went wrong and I were caught, perhaps you were wondering if I would do a lot of talking to make things easier

207

for myself. Give names . . . involve you and Benson here."

Unmoved, Mandel said, "I think you would find it impossible to involve Benson or myself. To involve a man you've got to give him a correct name and an address. But you would be involving Berners and Miss Vickers. Anyway, the question is an idle one. I don't think you would try and save your skin that way. If the thing goes wrong and you're caught, you've got nothing left except an automatic in your pocket. I know what you would do with it. Yes?"

"Maybe."

Raikes drained his drink and put the glass down. In his own mind there was no question of "maybe". In going over the plan in the last weeks he had often come to this point. Any plan had to envisage the chance of failure. If it should happen it had long been clear to him that nothing remained, nothing that he valued. Months ago when he had retired with Berners the position had been just the same. If a policeman had walked into his house he would have shot himself. If things went wrong on the ship and there was no hope for him, then he would do the same.

Berners stood up and for the first time spoke.

"There's no question of failure. In certain circumstances people are predictable. The Captain will be forced to co-operate. That is the key point. Once that happens the whole thing will go smoothly, because every move will be backed by the Captain's authority. So don't let's talk about it any more." He looked at Benson. "When do you want me in France to do these helicopter timings?"

Benson said, "It'll be a couple of weeks before we're ready for that. You don't just walk into a showroom and buy a Bell 205A like that. Not for this kind of job. And you don't just rent a furnished country house in Brittany by motoring round the agents. We've got plenty of time. We're not out of March yet . . ."

As they talked Raikes turned and looked out of the window at the river and the embankment traffic. Some black-headed gulls were scavenging in the mud banks, and pigeons were courting in the crevices of Waterloo Bridge above the brown water. He had a sudden picture of the Taw, gin-clear, and the white mouth of a trout showing as it levelled off to take a rising nymph. . . .

Mandel moved up to his side.

He said quietly, "It's a good plan. I'm sure it will work. The difficult part, of course, is yours. I've every confidence in you. Believe me, I'm sorry that we are working under these circumstances."

"You're forcing me to do something I don't want to do, Mandel. So don't give me any comforting talk. Because I've got to work for you, don't expect me to like you. I'm going to do it. Just be content with that."

Two days after the meeting with Benson and Mandel, Raikes went down to Devon. There was nothing further for him to do in London. His passport was in order and he'd got his entry visa from the United States Embassy. Belle didn't want him to go but he said that he had to fetch up the canisters and there were things awaiting his attentions at Alverton Manor. Apart from the fact that he wanted to get away from Belle for a while, he would have gone anyway. The salmon fishing had opened on the first of the month and the sea trout and trout season on the fifteenth.

He spent the first three days on the river and, for hours at a time, all memory of Mandel and the *Queen Elizabeth 2* went from his mind. Out of courtesy he rang Mary's home but was told that she was still away. The evenings he spent at home mostly by himself. He had plenty of invitations to go out but refused them. Most people by now knew of his break with Mary and he guessed that most dinner party engagements would have been planned with some suitable partner for him. He had no interest in women, and he knew that he would have none until this operation was over. At the moment he acknowledged frankly, even with a fading resentment, that he was in a trap, being trained to go through certain antics and until he had satisfied his trainer he would not be let out. And when he was let out it would be to an incomplete freedom ... pleasant, giving him everything he had ever wanted except the iron security which he had once thought he had arranged for himself. Well, he could live with it. But there were times when he could not stop himself—useless though he knew it to be—from brooding about Mandel and Benson, wondering if there were some way he could escape from them and from this project. It was then that he felt most trapped, then that he drank too much by himself, and sometimes, full of frustration, left the house in the dark and walked for miles. With him often went persistent fantasies of ways he could kill Benson and Mandel and escape, but always underneath ran a current of common sense forcing him to acknowledge that there was no escape. Sarling had been a fool, an overconfident fool and had invited death. But Benson and Mandel were well protected, and he had to accept the logic of their dictate. Years ago he had committed himself to a way of life that offered only one chance in a million of a future free of fear. He had thought that chance had come up for him. Now, he knew better.

Over the days, his thinking about Mandel and Benson faded. He found himself, almost with pleasure, lying in bed at night thinking about the ship, thinking about the moment that would surely come when he would stand on the afterdeck, above the tiled swimming pool and see out in the darkness the Very signal from the helicopter, see himself walking forward along the glassed-in run of the boatdeck to the Officers' quarters. He opened a door and the Captain's lounge was in his memory, clear and detailed, and he wondered how he would find him ... coming shirt-sleeved from his sleeping quarters, sitting at his desk, or sprawled back in an armchair with a nightcap in his hand ... ? He saw and heard himself talking to the man ... and although it was weeks ahead he could feel a nervous excitement rise in him, now, as he thought of it, which he knew would not be with him at the actual moment. From the moment of the first Very signal all emotion would be clamped down. . . .

But in those dark hours, watching the moonlight creep across the wall, hearing the steady tick of the bedside clock, the biggest irony always came to him. What he had done with Berners in the past he had enjoyed doing. He had been the master, had been delighted when a bait was greedily taken, and had known the full satisfaction of increasing his wealth and bringing Alverton Manor nearer. Now, he was the odd man out. He had known no true joy in the planning, was far from being his own master, would take no satisfaction from success and be indifferent to the additional money it would bring him. With him, too—arising perhaps from his ancestry—was a permanent disgust that they should be doing this to a beautiful ship on her maiden voyage . . . the whole conception was sacrilegious, an affront to tradition, a dirty insult to the Captain and his ship. But none of the others showed any sign of feeling this. Benson and Mandel thought only of the gold and their undercover trading profits; Berners—why had he never completely understood the man before?—was frankly greedy, had never wanted to retire, would always want more than he had to satisfy his lust for beautiful possessions . . . Yes, Berners had long forgotten that they were being forced to do it. Berners liked working under orders, being someone else's man so long as it made big money for him. And even Belle welcomed it . . . welcomed it in her stupid way because it kept him longer with her. Christ, what a crew . . . And then, in the dark bedroom he laughed out loud at himself. Who the hell was he to condemn them? What was he, what was his particular virtue, marking him out from them? Simply that he liked to be his own master. But after that there was nothing to be said for him.

At the end of the month he had a telephone call from Belle saying that Berners was back from France and wanted to see him. He went up to London, taking seven of the gas canisters with him. He got in just before lunch and Belle was waiting for him. She came into his arms as though he had been away for a year. Easily, as though the break from her had freshened him, given him a recharge of facility to play his part, he held her, kissed her and made a fuss of her and felt the happiness overflow from her, but as he held her and caressed her, he felt his own body stir, and although it had not been his intention, he took her into the bedroom and made love to her. Anything less, he told himself afterwards, would have disappointed her, but he knew it was not the full truth. In the moment of holding her and kissing her he had suddenly found himself wanting her . . . not her as Belle, but as a woman.

She made him a drink while he unpacked his suitcase, turning and watching him as he opened the safe and locked away six of the seven canisters. When he left one canister on the table, she said, "What's that one for, Andy?"

"You can drive me down to Brighton. On the way down we'll find a wood somewhere and I'll show you how to work it."

Belle put her drink down slowly. "You really mean that . . . that I may have to?"

"It could happen."

"But that would be killing people."

"So what . . . we've done it before. You haven't forgotten Sarling have you?"

"No, but . . . well, that was different."

"There's nothing different about death. It's death."

He came over to her smiling and picked up his drink. "Look, get this straight in your head. If I say you won't have to use it, I mean it. You won't have to, because this plan will work. But it's no good going into an operation like this not meaning what you say, not believing in your threats. It's a matter of a frame of mind. When I talk to the Captain he's going to know that I mean every word I say—because *I am going to mean it*, and it'll be plain to him. In the same way, you're going to be on that boat knowing that if things go wrong you're going to do everything you've been briefed to do. That's the only way we shall be successful. Unless you believe you're going to do it, know you will do it . . . then we could be in trouble. If you want to survive you've got to be ready to kill."

"But you told me I would never have to do it."

"Of course I did," he said patiently. "But this is something different. It's a question of attitude. When I go in to the Captain *I've* got to know you will do it, because knowing that makes everything I say to him the truth, and in those few minutes in his quarters anything except the truth will stick out like a sore thumb. Can't you get that?"

"Well, I suppose so, yes."

"Then you've got to know how to work the thing, haven't you?"

"Well, yes . . . yes, I suppose so."

"Then we'll take this one with us this afternoon and you can use it."

He turned away from her, drink in hand. A few minutes before he had been making love to her, taking her body willingly. Now, he was holding down his irritation with her . . . *Well, yes . . . yes, I suppose so.* This weak stumble as she came up against reality. She lived in a fairy-tale world, even a macabre, grim fantasy world, where she did outrageous things . . . shop-lifted, forged cheques, helped to kill Sarling, was appalled at the moment of action and then, within hours or days, assimilated or forgot what she had done, but only to be appalled and shocked again when she came up against the truth of her own capabilities. If something went wrong she would set off the canisters. She would do it dumbly, obediently, because he had told her to do it. Because now she was in love with him and she would do anything that 'Andy' told her, believe anything that he told her. Yet, if she had to do it and people died, she would begin to forget about it the moment she stepped off the ship at New York.

He turned back to her, smiling. "You've got nothing to worry about. Whatever happens nobody can touch you or trace any connection between us. You either throw the canisters over the side, or quietly place them in the places I've told you and then go back to your cabin and forget me. Nobody can touch you."

He didn't entirely believe it, for if things should go wrong then an enquiry would start that might eventually lead back to her, but if it did he would be beyond caring anything about her . . . beyond any caring.

She drove him down to Brighton that afternoon. They made a slight detour taking the Uckfield—Lewes road and, just before Uckfield, they stopped where the road ran across Ashdown Forest and walked a couple of hundred yards across a heath. He showed her how to work the canister and she pitched it into a clump of bracken where it exploded with a soft *plop*.

In Brighton she dropped him near Berners' house and drove off to park on the sea front and wait for his return.

Berners was waiting for him with a full report on the loading trials and the details of the French end. The trials had shown that by using four loading nets, each loaded net being swung inboard and unhooked and a fresh net dropped free to the deck for the next hoist, that the gold, from a waiting position on the foredeck, could be taken aboard the helicopter comfortably within forty minutes. This also included the time for Raikes to be lifted aboard. To this figure had to be added thirty minutes from the time Raikes went into the Captain's quarters until he and the Captain were in the wheelhouse and the order was given for the ship to slacken speed and come up into the wind. To this had to be added another thirty minutes at least for the bullion to be brought on deck. A total of an hour and forty minutes.

Berners said, "There's no question of our not being able to clear it from the deck in forty minutes. That gives you an hour's operating time aboard. What do you think?"

"It's generous, but not too generous. Bringing the stuff up from the Specie Room on the lift will be a quick job. It's carrying it across to the starboard side, through the crew's quarters and out to the foredeck that's uncertain. Call it at a maximum something like eighty single boxes between, say, four men at a minimum. That's twenty boxes each weighing twenty-five pounds. They're not bulky. Each man could carry two boxes—fifty pounds—that's ten trips a man. With another man on the foredeck to start loading the net the moment the bullion begins to arrive, the carrying time from the lift can be running concurrently with your lifting time. Yes, I'll accept an hour and forty minutes. It could work out less. I hope it does. What about the French end?"

"The moment we land that's Benson's headache. You and I go off separately and have nothing more to do with it. They've found a place on the Brest peninsula, west of a town called Loudeac. It's called Château Miriat."

"How far will that be from the ship's position between midnight and one?"

"From your timing from Le Havre she should be about ten or fifteen miles just north-west of Alderney in the Channel Islands. That gives us a distance of around two hundred and fifty miles out and back. That's an hour's flying time each way, and then the hovering time over the ship so we'll have to carry a full fuel load. That still gives us a safe margin. I'm going back this weekend and we're going to carry out a dummy night run to check everything. They've found a good set-up over there and Benson is very efficient." Berners made no effort to conceal the admiration he felt. "I must say, when you operate with the money behind you that these people have, the whole thing becomes too easy."

Raikes said, "You'll be telling me next that you'll be prepared to go in on other jobs with them."

Berners palmed his bald patch. "Well . . . if I ran short of funds I might. Let's face it, they're making no trouble for us and they're being generous. They didn't have to give us seventy-five per cent. We'd have settled for thirty in the circumstances."

"I'd have settled for cutting both their throats if it would have done any good."

"Well, we didn't have that choice, so why not make the most of this and be happy about it?"

"What about the pilot and the other man who is coming with you?"

"I've only met the pilot so far. The other man's coming in just before the actual day." Berners stood up and moved to the window. The afternoon was fast going and the sea was a gun-metal grey under the low clouds. With his back to Raikes, he said, "I never offered and you never asked me, but you know I would have done the ship part willingly. You don't think I couldn't have done?"

"I know you could. But I've always been the front man. Why do you bring that up?"

Berners turned, "Well, between ourselves in this room, we can be franker than with anyone else. It's the front place. It's the dangerous place. And the best plan in the world can go wrong. Oh, I know we long ago agreed not to have this kind of talk. But for the moment let's accept the possibility. What would you do?"

"If it went wrong?"

"Yes."

"If I got stranded on the ship and couldn't see a safe way out without involving you or Miss Vickers . . . couldn't see any future for myself . . . Well, you know what I would do. What I've always said. Finish myself."

"We could get away with the gold, but you could be finished . . . and that's what I want to ask you. I know nothing about your private life, but there would be your share . . . maybe there's someone in particular you would like it to go to. If there is, I would see to it."

"Thanks—but there isn't anyone."

"Well, it was just a thought. Not a nice one in origin, but there. . . ."

Raikes smiled, a sudden warmth in him for this man. Greedy he might be, but for God's sake what did that matter? They had worked together loyally for years, and those years had put them close, bound them into a relationship stronger in many ways than friendship. He said, "You just come flying in on that helicopter at the right moment and fire your little Very light. The stakes are higher than selling off a phoney business but beyond that there's no difference. We're just going to manipulate people as we did in the past. You and I—with a little outside help. Nobody can teach us anything about people."

He left Berners and went to find Belle. They drove back to London having dinner on the way. They slept together that night and he stayed in London for another three days before going back to Devon. The day after he went back Belle learned that she was eight weeks pregnant.

She sat in the kitchen. On the table before her was an untouched mug of coffee. A dirty dun-coloured skin had formed on top of it. She dropped her cigarette end on it and the skin slowly collapsed under the weight disappearing like a closing parachute.

Good old Belle, she thought. Always something cropping up and, as usual, not something that made her want to dance with pleasure. Her first hope had been that because of all this Cunard business coming up she had been upset and put off her course. But after a few tests the doctor had been certain.

How could it have happened? Always she wore a diaphragm and, when she had time or warning, she used a vaginal jelly . . . Yet here it was. She was going to have a child. His child. No wonder, considering the way he came into her sometimes and worked at her. It was enough to knock anyone's cap off. But what the hell did she do? Did she tell him? After all, he might want it, might even . . . No, he would never marry her because of it. They didn't have that kind of code. He had some kind of love for her. She was sure of that. But not her kind of love for him. She had money now and he would leave her to carry the baby if she wanted to go ahead with it. But did she want it? She lit another cigarette and tried to see herself as a mother— unmarried—fussing around with a child . . . well, it would be a new role. And why not? Once you got over the first stages of thinking about it, of knowing that it was there inside you, then you could go on to think of the good things. A child. His child. Something of him, anyway, that she would always have when she had lost him. And she was going to lose him. No question of that. He was in this with her because he had no choice. But once this ship business was over he would be away. Lots of girls she supposed lost a lover and were left with his child as a consolation prize. Did she really want that? Something that would always remind her of him? When he went perhaps it would be better to have nothing. Get your head down, Belle, and begin to forget him. Make an empty space in your head and your heart where he had been and then fill it up with any old junk that came along.

She got up and walked through into the lounge. There was a copy of *The Field* lying on a table where he had left it. That was his life. It could never be hers. That's where he was now. Down in his bloody Devon—and not a thought in his head for her. Hunting and shooting and fishing. The country frightened her. If she walked across a field and a cow turned a head towards her she thought it was a bull. Sometimes of an evening here, when he had had a few drinks, he would sit and talk to her generally about the country, about his river . . . but all the time she knew that he wasn't really talking to her. He was talking to himself, reminding himself of what he really loved. And what he really loved didn't include her. He took her body up here, enjoyed it, but he did it—she smiled to herself ruefully—like a mountaineer because it was there and he just had to get on top of it. And now she was pregnant. And only a month away was the time when she would go aboard the QE2. Miss Belle Vickers—unmarried mother to be (unless she got rid of it)— bound for New York, and sometime after midnight on the first night out she'd stand on one of the afterdecks with a big hand-bag full of those damned canister things . . . and, if the job didn't go smoothly, she'd walk forward dropping them here and there. She'd do it if it came to it because where he was concer-ned she had no will of her own . . . Never had had. Always been

218

told what she must do and doing it ever since she had first put her hand out for that two-bob tin of talcum powder or whatever it had been . . . If she had any sense she knew what she should do right now. Pack up, while he was away, get right out of here, hide somewhere, find herself a cottage or a flat up North, forget this nightmare about the ship, and sit back and either have the brat or get rid of it. That's what she should do. She had the money and the time. But she knew she would never do it. When the time came she would be walking aboard that ship, and she would be hoping, against a sure knowledge that it could never happen, that one day he would take her in his arms, holding her and not her body, and tell her that he'd been a blind, stupid fool and that she was the only one in the world for him. Bliss. Just like it happened in the bloody films. True love, after a shaky start and a bundle of Technicolor misunderstandings, shining through and filling the screen with a big close-up. Well, why not? For Christ's sake, surely it did happen just now and again—and somebody had to come up with the winning number? Why not her? She could believe it one moment, reject it the next. But she could never reject it entirely. Hope springs eternal, Belle. And now here she was with his child under her belt, and the telephone not six feet from her and all she had to do was to put out her hand and be talking to him, telling him what had happened . . . How did you know about other people? Maybe it would make all the difference in the world. He could be delighted and come rushing back to her with his arms full of flowers and his head full of happy plans . . . Couldn't she see it, just. Not on your bloody life.

She went to the sideboard, reached for the brandy and then changed her mind and poured a large glass of gin. Mother's ruin. But the moment she held it towards her mouth she put it back. It would just make her tight and give her a hangover. That's the way it would be with her.

She flopped back into an armchair, nursing a gentle misery and then within minutes it was gone. That was the damned trouble with her. Although there was more black than white, she couldn't look too long on the black side. Maybe she had got the whole thing twisted up and didn't really understand him. Perhaps until this ship thing was out of the way he was deliberately not showing her what he felt for her—except when they were in bed, and wasn't that barometer enough? In the height of passion he said things to her, nice things, crude things, but always things she welcomed. Maybe when all this was over. . . . She drifted away in a daydream. He had another house down there that he was going to move into. Why shouldn't she go with him, with their child? There was nothing wrong with her. She could learn to like the country. She dressed well, and, for Christ's sake, she didn't speak and act like a tart. She could mix. She could be whatever he might want her to be. Church on Sundays, a good mother, a good hostess. She could learn to play bridge . . . ride a horse (Oh, God, perhaps not that) . . . be a good wife. And anyway, there was this. If he married someone else then it would be a woman who would never know anything about this ship business. But who knew whether some time in the future things might not break badly, trouble come rushing up to the doorstep? It wouldn't be fair to do that to another woman. Have her discover that her husband wasn't all he looked to be . . . break her heart. But, she, Belle, wouldn't mind. She would be with him, stand by him. No shock to her. It was something they would share together for the rest of their lives and be ready to fight if bad luck brought the police. Wasn't that something he must eventually see, even if he hadn't seen it now? He had to, surely? Surely from the moment she had walked into his house with Sarling's note Fate had meant them for one another, sealed the contract that meant they always had to be together for better or for worse? That, for sure, would be something he would come to understand? Of course it was.

Cheerfully, she got up and poured herself a glass of brandy. You're just too gloomy, Belle. Always looking on the dark side.

She raised her glass, sipped and silently toasted herself. Here's to a long life and a happy one with the right man. But as she turned away from the sideboard, as though she had moved from a warm room into a cold one, draught billowing through an open window, she felt the glow of optimism begin to fade.

There was almost a month to go. He had no reason to return to London until a week before the ship sailed, unless something came up from Benson or Berners and then Belle would telephone him.

The country closed around him and no effort was needed to forget what lay ahead. The thing was fixed, planned, awaited only execution. There was no need to go over and over it in his mind.

He dropped back into the way of life which long ago he had known and which, soon, would become permanent with him. He fished the Taw, the Torridge and the Tamar. On the Torridge one cold and dry day, with the water in perfect condition, he took three salmon, the largest sixteen pounds, all of them with sea-lice still on them. Spring was rushing in. The blue-tit belled in the bank growths. Kingfishers, bright-coloured meteors against the young green bud-burst, flashed up the waters and the courting dippers bobbed and curtsied in haste to one another on the river boulders. Standing still in a Tamar pool one evening he had a mink swim by within two feet of him, a sleek, miniature seal. Coming home in the fading light later a dog otter crossed the gravel drive ahead of him, stopped, sniffed the air towards him, and leisurely moved away through the rhododendrons.

He was more social now, went out to dinner with his friends, let this life close around him, drawing strength and comfort from it. Mary was back but he met her only once at a friend's house and they were pleasant with one another, but it was clear that nothing remained between them as far as he was concerned. He was grateful to her that she had done for them what he knew in the end he would have forced himself to do.

All the work at Alverton Manor was now finished, but he

knew that he would not move into it by himself, knew, too, that he would do nothing about any other woman until after the bullion lift.

Sometimes of an evening when Mrs. Hamilton had gone, Belle would telephone him. Usually she was reluctant to ring off and he let her chat away without impatience.

Then in mid-April when she rang one night she said, "Berners wants to see you. When can I tell him you'll be up, Andy?"

"The day after tomorrow. Tell him I'll meet him in the R.A.C. for lunch."

"You'll be coming here?"

"Yes, of course. We'll go out to dinner."

He went up on the morning train and met Berners for lunch. To his surprise Benson was there, too. From Berners he learned that a dummy run had been carried out at night with the helicopter with an adverse wind on the outward leg of the flight, but even so there had been an ample margin of fuel.

Benson said, "I came along to tell you that from now on neither Mr. Mandel nor I will be in England. Berners is coming back to France two days before the ship sails. If anything goes wrong this end or if you want to get in touch you can use the Applegate number you've got. Also, to put your mind at rest, we've checked at least three City gold dealers and there will be consignments aboard of well over a ton. We've arranged a weather check when you get to Le Havre. We'll check it in the Brest area and Miss Vickers will receive a direct radio telephone call aboard ship from Berners. He'll talk generally for a few moments and then she will ask him how her aunt is. If Berners says she's much the same, that means the operation is on. If he says she's much worse than she was, then the operation is off. If between the time of the ship leaving Le Havre and midnight the weather gets too bad for the helicopter then it won't show up and, since you won't get any Very light signal, you won't go into action."

"And I'll be on my own. Aboard without a ticket."

Benson shrugged. "Well, that won't be very serious. You can say you couldn't bear to leave Miss Vickers and offer to pay for your passage."

After lunch Raikes walked up to Mount Street and stopped on his way at a flower shop in Berkeley Square. He went into the flat carrying a bunch of crimson carnations.

The flowers were too much for Belle. It was the first time he had brought her any and, as she held them after he had kissed and greeted her, she could not stop herself from thinking that the recent days of separation had forced upon him some recognition of what she meant to him; that he had truly missed her and wanted her to know this, not with words but with the show of flowers. This fantasy of thought on her part, and she knowing it was fantasy though half-believing it was not, broke her down.

She went into the kitchen and came back carrying the flowers arranged in a vase and put them on the table. She stood behind them and smiled at him and the news she had not meant to give him came from her, stumbling and awkward.

"They're lovely, Andy . . . It's like, almost, as though something might have told you . . . Well, you know, that it was just what . . . well, what *we* both wanted. Say it with flowers."

Raikes went towards his bedroom to put away his overnight case. "My father used to grow carnations in his greenhouse. Grew them for years and then he and the gardener had a flaming row about them . . . God knows what about. But they were always quarrelling with one another about plants. Anyway there were no more carnations."

She followed him to the door, knowing that he had heard nothing pertinent in her remarks. For a moment she hesitated. She could let it go or persist. Damn it, he had to know. For both their sakes he had to know. All right then, for her sake most. Perhaps this was the one thing that was needed to make him see what he felt about her.

"Andy . . ."

"Yes." He turned.

"Do I look different?"

"Different?"

He looked at her. He was used to her now and there seemed nothing different about her. Not even when she changed her hair style or wore a new dress was she ever more than Belle, the woman who was there, had to be there because that for the time being was the way things ran with him . . . Belle with the loose auburn hair, that long Burne-Jones face, not pretty or beautiful but not unattractive . . . Belle, long-legged, well-fleshed on the breasts and buttocks, slim-waisted, all familiar, well-known in love-making, but just Belle Vickers who at times with her *Andy* and her *supposes* and *well, yes, buts* could make him clench his teeth with suppressed irritation.

Gallantly, he said, "You look as lovely as ever."

Pleased, she said, "Perhaps that's it. You were all eyes for me. You should have listened to what I said, Andy. I said *we*, Andy. *We* were happy to have flowers from you. . . . Oh, Lord, do you want me to spell it out? I'm going to have a baby. Your baby."

He said nothing. He just stared at her. Curiously he was unsurprised. Not because it was something which, even in a passing thought, he had imagined could happen. He had never given it a thought. But in these few moments now he saw that this was how it had to be, this was part of the irony of life which had begun to operate from the moment months and months ago when he had put a red ballpoint tick against a fishing rod in a catalogue. From a position of strength and security, the future planned the way he wanted it, everything had to sway and tremble, threatening collapse, only to be held together by his own unyielding determination. For months he had been doing that . . . was almost on the point of restoring things the way he wanted them. And now this woman was carrying his child. He stood there, not thinking of her, but of Mary. Mary should have been the one, not this underbred, market hack. Christ—the thing he wanted most was held by her . . . an unfamilied slut, fumbled with by her own stepfather (Oh, yes, in the aftermath of passion one night she had lain and told him about herself, pouring it out), mucked about by boy-friends in shared flats, used in hotel rooms by some salesman crook ... used by Sarling like a willing or not housemaid in a top attic spreading her thighs for the master ... yes, used by him, too. But only for use. Not for carrying his seed. Not in her. He saw her lips tremble, knew the stupid, weak irresolution in her ... supposing he might be angry ... wondering was it all right ... and he knew exactly what she was going to say, and heard her say it.

"Oh, Andy ... I thought ... well, I supposed that you would be pleased. I'm sorry about it ... but, well, I did always wear a thing. It was no cheat and I swear—"

He went to her, put his hands firmly on her shoulders and cut off her words with a quick smile and a kiss.

"Stop getting worked up. Of course, I'm pleased."

"Oh, Andy, are you? You really and truly are?"

"Well, of course I am. But it's come at an awkward moment hasn't it? It just depends what you want to do about it. If you want to keep it, well that's fine. It doesn't make any difference to all this ship business. But if you want to get rid of it—"

"Get rid of it?"

"If you want to. It's for you to decide. But, if that's what you want, we can't risk having it done before this trip ... there might be complications. You might not be fit to travel."

Her voice trembling with anger, Belle said, "Why don't you say you don't want me to have it? Is that it?"

"Belle ... it's nothing to do with me."

For the first time, out of her disappointment and unhappiness at his response, she lost her temper with him.

"Listen—you put it in me. It's everything to do with you. Do you want it or not? I'm not asking you to make an honest woman of me. I'm just asking you whether you want it or not?"

"Be sensible, Belle. This is your decision, not mine. I've always been frank with you. I'm very fond of you. In a way, if you like I've a kind of love for you ...." He was picking his way delicately now because he knew that somewhere he had handled her wrong. "But I've always made it clear that I wouldn't

225

marry you. We've been thrown very close together in all this business and what has happened is what would happen between two normal people. But when it's all over we've got our lives to live separately. If you want to keep it, then naturally, I'll be financially responsible for it. I'll be happy for you to keep it, but you've got to think of yourself. Some other man will come along and there you will be with my child. Other men don't go too readily for that kind of thing. You must see, it's your decision not mine." As he spoke he moved up to her, put his arm round her and drew her against him. "Now come on, calm down. You've been waiting here to tell me this and now you've done it you're all worked up. But I've got to be honest with you. At least I love you enough to be that. If you want to keep it, then I'm happy for you, and happy for me. But if you want to get rid of it, then I can understand that. Whichever way, though, it's got to be your decision. Damn it all, Belle—it's your future. Now come on, simmer down." He turned her face up to his and kissed her.

As he held and kissed her, she knew it was no good expecting something which had never existed. Flowers she'd got (why?) but not because he'd known how she was. And honest common sense she'd got, because he was dead right about it being her decision. Love she'd got—of a kind; and right now as he held and comforted her she knew that limited though it was it was enough to smooth out all resistance or disappointment in her. At arm's length she could keep herself intact from him, but the moment he touched her he could have asked her to strip naked and stand on her head and she would have done it. Why? For God's sake why?

Moving from him, she said, "I'm sorry, Andy. Everything you say is right. I suppose, well, I sort of got myself worked up about it, not knowing whether to phone and tell you about it and all that."

"I understand. And I'm sorry, too, if I didn't handle it right. After all—" he smiled, the brown skin wrinkling round his blue eyes "—it's not a situation I've been faced with before. Coming

226

on top of all this other stuff I wasn't up to it. Am I forgiven?"

She nodded and came to him again. As she pressed against him, knowing where the touch and the embrace would lead, that she would be lifted from her feet and carried to a bed, and knowing there would be no fierceness in his love-making, but a slow, relaxing gentleness, she made up her mind. No matter what he wanted, no matter whether after this ship business he left her and she never saw him again, she would keep the child. Boy or girl it would have something of him, something that really and truly belonged to her, and with that she would be content. As he put her on the bed and began to strip her and she lay back with her eyes shut, feeling his familiar hands about her, she told herself, Be content, Belle. Be content with small scraps of happiness because that's all you're ever going to get. And let's face it, one way and another in this crumby life that's all most people get though you don't see them going round with long faces about it.

Two days later he went back to Devon. They were two days in which he had spent all his time with Belle, looked after her and been considerate and gentle, not from design, but because there had developed in him a new conception of her which arose from pity. Until now he had seen her as someone to be used and handled because she was part of a problem which he had to master. First of all in connection with Sarling, and now in this ship business. But all her life he realised she was going to be used and handled. For the first time in his life he was sorry for someone and the feeling was a luxury. But he knew that it was a luxury—so far as she was concerned—that he would cut off sharply the moment the helicopter lifted him from the foredeck of the *Queen Elizabeth 2*.

But in the following days in Devon while the kindness of thought towards her persisted, something else grew from it. Always he had been able to face the fact that if disaster struck then he would write himself off. It was no idle exercise in final heroics. He just knew that this would be, had to be, his way. He had known this almost from the moment of the success of his first swindle years and years ago. But now if he killed himself some part of him would be left behind, the child that Belle carried—and he knew that she would carry it and keep it. Through the child in Belle he would have continuity . . . but not on the terms he wanted. Was this then some further irony that the fates were threatening him with? The Raikes line would go on . . . but through a bastard fathered on a woman who never in a hundred years would he have dreamed of taking to Alverton Manor. So now he found himself thinking about the child more and Belle less, and there was an obstinate certitude in him which made him think of it always as a boy. He could see him, well looked after by Belle, but dragged about from flat to flat . . . ignored perhaps by any man she married, but more likely tolerated and indulged by a succession of lovers . . . growing up not as he would have wished. The thought hurt him. Things could go wrong and he would have to bow out knowing that all that was left of him would be the boy, unfathered, unplaced, knowing nothing of Alverton and the Raikes blood. It was then that, though he was now dead, a stronger hatred than ever for Sarling came back, a hatred that carried over into his feelings against Mandel and Benson who had picked up the weapon from Sarling's hands and used it still against him.

Three days before the ship sailed he went back to London. Belle was going down to Southampton on the boat train on the morning of the sailing. He went down to Southampton the day before to stay the night at the Dolphin Hotel which was quite close to the docks. There would be no contact between them until he walked into her cabin just before sailing time.

Over lunch together before he went down to Southampton, he said, "You know what you've got to do. We've been over it often enough. You've got nothing to worry about. While the ship's going over to Le Havre I'll take you over the ground. It'll be quite safe to do it together. People will be milling round getting settled and the stewards won't have got to the stage of recognising faces. It's after Le Havre that we'll have to be careful."

Belle nodded. He had drilled her often enough about her part, and she knew that she could do it and would do it. The moment you were really on your way things became easy. At this moment she was not concerned with any of the ship detail. She was thinking ahead to New York and after. She was staying there a week and then flying back. It was the moment of arriving back that was in her mind. What happened then? She wanted to ask him but knew it would be unwelcome. In fact she was almost glad that she couldn't ask him because she didn't want to hear him say, "Well, we'll meet a couple of times, clear up the financial end, and that will be that." And either you have the baby or don't, my girl, she thought. And have it she would. And he was going to know. The fact that she had it might bring him back some time. . . . Oh, Belle, she censured herself silently, for God's sake stop dreaming. . . .

He stood up briskly and moved to his bedroom for his overnight case. He couldn't take it aboard with him from the hotel. It held a new pair of unmarked pyjamas, a new set of toilet gear, six gas canisters, a Very light pistol and four cartridges, an automatic pistol and a small jemmy for dealing with the door of the Officers' quarters should this be locked. The next morning he would take a taxi to Southampton Station and leave the case, with only the pyjamas and toilet gear in it, at the Left Luggage depot and then go on to the docks with the rest of the stuff in his overcoat and suit pockets.

He came back, carrying the case and his overcoat and looked down at her, his face breaking into a slow smile. She remembered the first time she had ever seen him. Herself, as nervous as a kitten, and him, slitting open Sarling's note and reading it without any movement of face. She remembered how through her nervousness she had felt sorry for him and had tried to show her sympathy. What a waste that had been. He needed nothing from anyone that he could not take without help. Oh, yes, she loved him, was trapped by her love for him, but at least she understood him.

He put down his case and coat and she stood up and went into his arms. He gave her a hug and kissed her, and then with a boyish grin said, "Miss that boat train and I'll break your neck. Goodbye, love."

He went and she watched him through the window get a taxi. He went off without looking up, and it suddenly came to her then that ever since the day she had told him about the child he had never made any other reference to it. He was useless to her and she was making a bloody fool of herself over him. If she had any sense she would go and get a train now, to anywhere but Southampton, and trust to luck that neither he nor any of Benson's lot would ever find her. Go and live quietly somewhere, have the baby, and live happily ever after with her memories.

Going to her bedroom to make up her face, she had almost convinced herself that that was exactly what she would do. In the bedroom, lying on her dressing table was a bouquet of red roses which he must have smuggled into the flat. Propped against it was a note. *To you both—with all my love, Andy.*

She sat down on the bed holding the note, tears coming into her eyes. Surely, surely to God, underneath somewhere or the other, whether he knew it or not, what he had written must be the truth? It must be. Must be.

CHAPTER THIRTEEN

HE TOOK A taxi from his hotel to the station and left his
case. He came out and took another taxi to the docks. He had
the jemmy for the door, the Very pistol and four cartridges in
one pocket of his coat, the automatic and three of the canisters
in the other pocket and three in his suit pockets. He carried
nothing on him to identify him except his passport and American visa. Neither his suit nor any of his clothes were marked.

He paid off the taxi short of the Ocean Terminal. It was a
mild morning, a few high clouds being pushed up Channel by a
steady westerly wind. The boat train was not in yet but a lot of
passengers were arriving by car and taxi.

The *Queen Elizabeth 2* lay alongside looking as though she had
never moved since he had last seen her. He went into the
Terminal and up to the top floor, showed his boarding permit—
made out in a false name—at the visitors' checkpoint and then
went aboard into the Midships Lobby on Two Deck. As he
moved into the rotunda-shaped lobby a ship's photographer was
taking photographs of people coming aboard. Later these
would be displayed for purchase in the glass cases in the
Shopping Area. Raikes put a hand up, twitched at his nose
to hide his face and turned away from the photographer,
losing himself in the movement of people. He went up the
stairway to One Deck and then walked aft along the starboard
side past the Beauty Salon and the Barber Shop and then out
on to the One Deck Lido. Here he leant over the rail and
watched the movement on the quay below and the passengers
coming aboard. The boat train came in. He stayed, watching the

231

movement of people, waiting to spot Belle, a green hat and a yellow coat . . . she liked bold colours. All the way down in the train he knew she would have been nervous, but it would go when she stepped aboard. Away across the water on the French side, near Loudeac, Berners and his party would be up, preparing to pass a long day, living for the darkness and midnight. Leaning over the rail, other people around him, he felt detached from it all, devoid of personality and of urgent purpose. At midnight, when he would stand out here and see the signal light flare up redly into the darkness from the helicopter, he would come coldly and efficiently alive and move up past the quarterdeck and the upperdeck to the boatdeck where he would go forward to see the Captain. The plan had been made. His confidence was entirely in it. Standing there, waiting for Belle, there was no thought in his mind of the child she carried.

He hung around until long after the boat train was in, then he walked forward and took a lift down to Four Deck. He went along to her cabin on the port side and she let him in. He held her in his arms and kissed her, did it with a warmth he didn't feel, gave her the words she wanted, and saw as he stepped back from her that she was wearing round her neck a single row of pearls which she had worn when he had first seen her. With her, he knew, that would be from design not accident . . . but not, he was sure, because she felt that she should wear them now as a symbol of parting.

He locked the cabin door and waited while she emptied her suitcase, putting her things in drawers and the wardrobe. When the case was empty he put the automatic, the canisters, the Very pistol and cartridges and his coat, scarf, gloves and hat in it. Without a word, she locked the case and put it away.

He said, "Now I'm going to take you round and show you the ground. Remember it's easy to get lost on a ship like this, so we'll confine ourselves only to the parts which you will have to know. The whole ship will be milling like a beehive until long after she sails so nobody's going to notice us." He gave her a quick grin and then cupped her face in his hands and kissed her.

"From this moment you don't have a thing to worry about. It'll all go like clockwork." He slid his hands down and touched her pearls. "You wore these the first day I saw you."

"A bad day for you."

He shrugged. "In some ways. It made things a little more difficult. But nothing is ever entirely bad." His hands left her and he turned to the door, then paused and looked back at her. "There's something I want to tell you. I hope you'll agree. I want you to have the baby."

"Oh, Andy—"

"Have it. We can talk about all the rest later."

He opened the door for her. She went out, hiding her face from him, not wanting him to see her happiness, a happiness which she was projecting far ahead of this moment. *I love you with red roses*, and now this . . . Oh, yes, she knew he could be a devious bastard but not so deep that he would bother to say something like this when, so far as this plan was concerned, it was unnecessary. He knew she was his. He didn't have to do or say anything out of the ordinary to keep it that way . . . But he *was* doing it. Doing it because he couldn't help himself. Because there was something working in him which he couldn't ignore. Just be patient, Belle, she told herself, don't rush anything, and particularly not him. There's no need. It's there in him, growing all the time.

She walked round with him, his hand sometimes holding her arm, steering her, hearing his voice as he explained things and, out of loyalty to him, she pushed her happiness away and concentrated on everything he said. On paper, over diagrams, she had done all this before, but now she was actually aboard the ship and the blueprints were real and solid . . . wood veneers and blue carpets, cabin doors and stairways, stewards and passengers and visitors moving around, tugs hooting and gulls calling and, somewhere in the bowels of this ship, the gold bullion already aboard.

He took her forward to A Stairway and they climbed up to the boatdeck. Looking over the handrail she could look down the stairwell through the decks, a drop of almost a hundred feet. From the top of the stairway on the boatdeck he took her back along the length of the deck, showing her the 736 Club, the Coffee Shop and the Juke Box, the Theatre, the run of shops and the two-tiered Double Room at the stern and, although she knew she would never have to do it, but knew too—because this he had impressed on her—that she must know that she could, he pointed out to her the places where she could drop the can-isters, showing her where to stand, and where to toss them so that she could move unobtrusively away to safety herself. And while he spoke, casually, quietly, people moved around them laughing and talking. They went down the starboard side and then back along the portside to the top of the stairway.

He said, "Use this spot as point of reference. From here, you can get a lift down to Four Deck and then you're only a few seconds from your cabin. Or you can go down the stairway. On the deck below this—the upperdeck—is the Look-Out Room. It's a big lounge with a bar, and windows that look out over the foredeck. Tonight when all's going well you can go there and watch the bullion lift. There are little blinds on the windows to stop glare at night but you can pull them aside. When you see them lift me off the deck you can go back to your cabin and sleep without worry."

He took her down to the Look-Out Room and standing by the window showed her the foredeck. From here, he took her down to One Deck and along to the Deck Lido at the stern.

"This is where you'll wait with me tonight until we get Berners' signal. Then I shall leave you and you'll stay here until you see the first Very signal from the wheelhouse. You can't miss it because it will be high in the air. If it doesn't come within the time period you know what to do." He held her arm and looked at her. "We don't have to discuss that one again, do we?"

"No, Andy."

"Good. When you get the second wheelhouse signal, throw the canisters over, and then you can go forward and up to the

234

Look-Out Room and watch the lift. And remember this, after that second signal your job is done. You're just a passenger for New York and you know nothing. Now, you go back to your cabin. Call the steward and tell him you're a bad sailor for the first few hours aboard and you're going to rest and don't want to be disturbed. As soon as the ship's clear into the Channel I'll come along and be with you until about half an hour before we make Le Havre. And don't forget the cabin drill. If I'm in there with you and the steward ever knocks, we both go into the toilet compartment, turn the shower on and you stick your head out and call to the steward to come in."

Belle found her way back to her cabin without difficulty. Raikes went back to the Look-Out Room, ordered himself a drink and through the windows watched the preparations for the liner to be taken out.

A little after midday the *Queen Elizabeth 2* was warped and nosed free from her berth by tugs. From the ship passengers waved to their friends and the crowd ashore. A band played, and the coloured streamers between ship and shore tautened and broke as the water gap widened. Tugs hooted, sirens blew, and taxi drivers kept a finger on their horns in salute. The red and gold Cunard house flag stiffened a little in the breeze, gulls wheeled overhead, the sun edged through the high clouds, brightening the putty-coloured sun decks, and the lifeboats in their sage-green davits threw slow-moving shadows as the ship was manoeuvred. It was not just a ship that moved away from the quayside, but a holiday resort that moved and floated, a place and a world of its own. Down in the Look-Out Room a few tables from Raikes, a gentle alcoholic was served his fourth brandy on a white-topped Arkana table. In the Britannia Restaurant the figurehead stared straight ahead of her at the glass swing doors and had no thought of ancient sisters who once lodged beneath bowsprits and never had the salt taste of spume from their lips. In one of the cabins de luxe a

235

kleptomanic matron discovered that all the coathangers in the wardrobe were continental type and no use as keepsakes to steal thus saving the Company an average loss of eight thousand hangers a year. Some people, even before the lift and feel of the sea in the Solent had welcomed the liner, were already criticising the drab design of the Hardy Amies stewards' uniforms of khaki jackets and dark blue trousers, the incongruity of the stained glass window in the Q4 Room and the poor lighting of the perspex panels designed by Rory McEwen, and others were missing the grandeur and "Palm Court" atmosphere of the old Queens and of the days when Tallulah Bankhead had asked a steward, "What time does this place get to New York?" People were already buying souvenirs and presents in the shop arcades. There were four people at prayer in the Synagogue, and a small trickle going through the Art Gallery which held forty-five thousand pounds' worth of pictures. In the Grill Room a waiter dropped a set of salt and pepper containers designed by Lord Queensbury, and seasoned travellers who liked their travel to be leisurely and comfortable were already searching for the small bar and the friendly barman so that they could avoid the late night drunks in the main bars. But of the thousands of people who saw the ship move down Southampton Water, many of whom had seen hundreds of ships move down, the old Queens, the *Carmania* and *Franconia*, few were not moved by the sight and wished they were aboard.

So, to a ragged chorus of whistles, sirens and hooters, the great ship turned out towards the sea and her maiden trans-Atlantic run, and deep down in her Specie Room on Eight Deck lay three tons of gold bullion and a ton and a half of silver bullion, and the gentle drunk in the Look-Out Room leaned across his black banquette and said to Raikes, "They can keep their Jumbo Jets and their Concordes. When I travel I like to feel that it takes time. No snatchin' at drinks between here and there and a tasteless roast chicken leg served up in a cellophane bloody pack. No sitting on your bloody passport and ticket because there's just time to lose 'em and not time to look

236

for 'em. For my money a ship's a lady and a gentleman should always travel with a lady. And believe me, this one's a real thoroughbred. Modern, up to all the tricks, but a lady. Here's to her." He raised his brandy glass, found it empty, and called to the steward.

In her cabin, Belle lay on the small bed and day-dreamed, forgetting for a while completely the purpose of her presence aboard. Somewhere in Devon they had a house, the two of them, and there was a nanny for the girl. . . . Yes, she saw it as a girl to begin with. She wanted it like that, but she'd give him a whole quiverful of boys afterwards. It had to come to that. She loved him so much that it had to pass to him, was passing to him . . . she'd do whatever he wanted. Try not to irritate him with the way she talked. Put a plum in her mouth. Go to the best hair stylists and dress salons, make herself over with the right stuff. Tweeds, simple but expensive little dresses . . . hunting, shooting, and fishing . . . and learn to sit on a shooting stick and mark a race card, and stand by him like a tigress—she opened her mouth and showed her teeth at the cabin ceiling—if anything went wrong. Yes, she was it for him and he had to be it for her. And if he wanted her five times a day or only five times a year she would be happy. Mrs. Andrew Raikes. She reached out to the dressing table console and turned the radio on softly, then lay back and went on dreaming . . . bright lights, soft music, love triumphs.

When he knocked on her door two hours later she was sleeping but still dreaming.

He said, "I had some sandwiches in the Coffee Shop. You see you have some dinner tonight. Nobody can operate on an empty stomach."

He locked the door, took off his shoes and lay down beside her.

"If the steward knocks, don't forget—the shower."

He was asleep within ten minutes.

The place which they had rented was five miles from Loudeac.

It was a small château, beginning to be dilapidated, standing in its own grounds, tree-surrounded and with a large lawn behind the house where they had parked the helicopter. Although it carried no markings they made no attempt to camouflage it or hide it. By four o'clock the next morning the house would be empty and there would be nothing left which would help to trace them.

At ten o'clock Berners, sitting in the small study that looked out over the lawn, had a call from their man in Brest to report the weather. The wind was WNW, Force 3.

"That's twelve knots," Berners said to Benson who was with him.

At midday the report was the same. Cloud cover had thickened a little off the Channel Islands and dropped from three to two thousand five hundred feet. The report at four o'clock was the same.

Benson said, "Where would you rather be? Here, or out there on the ship?"

Berners smiled. "I am out there. Just as he is here, although he's never seen the place. I'm there because he knows he can rely on me, knows how I think and how I will act. The same goes for me with him."

"You've never known much about him, have you?"

"It's never been necessary. I've known him. That's enough. Where he lives or how many suits he has is of no importance."

"What will he be doing now?"

"Sleeping in Miss Vickers' cabin."

"You can't know that."

"I can. What you and Mandel got was the plan, the main details. But he and I have never done anything without going through everything. Within limits of say ten or so minutes I can tell you everything he's done on that boat so far. I could have put a call through to him at twelve-thirty and had him paged in the Look-Out Room."

Benson smiled. "You should have been twins."

"We are—when it comes to working."

238

"What will he do if things go wrong aboard the ship and he has to run for it?"

"He's got a passport and an American visa. He stands every chance of making New York. It's only a few days. People are always stowing away and making it. The hardest thing to find on a ship that size with all its bars and eating places is a well-dressed stowaway. It's the chap who hides in a lifeboat that gets caught. It's like any London club. You can walk into any of them if you're dressed right. They all have members who live in Ireland, Scotland or abroad who come in about once a year or less. The whole thing about being unquestioned is to look and act as though you have a complete right to be where you are."

"He still might be caught."

"Then it would be the end. You heard him say that. He means it."

"And you?"

Berners laughed. "I'm very fond of being alive—but on my own terms. I'd die in prison. So, if the need arises, I shall take good care to die out of it."

"Does Miss Vickers feel the same way?"

"I've never asked her, but I know she doesn't. She's the kind that puts up with life, just so long as it is life. They call it, and I'm sure she would, making the best of a bad job. Raikes and I would never settle for a bad job. Would you?"

Benson twisted the gold ring on his finger and then smiled, his white teeth flashing against the tanned face. "Frankly, no. Not now. You see I once did three years in a Turkish prison. It taught me a sharp lesson."

Berners said, "You wouldn't be thinking of making something go wrong aboard?"

Without surprise Benson said, "No. I wouldn't be talking like this if I were. I'm just interested in Raikes. You're enjoying doing all this. He's not. We're forcing him. Why couldn't he enjoy it, too?"

"Because he's got all he wants."

"And you?"

"There's no end—I've discovered recently—to the things I want. They're solid, tangible and beautiful and so many of them. But Raikes wants himself. Not the man he is now, but the man he missed being. He thinks he can have a second life. I've never been candid enough to tell him that he's chasing a dream. After all, why shouldn't he do just that? So many people do."

At six o'clock the wind was still in the same quarter, still at Force 3 and the cloud cover had risen five hundred feet and thinned but there were scattered rain storms in the Channel approaches.

At eight o'clock Berners put in a call to Miss Vickers on the QE2 at Le Havre. During the course of their very ordinary conversation she learnt that her aunt was much the same.

As Belle put back the telephone receiver, Raikes said, "All right. Now you go and have some dinner. Take your time. I'm going off now. If you happen to run into me you don't know me. The steward will be in to turn back your bed sometime in the next couple of hours. I'll be back here at half-past eleven to pick up my hat and coat and stuff. You join me on the Deck Lido of One Deck at a quarter to twelve."

He put out a hand, touched her face and went. A few minutes later he was leaning over the rail aft watching the passengers boarding from Le Havre. After a while a brief, heavy rain shower drove him inside. He bought a magazine at one of the shops and then went and sat in a chair on the promenade deck outside the Double Room. In all the restaurants and the Grill Room now people were eating and drinking, choices being made between a thick sirloin steak or *Suprême de Turbot*, waiters explaining just what was in a *Paella à la Valenciana*, recommending a wine to go with the *Kebab à la Turque* . . . hundreds of people, enjoying themselves while Raikes sat, untroubled, reading an article about the revival of interest in Pharaoh hounds from Malta and waited for the hours to pass.

He sat there for an hour and then moved forward into the Look-Out Room. The blinds were already drawn. At nine o'clock he went aft and watched from the rail as the liner blew a salute to Le Havre and then began slowly to move out into the Channel. The French coast and the lights of Le Havre dropped away in the growing darkness. He stood there until the night air began to make him cold and then he went through to the Theatre Bar and had a large whisky. As he stood there Belle passed him but they took no notice of one another. He watched her thread her way past him through the other passengers. She wore a plain black dress, a little scarf over her shoulders and around her neck were the pearls. Momentarily he was touched with a sudden affection for her. There was little about her he liked, her body most, and yet disconcertingly he was aware that there was something between them. Not only the child she carried, but a bond that came from the events they had shared in the last months. But more than that he was grateful for her loyalty. To him, he knew, no matter its source, she was completely loyal. And it was the same kind of loyalty as he knew with Berners. Berners would have said that it was because they were all the same kind, people outside ordinary society, their interests and welfare cemented by the simple fact of being different from other people. The odd thing was that he had never felt different from other people. Other people, fundamentally, were the same as he was. It was just that they had never found their lines laid in the strange places he had. Given the right pressures, given the moments of crisis and threat, then most people would lie and steal and kill. In fact, most people had a need for such activities. That was why they were happy in war. That's why they rioted and wrecked public places and trains after a football match. In him, in all of them, were the primitive instincts close to the surface, seeking some excuse for emergence. Yes, Berners was his kind, and so was Belle . . . and so—given the right circumstances—was every living soul on this ship.

For the next two hours he moved around the ship matching

his movements and his waiting periods to the plan he had carried in his mind for so many weeks. He hadn't eaten since his morning sandwiches and there was only one whisky inside him. His body craved nothing, not food, nor excess of alcohol, because his body had ceased to exist. He was Raikes, part of a plan and a routine.

At half-past eleven he went to Belle's cabin. There was little talk between them. He took his hat and put on his coat and gloves. Into the pockets—wiping them all clean of prints first—he stuffed the Very pistol and its cartridges and the small automatic.

At the door before leaving, he said, "I'll be waiting on One Deck Lido. Carry your coat over your arm and put it on just as you go out. And when you come back in take it off and carry it the same way so that it partly hides your big handbag."

She moved up to him and he was unsurprised by the clear, sharp movement of fear in her. It had to be there, to well up and then be banished before she was free to move.

"Andy . . . say something happened . . .? Well, I mean, just suppose?"

For once her sloppy speech didn't irritate him. It made him smile.

"Nothing is going to happen which we don't already know about."

"But if something did . . . just suppose it did? You would come to me for help wouldn't you?"

"If I want you or your help for something which isn't in the plan—then I'll come to you? Is that it?"

"Yes."

"If I want something and you have it then I'll come. You know that already."

He leaned forward and kissed her and then left her. Fifteen minutes later she joined him on the Lido Deck. They stood close together on the port side, looking out through the darkness towards the south, towards the direction from which the helicopter would come flying in. Like a lover he crooked his arm in

hers and they stared silently across the sea. The wind which had
been westerly when they had left Le Havre had gone round more
to the north. There was a slow swell running and mixed with the
wind noises came the steady hiss of water breaking away from
the ship's sides, streaming out behind in a pale, luminous wake.
A handful of other people walked the deck, coated and scarfed
against the wind and now and then a red cigarette end was
flicked over the side.

Belle, conscious of the warmth of his arm against hers,
thought, here we stand like a couple going off on their honeymoon trip. Like dozens of other couples that there must be
aboard. If life had been right, properly planned, this in truth
was how it should have been, even if not with him, but years
ago with some other man, he and the hardness of his body, and
the ungivingness of his spirit never to have been known by her.
And that would have been all right, because what you never had
you never missed. Him, as a man, that was. Not a honeymoon.
That she missed, would always miss, she guessed. No confetti.
No trousseau. No excitement. No going from here urgently to a
cabin to make love for the first time as married people. Life
had really dished it out to her, and a fine honeymoon couple
they made. He with his hidden automatic. She with a handbag
full of filthy canisters that could wipe out scores of people and,
somewhere deep down in the guts of this bloody great affair,
tons of gold. And, let's face it, that was what men were really
interested in having and getting—money. Women, marriage,
home and children were just sidelines to them. Decorations
round the great maypole of their lust for money and power
and position.

He turned his face a little toward her and kissed the corner of
her eyebrow and her heart jumped at the unexpectedness. It
couldn't be playacting for the benefit of anyone watching. It
had to be real. This thing coming out in him for her, to meet
the love she carried for him. Had to be.

At her side Raikes looked at his watch and said, "Ten past
twelve. They're late." It was said more to himself than her.

243

Let them be late, she thought. Just don't let them come at all. Let him be stuck here aboard with her, a stowaway to give himself up and pay his passage. From New York they could go off together . . . anywhere . . . find themselves a new life. Find themselves . . . their real selves. The two decent people they should have always been. Please God, let it be that way.

Suddenly, a quarter of a mile away on the port bow, a red Very flare streamed into life high up, hung burning for a while and then dropped and disappeared, leaving the blackness of the starless night blacker than it had been before.

Almost immediately his arm left hers.

He said, "Wait here until you've seen the next two sets of Very lights from the wheelhouse—then you can go to your cabin or watch from the Look-Out Room."

She nodded, and half raised a hand to touch his face but he was gone, moving away from her.

Now he moved automatically, no hurry in him, no emotion except the nullity of feeling which was emotion enough. He went the full length of One Deck, forward to A Stairway, and from there, hat in hand, he climbed the blue-carpeted flights to the boatdeck. The staircase finished outside the 736 Room. He went to the glass doors and looked through. There were quite a few people in there and beyond in the Coffee Shop. He looked at his watch. Twenty minutes past twelve. He moved to the starboard side down a short alleyway and without trouble jemmied open the door into the Officers' Quarters. Memory served him faithfully, but not nostalgically. Long ago he had moved in here, watching, noting, ready to substantiate his presence. On his right a bedroom door was open, a cup and saucer and magazines on a low table and he heard a man whistling gently to himself. He passed down the runway and turned left up the stairs to the Senior Officers' Quarters. At the top of the stairs he moved forward, past the quarters of the Staff Captain on his right, and the door to the Captain's

244

quarters faced him. He paused, put on his hat, pulled his scarf from his pocket and wrapped it around the lower part of his face. He took the automatic in his gloved hand, opened the door and went in and let the door close quietly behind him.

The room was familiar to him. The desk before him still had its little collection of dictionaries in their book-ends. The jar of pencils and pens seemed untouched from the last time he had seen them. The standard lamp at the side of the desk was on and a few lights burned around the walls above the green leatherette chairs and banquettes. There was no one in the room. On a low round glass table to his left stood a potted dusty-pink azalea where once had been the flowering cactus. Farther away to the left and forward the door to the Captain's sleeping quarters was open. As he looked towards it the Captain came through. He was bare-headed and fully dressed, the gold buttons of his jacket undone so that it swung comfortably open.

The Captain came a few steps into the room, humming to himself, before he saw Raikes. He stopped. His bearded chin jerked up questioningly and Raikes saw the web of lines at the corners of the eyes grow and deepen. Many times he had seen that face in photographs. Many times he had seen himself here talking to this man . . . this strongly built, greying-haired, pugnacious-looking, solid figure of a bearded sea captain.

In a surprisingly gentle voice, even a touch of gruff humour flowing into it perhaps at the thought that this was some fool of a passenger who had lost his way, the Captain said, "Who are you, and what are you doing here?"

Raikes moved farther into the room and raised the automatic.

He said, "I'd be glad if you would be kind enough to sit down and listen to me."

The Captain looked from the automatic to the scarf round the lower part of Raikes's face. Raikes had the impression that he was noting them as he would have noted sloppy dress in his officers or some breach of rules by a seaman, framing already some sharp reprimand. Before the reprimand could come,

Raikes went on, "I'm a very serious and determined man, Captain. Let me assure you that if you don't listen to me and do as I say without fuss then a great many of your passengers are going to be killed. So will you please sit down and keep your hands where I can see them."

The Captain said nothing. He looked from Raikes to the door behind him and then slowly buttoned up his jacket and sat down.

"Thank you."

"Don't waste your civilities on me, man. Just say what you have to say." There was a hard, controlled anger in his voice, and Raikes could understand it, and even in his own mood of emotionless movement and intent give a passing sympathy to it. This of all the plan was the hardest section to work through for he was talking to a man for whom—though he knew nothing significant of him personally—he had the greatest respect and admiration. He was talking to a professional man in the fullest sense, a man whose profession was his life, a man who had joined the Cunard Company thirty-odd years before as Third Officer of the *Lancastria*, served through the war in armed merchant cruisers, with coastal forces in motor launches, and in corvettes in the North Atlantic and on Russian convoys. His first Cunard command had been in 1954 as Master of the *Alsatia* and his first passenger ship command the *Carinthia* four years later, and since then he had commanded nearly all the ships in the Cunard fleet and now sat, at the beginning of duress, the Captain of the latest and greatest of the fleet.

"What's the matter? Have you lost your nerve and your tongue?" Anger now held contempt.

Raikes shook his head. "No. Now listen. This ship is carrying gold bullion. I have a helicopter hovering a quarter of a mile off your port bow, waiting to come in and lift a ton of that bullion off your foredeck. You will give all the necessary orders for that to be done without incident."

"I'll see you in hell first."

"If you don't do as I say, and make the correct signals

246

which I'll explain, I have an accomplice waiting aft who will walk forward through the public rooms of one of the decks and a lot of your passengers will die."

Under lowered eyebrows, the Captain looked at him and rubbed a forefinger along his lower lip, and Raikes knew that these were the moments of responsibility; of weighing and calculating so many things in the depth of his, Raikes', own intent; the awareness in the Captain's mind of all the passengers aboard in his trust and care, and more important the real truth of the situation, the truth that was firm and inflexible in Raikes and must show—did show—that it was unflawed. The words that came now showed him that the Captain understood the position.

"How will they die?"

"At least six gas canisters, fifteen-second fused will be dropped. I won't bother you with the chemical name of the gas—it was stolen from an Army depot some months ago—but I assure you that in an enclosed space it is almost immediately lethal. If you refuse to do what I ask some passengers will die."

"If I refused, so would you. You'd never get off this ship."

"That's true. But then I am prepared to die—if my deductions are wrong. You're not interested in my death, but you could never justify the saving of gold bullion against the loss of passengers."

The Captain rubbed his hand across his beard for a moment, and then said, "Go on. But make it short. Your kind are becoming too common in this world and I'm not enjoying your company."

"Very well. The bullion is in the Specie Room on Eight Deck—"

"I said make it short, man. You don't have to instruct me on the layout of my own ship."

"The keys are here in your safe. You'll get them out. We'll go up to the wheelhouse and you'll give the necessary instructions for the ship to reduce speed and come up into wind so that

247

the helicopter can come in and hover over the foredeck to winch up the bullion. The bullion is packed two or four bars to a case. Anyway, I want the equivalent of eighty bars brought up in Number One freight lift, which is opposite to the Specie Room, to One Deck and from there carried out on to the foredeck. I want four men for carrying the gold from the lift and another one on the foredeck to load it into the helicopter lifting nets. When the last load is up the helicopter will take me off. Until I'm lifted off the threat to your passengers remains."

"Is your accomplice going with you?"

"No."

"That means your accomplice is a bona fide passenger and you're not?"

"You're very quick, Captain. Yes." He moved back a little. "Right, are we ready to go?"

Unmoving, the Captain said, "I don't know that we are. What happens if I sit here and do nothing? Call your bluff?"

"There's no bluff to be called." Raikes brought the Very pistol from his pocket. "If a signal isn't fired from this from the bridge wing within the next fifteen minutes then my accomplice begins to walk forward, dropping the canisters."

"So you say."

Raikes shrugged his shoulders. He understood that the man had to probe this line, but there was no future in it. "It's out of my hands, Captain. No signal and the walk begins. Passengers die. And, so do I."

The Captain nodded at the automatic. "And me?"

"No. I have nothing against you. You'll live—and have to explain what happened. Explain why you set a ton of gold against fifty, sixty lives."

The Captain considered this for a moment or two and then he stood up. He picked up his cap from a nearby chair, put it on and then walked to the bulkhead behind the desk and fished in his pockets for his key ring. From the safe he took out the ring with the Specie Room keys on it. Without seeing them Raikes

248

knew there were three keys on the ring, one for the main door lock and two more for the additional two Union locks on the door. Berners, purely as an exercise in acquiring information, had amused himself with picking up details of the Specie Room from his own sources.

Raikes said, "There's a padlocked dead arm across the front of the lift on One Deck. I presume there is too across the lift entrance on Eight Deck."

The Captain turned and a shaggy eyebrow lifted.

He said, "It's a pity you haven't done your homework in some worthier enterprise. The Second Officer has those keys. He'll be in charge of the bullion party. Personally I'd like to be in charge of a firing party with you at the other end."

He began to walk across the salon to the door on the port side. Before he reached it, he stopped and turned to Raikes, nodding at the automatic in his hand. "Put that away. I'm not going on to my own bridge with that at my back."

Raikes slid the automatic into his pocket. Without another look at him the Captain turned and went through the door. Raikes followed and then moved up the narrow portside stairs to the entrance to the wheelhouse.

The wheelhouse was lit by shaded lights and the reflected glow of panels from the big console under the forward windows. There were four people there. The First Officer, a white silk scarf about his neck, who stood by the console, looking out of the central window, a Third Officer who leaned over the chart table laying off bearings on the chart, a Quartermaster, in white jersey and blue trousers, who was manning the wheel immediately behind the console, and a bridge boy who was wiping down the inside of the port windows.

As Raikes and the Captain entered, the First Officer turned towards them. He looked momentarily surprised to see the Captain.

The Captain said, "Good morning, Mr. Dormer."

"Good morning, sir."

The Captain said, "Mr. Dormer, I can't introduce you to

249

our guest, except to say that he's unwelcome. However, I can say that because of him a situation has arisen aboard which could well endanger the lives of many of our passengers. Because of this, I must ask you to carry out the orders I give, even though they may seem very odd and you may not agree with them. Is that understood?"

"Yes, sir."

Raikes saw the First Officer's eyes move to him.

The Captain called the bridge boy to him. To Raikes, he said, "Give him the pistol."

Raikes took the Very pistol from his pocket and fitted a cartridge and then handed it to the boy.

The Captain said, "Get out on the port bridge wing and fire it."

"High in the air," said Raikes. "Straight up."

The boy took the pistol and went through the door to the port wing.

A few moments later, standing in the stern still, Belle saw the green flare burst high in the dark sky forward. The slow tension which had been building up in her suddenly drained away. She turned away from the rail and lit herself a cigarette.

A quarter of a mile away on the port bow, a thousand feet up and well below the cloud level, Berners and the man with him in the stripped main cabin of the Bell 205A saw the flare.

Over the roar of the main rotor and the Lycoming gas-turbine engine, the man leaned forward and shouted in Berners' ear, "Thank God for that. You know I never thought this crazy stunt would ever get off the ground."

Berners said nothing. Away in the distance he could see the white steaming light at the QE2's masthead and as the heli-copter swung a little, he caught a glimpse of the red port light on the bridge. Aft of the bridge the liner was a blaze of lights from cabins and public rooms, bright jewels flaming across the face of the night. And Raikes was on the bridge at this moment,

250

untouched, unmoved, all feeling deliberately frozen, moving inexorably step by step through the performance which he had drilled into himself in the past weeks. Berners looked at his watch. It would be a good twenty minutes to half an hour before the first of the bullion was on the deck and ready for loading and the second signal went up for them to come in.

CHAPTER FIFTEEN

WITHOUT WAITING FOR the boy to come back, the Captain moved across the wheelhouse nearer the First Officer. Raikes followed him but stopped after a few paces so that he was able to keep all four men in view. He saw the Third Officer, back to the chart table, watching him woodenly. The Quartermaster looked neither to right nor left. All these men, he thought, all knowing that something was very wrong, but all held by the power of the Captain's authority, and the Captain held by the power of duress. Men fashioned their own chains out of the good steel of order and respect for authority.

The Captain said, "Mr. Dormer—put the engines on Stand-By. Tell the Turbine Control that . . . well, say visibility is deteriorating and we'll be reducing speed immediately."

"Very good, sir." The First Officer picked up the talk-back microphone from the console. Just for a moment his eyes ran over Raikes and his mouth twisted a little pugnaciously. Then he spoke into the mike. "Turbine Control. Bridge here. We'll be going on to Stand-By immediately owing to poor visibility."

The boy came back from the wing and Raikes moved a little and held out his hand for the pistol. The boy gave it to him.

The Captain ordered, "Stand-By Engines and reduce to manoeuvring speed."

"Very good, sir." The First Officer reached forward to the console and pressed the Stand-By button for each engine. A few seconds later a buzzer sounded as the Turbine Control Room repeated the order. Behind him, briefly remembered from his conducted tour, Raikes heard the chatter of the Engine Telegraph Teleprinter logging the order and its time.

Into the mike the First Officer said, "Turbine Control Room, this is Bridge. Reduce to manoeuvring speed. 100 revs."

Over the talk-back system Raikes heard the engineer's voice repeating the order as the Captain moved closer to the First Officer and said, "All right, I'll take it from here, Mr. Dormer. What ships have you around?"

"Nothing to worry us, sir. That one over on the starboard bow will pass about three miles to the north of us. Our course is 270 plus two degrees for set. Gyro Course 272."

The Captain nodded and then ordered, "Half ahead both engines."

"Half ahead both, sir."

As the orders were passed through and the engine revolutions dropped well below the hundred mark there was the loud blare of escaping steam from the funnel top outside.

Over the noise the Captain said, "Where is the wind now?"

The First Officer said, "WNW. Force 3, sir."

The Captain turned to the Quartermaster. "Steer two-eighty."

As the Quartermaster acknowledged and obeyed the order, Raikes felt the swing of the ship as she came round on to her new course.

Raikes said to the Captain, "What speed are we doing now?"

Without looking at him, the Captain said, "Tell him, Mr. Dormer."

The First Officer said, "We're at 60 revs. About ten and a half knots."

Raikes said, "I shall want the foredeck lights on."

Ignoring him, the Captain turned to the Third Officer and said, "Call the Second Officer on the phone. Tell him to come to the bridge immediately. Then call the Night Security Petty

Officer and the Bosun's Mate of the watch. They're to stand by with five seamen outside the Specie Room."

On the last two words, Raikes saw the quick jerk of the First Officer's head in his direction.

"Yes, sir," said the Third Officer and he moved to the telephone by the port entrance to the bridge, passing close to Raikes. He moved by him without looking at him, ignoring him, and Raikes knew that in the man's mind, in everyone's mind here, he was already branded and outlawed, that they did what they did because the Captain ordered it and they were now in no need of explanation for the orders. The duress had moved to them. Hold them by it for too long and they would begin to question it, work to find a way round it, and perhaps, one of them, stupidly try to destroy it. There was a long time to go yet.

The Captain said, "Mr. Dormer, switch on the for'd deck lights."

The First Officer moved to the light switch panel at the rear of the wheelhouse and threw a switch. Through the centre window Raikes saw the foredeck jump into brilliant detail from the night shadows.

From the helicopter Berners saw the lights of the ship angle away from them as it changed course and slowed speed. Now as the helicopter moved keeping station with it, he saw the deck lights come on.

The man behind him shouted, "Everything going like clockwork. Better get your body harness on because when we go in and start lifting you can go through that hatch like a dose of salts if you slip."

On One Deck Lido Belle had felt the ship swing round and slow, heard the noise of escaping steam from the funnel and knew that it all meant that somewhere up there things were going the way Raikes wanted them. It was late now and there was no one else on the deck. She pitched her cigarette over the

254

side and moved into the shadows near the entrance to the cabin run on the port side.

The Second Officer, looking a little weary at being called from his sleep, was on the bridge and was being addressed by the Captain.

". . . I don't want any questions. What I am ordering you to do is directly concerned with the safety of our passengers. The Night Security Petty Officer, the Bosun's Mate of the Watch and five seamen are standing by the Specie Room. Here are the keys of the Room. I want—" he looked for a moment at Raikes.

"Eighty gold bars, I want. They may be packed anything from one to four a box. Just make up the load as fast as you can."

The Captain said "Forty double boxes. Put them into Number One lift and have them brought up to One Deck and then get the men to take them out on to the foredeck."

For a moment the Second Officer hesitated, began to open his mouth to say something and then thought better of it.

The Captain turned to the First Officer. "Give the Second Officer a walkie-talkie, Mr. Dormer." Then to the Second Officer he said, "Report to me when the load is on One Deck."

The First Officer handed over a walkie-talkie set and gave one to the Captain who tucked it in his pocket.

Raikes had been shown one of the sets when his friendly officer had taken him over the bridge weeks before. They were Stornophones No. 5 with a two-mile range.

The Second Officer left the bridge. The First Officer stood at the console, staring down at the lighted foredeck. The Quartermaster stood at the wheel, a white and blue statue, and the bridge boy moved a cleaning rag busily over and over the same window, knowing there was something wrong, remote from it and still wrapped in the aftermath of pleasure from firing the Very pistol. The Captain, ignoring Raikes, walked to the chart table and with the Third Officer made a check of the ship's position.

For the first time in his life Raikes knew the real meaning of isolation; the coldness of its grip, colder than his own tightly controlled emotions, a coldness that was intellectual and shaming. Every man on this bridge, dedicated to the service of this beautiful ship, had rejected him utterly. They tolerated his physical presence because they had to, but they had consigned him as a person to limbo. He was the violater, the unspeakable defiler of the one thing which filled their lives with pride. They no longer wished to see him and, when they heard him, they heard him as a voice without humanity or decency. Isolation he had thought he once loved, the sweet, time-eating loneliness of the river, the isolation of his own dedication to revenge his father and return to Alverton . . . but none of these he knew now began to be isolation. This was isolation, here and now on this bridge. The thought flashed through his head, too, that were his brothers here now, seeing and hearing him, knowing the ultimate blasphemy that he was practising, then they too would have rejected him, turned from him and made his name a sound of horror to them for evermore. . . . For the first time in his life he was lonely and hated it and hated himself. And for the first time in his life, even as he crushed the thought, strangling it before it could move to full birth, he knew that he was an evil, twisted caricature of a man.

Surprised at the strangeness of his own voice he said, was forced to say to beat back the iciness that surrounded him, "Captain, when I go down to the foredeck I want you to come with me."

He could have spoken to the dead. Not a head turned his way. There was not the slightest movement of acknowledgement.

It was with gratitude that he suddenly heard the walkie-talkie in the Captain's pocket announce, "We're at the Specie Room now, sir, and loading."

The Captain lifted the instrument and said, "Very good." Then he moved across to Raikes, stood in front of him, a head shorter almost, solid, his eyes almost hidden as they narrowed in contempt, and said, "There's no need for you to stay on my bridge any longer. We'll go down to One Deck." He looked back at the First Officer. "Take over, Mr. Dormer."

"Very good, sir."

"Keep her as she is."

Raikes, anger now stirring under his control despite all his power to contain it, said, "There's still the second signal from the wing. Two Very lights when the bullion is on deck."

Without a word the Captain held out his hand. Raikes put the pistol and two cartridges in it. The Captain moved back to the Third Officer.

"When the first of the bullion comes out on deck, fire two shots from the port wing."

"Yes, sir."

The Captain came back, passing Raikes. As he reached the bridge door he said, without looking back, "Your signals will be fired."

Raikes followed the Captain from the bridge. They went out through the Officers' Quarters to the main stairway outside the 736 Room, and then down to One Deck. There were one or two passengers about still and they looked curiously at Raikes and the Captain as they passed.

On One Deck the lift door was open and three seamen were already unloading wooden bullion boxes under the super-vision of the Bosun's Mate of the Watch. Raikes and the Captain went by them without a word. As they moved across to the starboard side to pass through the crew's quarters to the foredeck exit, the walkie-talkie in the Captain's hand broke into life.

"Second Officer here, sir. The first boxes are on the foredeck now, sir."

"Thank you." The Captain answered not breaking his walk. Behind him Raikes could have been non-existent. They turned

257

down the alleyway, past the Stewardesses' Mess and Recreation Room and out through the iron door on to the foredeck. As they did so the wind came full into their faces and there was a faint lick of passing rain with it. Behind them from the port bridge wing a green Very signal flared in the sky and then another. A voice inside Raikes said coldly, It's going as it should, as it must. Go with it. Don't think of people except as bulk and movement. Don't be touched by the solid, rejecting, condemning figure ahead. This is not you, not Raikes, moving and commanding here. It is a man being forced as much as any of these other men. In a few hours you will be free, and alone in the only kind of isolation you understand.

On One Deck Lido Belle saw the two green flares hang lurid against the dark sky. There was nothing in her now of anxiety or of relief. It was going as he had said it would. That was his genius. You planned and the plan became fact. You took people and you used them. That, maybe, was his only real strength. That he knew how to capture and hold people and make them his puppets. Could there ever be any true tenderness in him, any core of softness that would feed and strengthen love . . . love for someone else . . . for her? Maybe, yes, now; now that this was all moving smoothly to an end. Maybe after this the growth would stir and spring fast to blossom. . . . Oh, God, she hoped so. She hoped so.

She eased her large bag to the rail, snapped it open and one by one dropped the canisters over the side. She went inside from the Lido and made her way up to the Upper Deck and forward to the Look-Out Room.

She had no need to pull aside a blind from one of the windows. Two of the blinds were up and a small knot of passengers was gathered round, looking out at the foredeck. She saw him at once, tall, hatted, and the overcoat swinging a little loose in the wind, just as the helicopter came swinging in over the bows, the roar of engine and main rotor breaking

258

through into the room. She saw seamen coming out, crabbed and bowed with the weight of bullion boxes, and three officers, one of them short, with four rings on his jacket cuffs who she knew was the Captain.

Someone said, "What's it all about? What's happening?"

"Some emergency I suppose. Or perhaps it's a publicity stunt."

"At this time of night—and no cameras? What do you think, barman?"

And the barman who had come to the window looked and said, "Dunno. Whatever it is it's all in order. That's the Captain and the Security Petty Officer."

"Who's the civilian? What are those boxes, anyway?"

She could have told them. But looking out she suddenly knew that she couldn't stay even to watch. He was out there, a thousand miles remote from her in his mind at this moment, and when he was lifted off the thousand she feared would stretch to two, to three thousand, to infinity. He would be lifted off and she would never see him again. And, because the conviction was now so strong in her, she knew she could not wait to see that moment come. It was better to go away and force herself to a hopeless hope rather than have for ever a picture of his passing from the lit deck, from her life, up into the blackness of the clouds.

She moved away from the group of people and went to her cabin.

The bullion boxes were being stacked around the housing of the telescopic mast, now withdrawn, forward of the capstans and the two raised anchor chain runs. The noise from the helicopter was deafening as it hovered steadily above. Looking up Raikes saw the side hatch door open and then the arm of the external hoist on the helicopter's roof swing out and the cable drop a few feet. A man, unknown to him, stood in the hatch-opening and dropped a net to the deck and the hoist cable began to run down smoothly, snaking gently in the swing of helicopter and the wind. As it came down Raikes saw Berners' face move palely into sight in the hatchway. Berners saw him and he saw Berners but they made no signal to one another.

Raikes said to the Captain at his side, "Not more than ten double boxes, or the equivalent, in each net."

Without acknowledging him the Captain looked at the Second Officer and nodded to him when he saw that the man had heard Raikes.

"Ten double boxes in each net, men. And watch that cable."

The net was spread, the boxes loaded and the sides of the net drawn up and caught on the hook at the end of the cable. Raikes looked up, raised a hand, and the cable went taut, took the strain and the net rose swinging up from the deck. The down draught from the main rotor as it speeded up blew a seaman's hat across the deck, sending it rolling in white-topped cartwheels.

Up on the bridge the First Officer, Mr. Dormer, looked down at the group on the deck, his eyes singling out Raikes and he thought, Why don't they just jump him, the bastard?

Someone looking out through the Look-Out Room window said, "Those boxes are bullion, I swear. You think this is a hold-up?"

"What, with the Captain and other officers out there? Don't be an ass."

"But that other chap, the civvy—he's got a scarf round his mouth."

"Toothache."

"No markings on that chopper . . . "

Level with the hatch door the net was swung inwards by the turn of the hoist arm and Raikes saw Berners and the other man grab it, swing it for momentum and then draw it in. Almost immediately another net was dropped free to the deck and the seamen began to load it. A few moments later the cable snaked down towards the deck.

As it went up loaded with boxes, Raikes looked at his watch. They were running slightly ahead of the best time he had hoped for and nearly all the boxes were out on the deck.

260

Up in the wheelhouse, the bridge boy had moved to the centre window on the port side and was staring out, one hand idly holding a rag against the glass. The helicopter was almost level with him sixty yards away. He could see the pilot at the controls and the two men handling the net. He was a bright boy and it puzzled him to try and make out who was handling the operation of the hoist mechanism. As the cable went down for the third time, he saw that the two men in the main cabin were busy hauling farther inboard the second net with its load, dumping out boxes and making room for the third load to come up. They weren't doing anything about the cable, so the pilot must be operating it for them. Blimey, fancy sitting up there like a bloody buzzing mosquito, keeping her steady over the bows and having to watch that cable, too. A rain squall pock-marked the windows briefly. Without being ordered the boy moved and switched on the wipers and the scene cleared below.

Down in Belle's cabin, the steward had long ago been in and turned down her bed. Her nightdress lay across it. It was flame coloured silk, a baby-doll affair with brief pants to match, bought for the trip. Raikes had never seen it.

She began to undress and when she was naked she stood back from the dressing table mirror and looked at herself. She wasn't showing yet . . . or was she? Perhaps a little, but in a way that did something for her. It was like that in the early stages. Just gave you that something extra, they said. Well, if anyone needed something extra to get what they wanted, she did. Something extra not around the body, but inside . . . something that would be there to hold him when bed wouldn't. She put her hand over her navel and wondered when it would begin to kick. Ages yet. He'd said he'd wanted her to keep it. That must mean something. She reached out for her nightdress and pants. Perhaps the colour was a bit tarty, but hell, wasn't that what men liked in bed?

In the helicopter Berners was sweating. He had the unobtrusive strength of small-framed, wiry men, but humping the heavy boxes just far enough to make room for others, stacking a few here and there was taking it out of him and the other man. Perspiration fogged his eyes as it trickled from his eyebrows. And the noise was deafening. The rain was thickening up now, coming in longer squalls. The deck below was smooth, glistening putty.

The fourth and final net was coming up and he knew without looking at his watch that they were doing well for time. An hour back and then no dawdling. By six in the morning he would be motoring well south, through Nantes and on to Limoges. . . . He began to think of a catalogue illustration he had seen of a thirteenth century Limoges enamelled copper candlestick. Beautiful . . . So many beautiful things he would like to have . . . would have . . . Perhaps he would never go back to England. Well . . . just to clear up and sell up maybe. Not like Raikes. England was for him. Rivers and all that fishing and the hordes of officials riding your back more and more. He looked down, past the upcoming last net at Raikes. Through all the operation he had stood there, alongside the Captain, the Captain his hands half in his jacket pockets, rain meaning nothing to him as it wreathed the deck run now and then; Raikes, raising his hand each time they were ready to haul . . . and everything going like clockwork, matching the clockwork of their minds, his and Raikes' . . . and people so easy to manage, to gull and rob, never expecting a wrong until it was done and past and then cursing or wondering how they could ever have been taken in.

The net was level with the opening and the hoist arm swung it in. The man at his side, as they hauled, panted, "Thank Christ for that. I wasn't built for hard work."

Quickly they unloaded four boxes from the net and then between them hauled the partly loaded net clear of the opening.

"That'll do," said the man. "Unship the cable and put the sling on the hook and we'll send it down for him. Mr. Him, eh? Like you. No names, no pack drills."

Berners turned from him and bent over the collapsed net to

262

free the hook. As he did so, the man behind him reached to a cabin support and snapped free the working length of Berners' harness. Berners heard the sound and glanced round. The man was holding an automatic a foot from his eyes.

He said, "Sorry, chum, but orders is orders."

There was no time for Berners to make any move; only a flash of bitter irony in his mind as he acknowledged the end . . . fitting, a falling from a dream of so much beauty to be possessed to crash on the deck at Raikes' feet.

The man fired and the bullet smashed into Berners' temple. The force of the blow took his body backwards, half out of the helicopter. The man raised a foot and pushed the body over the side, holding the edge of the hatchway as he watched it. Berners sailed down, arms and legs widespread, and crashed across the end of the port anchor chain mounting and hung there, back broken, the pulped face turned up to the little group of seamen four feet away, the working length of the safety harness swinging gently, just brushing the deck. Above, the helicopter lifted fast, filling the night with noise and began to crab away swiftly southwards.

Coldness went, but not control. Understanding, swift, needing no sequence of thought to stimulate the mind, flooded like a great warmth through him. For a moment there was deep pity, that even before the surprise, and then pity and surprise were gone, and the facts, the altered shape of situation and attendant movements, formed smoothly in his brain as he saw the pulped face, the broken marionette stir of the body and the loose swing of the body strap. Before anyone else had moved, before even a man had mouthed any cry of shock or horror, he had pulled out his automatic and was running, back across the deck to the entry to One Deck.

He ran through the alleyway leading to the crew's quarters and then turned sharp to the right along a small passage-way and came out, tugging off his overcoat, on to the stairway

263

landing at the head of Number One lift. The door was open still but no one attended it. He ran down the stairs to Two Deck and as he went he dropped his hat and coat over the blue handrail for them to fall clear to the bottom of the stairway on Six Deck. A man running in a hat and coat would be noticed. He pulled the scarf from his face and put it in his pocket with his automatic as he turned off the landing on Two Deck and dropped at once to a slow walking pace.

Now he was a passenger, any passenger going late to bed. Unhurried, thinking ahead calmly, he walked aft to the Midships Lobby and then took the midships stairway down to Four Deck. There was no question in his mind of where he was going. For the moment he had to be out of sight, have a few hours' sanctuary and only one person could give him that. On Four Deck he left the stairway and walked forward along the port alleyway past the cabins, right forward until the alleyway ended and then he turned left down the short angle of corridor to the facing door of Belle's cabin.

It was then, only after he had turned off the long cabin run down the port side into this small branch which held the doors to two cabins only, 4002 and 4004, which was Belle's, that some of the pressure went from him. For a moment or two, isolated here, Belle waiting for him only a few feet away, the time now well past one o'clock and no one much about, and certainly no one likely to turn the corner and see him, he could pull himself up, take the curb off a primitive desire to run and run blindly instead of forcing himself to a slow, late promenading passenger walk. He leant against the wall and ran a hand over his face and was surprised to find that he had been sweating heavily. What now? Berners had been shot and pushed out of the helicopter. He himself had heard the sound of the shot over the rattle of helicopter noises, heard it and seen Berners' smashed-in face. He and Berners had been betrayed, and that was the one contingency they had never allowed for in their plans. He and Berners, he thought bitterly . . . the one thing which had never troubled them. They had been gulled as hopelessly and completely as any of their victims in the past. Out there on the foredeck he had panicked and run. A controlled panic, but desperate, bridled flight it had been, bringing him straight to this point, straight to the only immediate sanctuary that offered. Now, immediate crisis ebbing, he asked himself whether he had the right to move the few feet ahead, open the door and involve Belle? Long ago he had involved her and she had played her part. Had he the right to involve her again—and this time offer nothing but moment to moment expediency against danger? He didn't have to ask her the question, because he knew what her answer would be. She loved him and there was nothing she would refuse him. But tonight, up on the bridge he had for the first time seen something of his true self, and seen more of himself as others saw him, and the impression was hard on him that maybe, for all his self-sufficiency and strength, his time was running out, that total rejection lay close to him. And the answer to it in his present state of mind seemed brutally simple. Not only men, but the gods were turned against him. Men had been able to do little against his arrogance, but the gods had turned against him—first with that small red ballpoint mark and now with Mandel's unexpected treachery—in order to humiliate and reduce him. They had let him stand on the verge of all he longed for and then had pulled him back. Now they still beset him, demanding perhaps some real form of contrition, some genuine penance from him which would be absolute and all absolving. He still had the resources of his own wit and strength and cunning to carry him out of this moving, sea-borne trap, but none of these would override the wrecking finger of the gods if they were still against him. So, before he went in to Belle, he knew—the instinct streaming through him from his mother, from the long line of ancestral superstitions—that he had to make his gift to the gods if in return he wished for their protection. And the gift could never be recalled, or shabbily snatched back. Made, it was made for ever. And, the thought flowing unbidden, as though some unseen presence in

265

this gloomy cabin run dictated the terms, he knew what the gift must be. The woman in there carried his child, the wanted loin-springer. It must open its eyes to January snows and frosts, see the yeast of rain clouds over the Taw valley, hear the rush on still nights of the waters where spent salmon and sea trout turned from the redds, they too ancestor-shot, the blood lines from moorland, narrow, shallowed waters to salt-sharp estuary floods and still, green-cool, food-rich Atlantic depths ensured, and that ensurement their only purpose. The child he wanted, but not her. But the gift must be made and he made it, vowed it to them. Let him but get safely off this ship and he would take her, make her his wife, love her with all the willingness there was in him to love, and bring her as mistress, wife and mother to Alverton Manor and guard and protect her there as though she had been the woman of his own free choosing and desire. This he would do and, as the vow was made, he moved forward to meet her.

He put his hand out and the door handle turned, unlocked. He went into the lighted cabin, shut and locked the door behind him, and turned to where she lay on the narrow bed. And looking down at her, he knew at once that the gift had been refused and that he, Andrew Raikes, was doomed because he had come to make it too late.

CHAPTER FIFTEEN

SHE WAS LYING diagonally across the bed on the down-turned covers, flat on her back and wearing only a pair of flame-coloured silk briefs. Her head was turned a little to one side, and her posture had made her right, full breast sag a little against the flesh of her bent right arm. Her left arm was out-stretched, as though she had flung it out in sleep, and hung halfway over the side of the bed, the fingers widespread. On the floor below the top half of her nightdress was lying in a scarlet mound, the cabin lights marking black shadows in the valleys of its creases and flounces. Her auburn hair was tied back for the night in a red ribbon, her eyes were open and there was a neat hole drilled with symmetrical exactitude half an inch above the bridge of her nose. A thin trickle of blood had dried from it to mark a slanting line to the top of her left eyebrow.

He looked from her away to the right, to the man who stood with his back to the porthole, and he made no effort to reach for his pocket and his automatic. The man stood, tall, grey-white haired, shoulders hawk-stooped under the dinner jacket, eyes shadowed by thick brows, his right hand holding a gun with a silencer fitted to it. In his lapel was a white carnation. He stood there rock-still, watching Raikes and the long face, hawk-nosed, was carved, pale alabaster.

Raikes said, "Why?" The syllable was thick and agony-loaded.

Mandel said, "Because she was part of you. Just as Berners was. You don't think this is a simple exercise in treachery, do you?"

"I trusted you. I did the job for you."

"Without a hitch, as I knew you would. I came aboard at Le Havre. I've watched the whole thing—with admiration."

"Then why kill us? Why?"

Mandel moved forward, knowing the shock in Raikes, knowing perhaps the grief and the weight of resignation that locked his body, knowing perhaps, too, that he was as close to deserving human compassion as he had ever been in his life. He put the muzzle of the gun against Raikes' breast and then reached into his right-hand pocket and took out the automatic. He stepped back and put the automatic in his own pocket and stood in the shadowed angle made by the wardrobe and the shower compartment.

Mandel said, "Because of Sarling. Look at this face and you'll see for the first time something of what his was once like. We were seven brothers and he the closest to me. The only one. We all went our ways but long ago he helped me to mine. And later when he needed it, I helped him. But I never knew anything of his affairs. Between us—alone in our family—there was love. Out of my love I have begun to pay for his blood. The only sorrow I have is that I could not personally kill Berners. But the woman has gone. And now you. I saw her first at the funeral. She never saw me. She had no idea who I was when I stepped in here tonight."

"She carried my child." And for that, for the now slow-dying other life inside her dead body Raikes knew that he was going to kill this man. Knew, not how, but knew.

"She helped kill my brother."

"He asked for death from the first day he knew about me."

"He dreamt a dream, and only after his murder did I know from you what it was."

"It was a dirty dream."

"It was his dream."

"It was his dream or mine. And his dream was dirty. Just as your love for him is dirty. You could have killed me long ago without bringing us all to this. You could have spared her and

268

Berners and killed me. But you had to have your profit on the gold deal as well. You know less of love than I do. For the first time I've found a man I can pity more than myself. Mandel, Sarling, filth!" Raikes spat at the man's feet.

Mandel smiled, a quick unfreezing of face muscle, and said, "My brother would have understood. No matter what you do in this life, combine it with profit if you can. Goodbye, Raikes."

He raised the automatic and fired as Raikes moved to him. The bullet smashed through Raikes' left shoulder, high up and close to the neck and he was flung to his right and fell. As he fell, his mind a red flame of shock and pain, his hands went out, seeking, and caught Mandel's right ankle as he hit the ground before him. Feeling leather, and material and hard flesh Raikes rolled and pulled, not for the moment knowing he rolled and pulled, holding in a fierce one-handed grip the only security left to him. He heard the second muted explosion and with a far detachment felt his body leap and twist as the bullet went home, smashing through his back above his left hip. But then Mandel was down, hauled down, pulled down, dragged down to him and, sightless with pain for a while, he grappled the length of the man with his hands, clawing and seeking and then found, lean and warm and taut with stretched tendons, the man's neck. His fingers closed on the flesh and squeezed, strong fingers and hands that from boyhood had lifted and pulled, taken him up trees, mad-swinging along masonry cornices at Alverton, hands that had cornsack-lifted and stag-hunting horse curbed, pushed and pulled tirelessly on the double saw with Hamilton, boat-rowed for miles up lochs against wind . . . and now, tightening, they slowly throttled the life from Mandel whose body lashed and kicked against him as a great salmon's body lashes and kicks and leaps free from the gaff on the boat boards . . . and then there was no more lashing, no more movement.

Raikes lay breathing and bleeding, his breath, half saliva, staining the carpet close to his mouth, and then he opened his eyes and the cabin's unwelcome world came back.

He pulled himself up, took the gun from Mandel and, wanting in this fast out-running spate of time to have no doubt clog his mind, he held the gun to the man's head and shot him where Berners had been shot and where Belle had been shot. Then he dropped the gun and there were only two thoughts in his mind, that he must go clean, leaving no dirty trail to wind anyone back to Alverton, that there must be a sharp-cut finish of all that said Raikes, said family, said ancestry, and that with the finish there should be profit for no one.

He moved, feeling the clam and pull of the blood sticky under his clothes, to the dressing table, found paper and then in Belle's handbag a ballpoint pen . . . a ballpoint pen, and the gods who had rejected him, added the final irony, for it wrote in red to match his own blood. . . . Slowly he formed the words:

From your unwelcome bridge guest. Tell the French authorities that the bullion will be off-loaded at the Château Miriat, Loudeac, Brittany within the next hour. Confirmation source this message, Cabin 4004.

Slowly, feeling the strength going from him, he folded the note in four and on the outside wrote, *Urgent. Captain William Warwick.* Then he stood up and went to Belle. Looking down at her, note in hand, he bent forward and took up her left hand and kissed it, and the flesh was still warm, and he knew only the truth that, although he would have never known how to love her in the way she would have wanted love from him, he would have taken her to Alverton and cherished her and loved the child and with that she would have had more happiness than she could ever have dreamt she could have had with him, or perhaps with any other man.

He turned to the console under the dressing table mirror and pushed the bell for the steward. He went to the door and out to the alleyway. He shut the door and trapped the note against the jamb just above the handle as it closed so that the steward could not miss it.

He turned into the main run of the portside alleyway. The whole of this deck was cabin accommodation and as far ahead of him as he could see the alleyway was clear, though he knew that all over the ship now the search would be under way, and messages would be thick in the air to shore stations. The Chief Security Petty Officer would be organising a search of all public rooms and the lifeboats, and the Night Hotel Officer would have alerted the bedroom stewards to make as many discreet cabin checks as they could. But he had no fear of being found because he walked now, forcing his left side to obey him, under the absolute protection of those who ten minutes ago had rejected his tardy gift. He walked down the narrow, quiet chasm between the cabins and went into the furthest aft lift and rode up to One Deck and from there walked out into the night and a thin lash of rain on the Lido Deck.

He went to the starboard rail and leaned over, alone on the deck, but with him was the thought of Berners and of Belle, and then thought of them faded as the dark surge of foam-flecked water below brought back water memories, river memories, brother memories, and there was a curious happiness in him and a great calmness as he climbed the rail and let himself drop over. Before he hit the water, he heard his father's voice come back over the years, the gentle, patient voice, saying . . . *Fight the water and it's your enemy. Go with it and it's your friend.* He dropped into it and let himself go . . . drifting away, soon to be spent and softly drawn down.